GUARDING WHAT'S MINE

LOGAN CHANCE

Copyright © 2025 by Logan Chance

All rights reserved.

No part of this book may be reproduced in any form or by any electronic or mechanical means, including information storage and retrieval systems, without written permission from the author, except for the use of brief quotations in a book review.

Cover Design By: Kim Lehnhardt

For my Greedy Girls—Kim L., Valerie, Lorey, Kim S., Tiffany, Rochelle, Maria, Stacey, Lisa H., Kasey, Lisa A., Maritza, Amy, Julie, Shaunna, and Kim G.

Self defense is not just a set of techniques, it's a state of mind that begins with the belief that you are worth defending.

Anonymous

A Gift

WANT MORE SEXY ROMANTIC READS?
Sign up for my mailing list and receive a FREE copy of my novella RENDEZVOUS.
CLICK HERE to claim your book.

Maddox Security

Please Read before Continuing

The first chapter of this book is a meeting of the Men of Maddox Security. Each book will showcase this SAME meeting, but from each hero's perspective in their book.

So, in this book the meeting will be shown from Boone's point of view.

In the next book, Taking What's Mine, the same meeting will be shown from Lincoln's point of view.

Etc…

The Men and Women of Maddox Security

Dean Maddox- Owner of Maddox Security. A total badass who's completely in love with his wife, Sophia. (You can read their love story in Stolen By The Boss)

Isabel Maddox- Dean's younger sister. She runs the business with her brother. She takes care of the day-to-day running of things.

Ranger Cole-ex-Navy SEAL and one of Dean's top security specialists. He specializes in negotiation tactics. Hard working, and loyal to those around him.

Lincoln Zane- ex- Navy SEAL. He's been working for Maddox Security since its creation. Specializes in communications and leadership. Don't let his quiet demeanor fool you, Lincoln cares deeply for those he's sworn to protect.

Orion Locke- Orion's got his own style of security and has been working in the law enforcement field since he turned eighteen. A complete loner, he takes his job seriously.

Boone Porter- A man who thrives off the grid. Ex-military, and a pure mountain man. He's skilled with his hands, and bush crafting skills.

Asher Hawke- the newest member of Maddox Security, and the youngest. He's eager for a chance to prove himself worthy of being one of the elite Men of Maddox Security.

Chapter 1

Boone

Today promises to be a good day. Not only do I get to travel for work—a perk I'm always excited about—but I'll also have a chance to escape to my cabin tucked away in the Tennessee woods just outside of Nashville. That place has been my sanctuary since I left the military. Something about the pine-scented air, the hush of the forest, and the satisfaction of chopping your own firewood speaks to a part of me that Saint Pierce's salty breeze never quite reaches.

This upcoming job is exactly what I need. Dean hinted last week there might be an assignment near Nashville, and he knew I'd be perfect for it—maybe because I'm ex-military and more than capable of handling tough situations, or maybe it's because I look the part. My beard's grown in thick and full lately, and I have to say, even though I'm more used to deserts and jungles than mountains, I've embraced the rugged look. The grizzly mountain man look.

I flash a quick grin to the blonde receptionist behind the front desk in the gleaming lobby of Maddox Securities, perched on the thirtieth floor of one of the tallest buildings in Saint Pierce. Then I step into the elevator. As I ride up, I can't stop myself from picturing the Tennessee wilderness, the crisp air, and the logs stacked neatly beside my cabin's porch. It's exactly what I need—a reprieve from Saint Pierce's relentless heat and an excuse to indulge in the kind of hands-on work that makes me feel alive.

When the elevator doors glide open, I stroll into the sleek, glass-walled conference room. "I'm here," I announce, rubbing a hand over my beard, letting a slow grin spread across my face. "The meeting can begin now."

A few of the guys chuckle, and I drop into a seat, nodding at Ranger. His expression is tight, like something's weighing him down. I remember what he told me last week—about his sister—and my tone shifts as I murmur, "Sorry to hear about your sister."

He gives me a brusque nod. "It's fine."

But I can see from the tense line of his jaw that it's anything but fine. Greta's a good woman. The thought of her hurting over some scumbag's betrayal sets my teeth on edge. I fold my arms over my chest, the protective instinct I honed in the Marines kicking up a notch. "If you need me to knock that motherfucker out," I offer, letting my voice go cold, "just say the word."

Ranger's gaze flicks to mine, appreciation in his eyes. "Thanks, Boone. I'll keep that in mind."

Across the table, Lincoln raises an eyebrow. "Knock who out?"

Ranger explains how his sister's long-term boyfriend cheated on her, leaving her heartbroken—and with little faith left in men. The reminder pulls at a part of me that's hardwired to protect the people I care about. Greta's off-limits when it comes to heartbreak, at least if I have a say in the matter.

I push a breath through my nose, cracking my knuckles as I consider the possibilities. Nothing makes my blood boil like someone who preys on a woman's trust. Moments like this take me back to my military days—guarding bases, escorting civilians through danger zones. I've seen enough ugliness in the world to know you can't stand by when someone you care about is in trouble.

"She's been devastated ever since," Ranger mutters, his voice low and pained. He laces his fingers together on the table, as though trying to keep himself calm. "It's probably why I'll never fall in love."

I feel a pang of sympathy twist in my chest for his sister, but I also get where Ranger's coming from. If I had a drink in hand, I'd raise it to toast that sentiment. I'm about to agree when Dean clears his throat.

"Love isn't all bad," he says, in that confident way he has of looking on the bright side.

A laugh escapes me. "I'm surprised you're even here, Dean," I tease, my tone lighter than the tension in the room. "Figured you'd still be holed up with your girl."

Dean's expression softens immediately. He starts talking about Sophia—this woman who turned his entire life upside down. The story is wild, even by our standards: the job was supposed to be a simple extraction, kidnap one of the Four Families' daughters, only for him to discover Sophia in her place at the last moment. Suddenly, he found himself pretending to be married to her, all so he could lure out Bishop Blackstone, a notorious mob boss. And now here Dean is, grinning like a fool because he's clearly head over heels.

"I've never seen him like this," Ranger whispers, nudging me. And he's right. Dean's happiness is so obvious it practically fills the room.

Then the door bangs open, interrupting the moment. Orion staggers in, his hair disheveled like he just tumbled out of bed. Honestly, knowing him, he probably did. He yawns, settles into a chair, and props his feet up on the table—unapologetically Orion.

I turn back to Ranger, who's rubbing the back of his neck. Seeing the hint of worry in his eyes reminds me why I'm closest to him out of everyone in the group. He's solid. Dependable. And he's the reason I'm even here. We met a couple of years ago. As soon as we both got out of the military, Ranger talked to Dean on my behalf, and got me this job at Maddox Securities.

It was exactly what I needed at the time—an outlet for that military readiness that never really leaves you, but without all the red tape. Dean built Maddox Securities from scratch, first dealing in high-tech security systems before branching into personal security. Now, he—and by extension, all of us—have flown around the globe, working with mafia families and all sorts of clients most people wouldn't touch with a ten-foot pole.

Of course, we keep our mouths shut about the specifics. That's part of the deal. Anyone who can afford the high price tag of Maddox Securities wants the best, and the best requires absolute discretion. We're a tight-knit, elite group, which suits me just fine. I'd rather keep my head down, do the job, and get paid well for it than deal with the nine-to-five grind.

Still, I can't help but notice the faint slump in Ranger's shoulders whenever someone brings up his sister. I remind myself that when push comes to shove, I've got his back—both on the clock and off. It's just who I am.

"Why do you schedule these meetings so early in the morning?" Orion complains.

Dean looks at his watch and shakes his head. "It's nine a.m. That's hardly the crack of dawn." He chuckles, clearly amused at Orion's theatrics.

Ignoring Dean, Orion presses his forehead against the polished cherry-wood table, letting out a long groan. I arch an eyebrow at the sight.

"Rough night?" I ask, my tone playful, though I already know exactly why he's so wiped—and unfortunately, it's not because he got lucky. Given how dedicated Orion is, he probably spent half the night chasing down leads or combing through files on our latest client. Still, I can't help wishing he'd had a more enjoyable reason for the dark circles under his eyes. The guy deserves a break. Hell, we all do.

But he only grunts in reply, which sends a ripple of laughter through the rest of us.

A moment later, Asher enters, his dark eyes flicking around the table, quietly taking in the scene. He's our newest recruit, and I don't know much about him yet—other than the fact that he's as sharp as any of us, and Dean seems to trust him implicitly. That's more than enough to put him in my good graces.

Dean clears his throat, gathering everyone's attention. "Thanks for being here. I know the past couple of months have been rough with me on the hunt for Bishop." His gaze drops to the stack of papers in front of him. He flips through them, the seriousness of his expression taking hold of the room. "I can't thank you all enough for the roles you played in tracking him down. Hopefully, now we'll have a little peace."

I nod in agreement. It's no secret that Lincoln and Isabel ran themselves ragged to keep things running smoothly while Dean was away. We all did our part, but those two especially carried a heavy load.

Dean continues, "And I owe Isabel a lot, too. She's been a huge help. Having a sister who's also a part of this operation is...well, I'm damn lucky." He smiles briefly, then glances at Lincoln. There's a flicker of something there—appreciation, maybe gratitude. I wonder if he'll acknowledge the extra mile Lincoln went. Or if there's something else going on behind the scenes.

Before I can dwell on it, Dean's all business again. "All right. Now that the dust has settled, I've got some new assignments to hand out. Let's get to it."

My pulse stirs. Nashville. I already know that's where I'm headed, but I try to keep my eagerness under wraps. I haven't been to my Tennessee cabin in too long, and just the thought of breathing in that crisp mountain air has me itching to head out.

Dean shuffles another stack of folders and picks one off the top. "Ranger, I'll start with you." He hands Ranger a slim file. "This is Tory Ann."

Ranger opens the folder, his brow furrowing as he scans the contents. "Is she attending the summit?"

Dean shakes his head. "No, her father—Frederick Malser—is the one attending. He's a world-renowned scientist and one of the keynote speakers at the G-Summit this weekend. He'll have his own personal security detail, so he wants separate coverage for his daughter."

Guarding What's Mine

Ranger arches an eyebrow. "Why not just let his own team watch over her, too?"

It's a fair question, and one that makes me lean in, interested to hear the explanation. Dean folds his arms, preparing to elaborate, and I can't help but notice how the tension in the room builds again—like we're all bracing for whatever surprise might come next.

"Frederick's been receiving threats related to his presentation at the Summit," Dean explains, tapping the file on the table. "He doesn't want anyone knowing his daughter will be in town. He wants to keep it all under wraps—especially since he isn't completely sure he can trust everyone on his own security detail."

Ranger grimaces. "That sucks."

Dean nods in agreement before continuing. "You'll take his daughter to the safe house: SEASHELL, and keep her there until the Summit is over. Minimal contact, minimal movement."

"Sounds good," Ranger mutters, though his expression suggests he knows it won't be that simple.

Dean's gaze slides over to Orion, who's half-dozing in his chair. I give the leg of his chair a good kick to jolt him awake.

"Orion," Dean says, "this is for you. Her name's Briar Green—the daughter of socialite Minnie Green. She has an ex-boyfriend stalking her. Her mother wants to ensure she's safe going to and from work."

"Ex-boyfriend?" Orion echoes, lifting his head. He flips through the file, eyes still heavy with fatigue. "Can't I just beat him senseless, scare the hell out of him, and call it a day?"

Dean's lips twitch with a hint of a smile. "It's never that simple, my friend. We need a more…subtle approach this time." He slides the folder fully in front of Orion.

"It never is," Orion grumbles, but he seems more alert now, scanning the details of his assignment.

From the corner of my eye, I notice Dean glance at Lincoln. Dean mentioned earlier that Lincoln already has his assignment, but there's a flicker of tension between them that piques my curiosity. Something else is going on there, but it's not my place to pry—yet.

Finally, Dean turns to me. I straighten up, anticipation coursing through my veins. "Boone," Dean says, sliding a manila folder across the table. "Here's yours. I gave you a quick preview last week, but now we have more details."

My pulse quickens as I pick up the file. Nashville. I'm already picturing my cabin nestled in the Tennessee woods. But the photo clipped to the first page stops me in my tracks. A woman's face—delicate features, fiery amber eyes, and hair a shade of red that practically smolders off the page.

"Wow," I breathe, before I can stop myself. "Who's this?"

"Aubree Ryan," Dean responds, leaning back in his chair. "She's got a stalker, too. We don't know who it is yet, but it sounds serious. She needs to get out of Nashville until we can figure out who's behind it."

I glance at the photo again, something tightening low in my gut. It's unexpected—this surge of protectiveness. I've guarded plenty of women before without blinking an eye. But there's something about Aubree that's already under my skin.

"Right," I say, clearing my throat. "I'll take her to my cabin nearby. That should keep her off the radar."

"Good." Dean snaps another file shut. "We'll coordinate the details, but you'll head out as soon as you can."

I barely hear him. My mind's already drifting to that tiny stretch of forest I call home, imagining what it'll be like to have this striking, vulnerable woman tucked away with me—hidden from the rest of the world.

What's wrong with me? This isn't the first time I've protected someone. Yet the sight of Aubree's photo has my thoughts scattering in a way they never have before.

I let out a low breath. Has it really been that long since I let anyone get close? Because one look at her, and I can feel my carefully constructed walls start to shift. And that…well, that might be a problem.

I swallow hard and force my features into a neutral mask, hoping Dean doesn't notice the spark of interest flaring inside me. It's not exactly professional to react to an assignment this way. But, damn it, seeing Aubree Ryan's photo triggered something I wasn't expecting—a twist of protectiveness mixed with an undeniable attraction.

This is fucked up, I tell myself. *Keep it together, Boone.*

I glance across the room at Orion, who's also flipping through his file with a furrowed brow. It's always something new with that guy, and by the way his eyes widen slightly, I can tell his current assignment isn't a walk in the park either. I make a mental note to check on him later, see if he needs anything.

Dean dismisses the meeting, and we all file out of the conference room. I catch a glimpse of Asher being asked to stay behind, probably for a private update on his own job.

Once we're in the hallway, I run a hand over my beard and smirk at my friends. "We all need to catch up soon," I say, remembering the last time we hung out. It ended in far too much whiskey and just enough laughs. "Last time was a damn good time."

Orion yawns, but there's a mischievous light in his eyes. "Maybe once I'm done protecting a girl from her psycho ex, we can do a guys-only poker night."

Ranger chuckles. "I'm definitely in."

Of course he is. Ranger kills it at poker; the man's practically a human lie detector. I still remember losing five hundred bucks the last time we squared off. Stubborn pride and a poor bluff are a lethal combination.

"I'd love some more free money," Ranger says, crossing his arms with a smug grin.

"No way I'm playing with you again," Lincoln cuts in. He shakes his head like he's still nursing that old wound. "Besides, my own assignment isn't exactly a cakewalk."

He shoots a quick glance down the hall, and I can't help but wonder if his job has something to do with the big meeting Dean had earlier. Ranger cuffs him lightly on the shoulder.

"Yeah, I figured," Ranger says. "Dean asked to see you before all of us earlier. What's going on?"

Lincoln blows out a breath. "It's Isabel," he admits, lowering his voice. "She's been threatened."

A heavy silence settles over us. Isabel is Dean's sister, and as long as I've been with Maddox Securities, I know one thing: family is off-limits. That makes whoever is messing with her a dead man walking.

"Who is it?" I ask quietly.

Lincoln shakes his head. "We're not sure yet. Dean has a few leads, so while he's looking into it, I'm basically glued to Isabel's side."

"Good luck," Orion says with a half-laugh. "You know how she gets when she's pissed."

We all nod in agreement. Isabel's not a woman you want to cross. And sure enough, the rapid click of stilettos against marble tiles echoes down the hallway. She comes into view, her gaze locked onto Lincoln like a heat-seeking missile. The fury in her eyes says she's well aware of this new 'protection detail,' and she's not happy about it.

Before she can level her wrath at the rest of us, we scramble to make ourselves scarce. I head for the elevators, shaking my head with a mix of amusement and pity for Lincoln.

That's life at Maddox Securities—constant danger, complicated assignments, and sometimes a little heartbreak. But we stick together, even when we're butting heads or chasing down leads.

Stepping into the elevator, I think of the folder tucked under my arm and the redhead who's about to turn my life upside down. I need to get a flight and meet Aubree Ryan. Keep her safe. Keep my head on straight.

I let out a slow, steadying breath. It's time to handle business, the way I always do—like a professional. Even if my gut twists every time I remember those fiery amber eyes.

Chapter 2

Aubree

"One more pie and then we're done for the day," Stuart calls out, brushing a stray lock of sandy-blond hair away from his forehead. I can't help but smile. If I could clone this kid, I totally would. He's only a teenager, but I swear he's got more hustle and heart than some of the grown-ups I've hired and fired.

"Let's make it the best pizza Earl's ever had," I say, rinsing off a ladle before tucking the last container of sauce into the fridge. The clang of metal and the sweet tang of tomatoes fill the air. I never get tired of that smell.

Earl's one of our regulars—he's been coming to Slice Slice Baby since the day I opened the doors. Seven years ago, my mom convinced me that a pizza joint next to the high school was the perfect idea. And boy, was she right. Every lunchtime and after every football game, we're flooded with hungry teens and their parents, clamoring for a slice of something cheesy and delicious.

Not that it was easy getting here. Sometimes I think my blood might actually be marinara at this point, considering how many hours I've put into this place. I've cried over everything from supplier issues to broken ovens. But after all the tears, I'm proud to say Slice Slice Baby is my life's work—and my absolute pride and joy.

"Dough's the key," I murmur, watching Stuart work his magic. He's kneading that dough like it personally offended him, which is exactly how I taught him. "If the crust isn't perfect, the pizza won't be perfect."

I've got a little secret to make sure our crust stands above the rest: I ship in water from a natural spring in Montana. Crazy? Maybe. Over-the-top? Definitely. But it's the only way I can recreate that same crisp and airy crust every single time. And if you ask me, it's worth every penny.

I also ship in the best flour from Italy. Organic tomatoes from California. And I only use the best products.

Okay, so my pizza isn't exactly famous yet—there aren't any shiny trophies lining the walls. Still, I dare anyone in Tennessee to find a better slice. Someday, I'm hoping to snag a few awards to prove my pizza prowess once and for all.

Stuart finishes stretching out the dough and starts layering on the sauce and cheese. He's done this a thousand times, but I still hover behind him, making sure each swipe of sauce looks just right.

"This is Earl's order, yeah?" I ask.

"Yep," Stuart replies. "Pepperoni, mushrooms, and extra black olives."

"Right. Extra is good, but let's toss on a few more, just in case," I say with a grin. Earl loves his olives—every time, he insists I dump half a can on his pie. "Let's really blow his mind."

Stuart snickers and sprinkles on more of the salty black orbs. "Sure thing, boss."

I watch him work, feeling a rush of fondness for this little pizza family I've built. We might not be the biggest pizzeria in town, but we've got heart—and, in my humble opinion, the best crust in the entire state.

Once Stuart slides the pie into the oven, I'm already imagining Earl's delight when he cracks open the box. Moments like that—seeing the joy my pizzas bring—are why I keep fighting the good fight…dough under my nails, sauce stains on my apron, and a smile on my face.

Sometimes I wonder if this is exactly what I was born to do: feed people, make them happy, and maybe give them a delicious memory or two. After all, if you can't find joy in a gooey slice of pizza, are you really living?

"Thanks for a great day," I say, patting Stuart on the back. "Now let's finish strong and get this bad boy to Earl. Then we can finally call it quits."

With the final pizza baking, I take one last glance around the shop—at the red-checkered tablecloths, the cheesy pizza-themed décor, and the high school kids laughing as they walk out the door after getting their orders. It's all mine, and even on the hardest days, it's totally worth it.

I smile as I make my way toward the back of Slice Slice Baby, weaving through the kitchen and into my cramped little office. It's more like a glorified closet with a desk, but I cherish every corner of this place. Settling into my squeaky office chair, I boot up my computer to run the end-of-day reports. My eyes land on the inbox, and my stomach twists the second I notice an unread email from an address I don't recognize.

Great. Probably another spammy message, I think, though unease prickles at the back of my neck. For the past few months, my inbox has been a minefield. A little voice in my head whispers that this might not be spam—it could be the latest threat from whoever's been targeting me. I feel my breath hitch, but before I can even click on it, a thunderous crash echoes from the front of the pizzeria.

My heart plunges into my stomach. "Stuart?" I call, launching out of my seat.

I sprint across the kitchen, flinging open the swinging doors that lead to the dining area. The entire space is littered with shards of broken glass. My eyes land on Stuart, who's standing near the front window, looking more than a little rattled.

"I'm okay," he assures me hastily, though his voice wavers. "Everything's okay."

I step closer, taking in the horrifying sight. Our big front window is shattered, and a cold draft whips through the shop. "What happened?" I ask, trying to keep the panic out of my voice.

Stuart moves toward me, clutching a brick in his hands. "I think...it's a brick," he says, his expression unsure, like he's still trying to process it.

I gingerly sidestep the glass crunching under my sneakers. "Be careful," I warn, quickly checking him over. No cuts, thank goodness. Then I notice something else: a piece of paper wrapped around the brick, held by a rubber band.

Stuart extends the brick. "I'm so sorry," he murmurs, guilt pooling in his eyes.

I take it from him, carefully sliding off the note. My fingers tremble as I unfold the paper. Two words stare back at me in thick black marker: *Die bitch.*

I swallow hard, my vision blurring with tears. I refuse to cry in front of Stuart—he's only a teenager, and I'm supposed to be the adult holding it all together.

Suddenly, Earl, my most loyal customer, appears in the doorway, clearly alarmed. "Oh my God, what happened?" He rushes over, and I silently hand him the note. The expression on his face darkens as he reads the words. "I'm calling the police," he says, already dialing on his phone.

Before I can protest, Stuart gasps. "Earl, your pizza!" He dashes behind the counter and flings open the oven door, pulling out Earl's order. Smoke puffs around him, and the smell of toasted cheese mingles with the metallic scent of broken glass.

Earl waves him off. "Don't worry about that." Phone pressed to his ear, he rattles off details to the 9-1-1 operator. Meanwhile, I'm still standing in the center of shattered glass, trying to wrap my head around what just happened.

The threats started three months ago—anonymous emails, weird phone calls at odd hours, stuff that made me anxious but never truly scared. At first, they were mild: telling me I should 'watch my back,' or claiming they didn't like my pizza (which, obviously, is a crime in and of itself). Over time, though, they've become bolder and more hateful.

My mom has been insisting for weeks that I hire professional security, going so far as to use her credit cards to snag "the best money could buy," in her words. I wasn't thrilled at the idea of having a bodyguard—who wants to feel like a criminal in their own pizza shop? But tonight's incident changes everything. I can't deny it anymore: I'm not safe, and neither is anyone around me.

I take a shaky breath and look at Stuart, who's staring at me with worried eyes, and at Earl, who's doing his best to calmly explain the situation to the police. My pizzeria, my safe haven —it's all under threat. And as much as I hate to admit it, maybe my mom was right. Maybe I do need help…someone to protect me until we figure out who's behind these threats.

Brushing away an errant tear, I steel myself. First, I need to clean up this mess and make sure Stuart and Earl are okay. Then I'll call my mom and let her know she was right—about everything. If it means keeping Slice Slice Baby safe, I'll swallow my pride and deal with a security detail. Because no matter what, I won't let some faceless coward run me out of my own life.

A man with a deep, gravelly voice steps into the pizzeria, stopping short when he sees the shards of broken glass littering the floor. "What happened here?" he demands, scanning the room like he's expecting a battle at any second.

Earl, my loyal customer, tucks his phone away. "Are you with the police?"

The newcomer shakes his head, flashing a badge that reads Maddox Security. "I'm Boone Porter." His gaze swings between Earl and me, narrowing slightly before his voice rumbles, "I'm looking for an Aubree Ryan."

"That's me." I hesitate for a split second, then take a step closer. My heart thuds in my chest as I lift my eyes to meet his. "Mr. Porter?"

He nods. "I'm with Maddox Security." He's not at all what I expected when my mother said she'd hired 'top-notch' security. He's... well, gorgeous. He's tall and broad in a way that makes him look built for protection—like the walls in this shop could cave in and he'd keep me safe from the rubble. His dark beard is thick and full, framing his jaw and making him appear a little dangerous. And his eyes—an intense, almost chocolate brown—feel like they're boring straight into my soul.

I flush, remembering to breathe. The strangest thought flits across my mind: the sensation of that beard brushing against my skin, maybe somewhere far more intimate than I should be picturing in a moment like this. My face warms, and I give my hand a quick shake before I offer it to him.

When he takes my hand, his grip completely engulfs mine. It's firm, controlled—just like the rest of him. I do my best to act normal, but my pulse is hammering like I've just run a marathon.

Stuart steps in, saving me from babbling. He recounts the entire story—how the brick came crashing through the window, how we found the note with that awful message. I stand off to the side, arms crossed over my chest, trying to keep from trembling. This is really happening. My safe, cozy pizza shop feels like ground zero for something horrible.

"I can't believe this is happening," I whisper under my breath. Earl moves beside me and slips an arm around my shoulders in comfort. That's when Boone's gaze snaps in our direction, his jaw clenching. I hear the low rumble of a growl slip from his lips, so quiet I almost wonder if I imagined it.

"Can I speak with you for a moment?" Boone asks, directing his question pointedly at me. His eyes flick to Earl, then back to me.

"Oh, okay," I manage. My voice sounds smaller than I'd like. I gently disentangle myself from Earl's side-hug and follow

Boone a few steps away, the broken glass crunching under my sneakers.

When we're far enough from the others, Boone folds his muscular arms across his chest. "Who is that man?" he asks, tilting his head toward Earl.

I bite back a laugh. "Earl? He's harmless. Just a regular customer—he's been coming in since we opened."

Boone sizes Earl up one last time before turning his intense gaze back on me. "You're closing your shop for a few days."

My jaw drops. "Excuse me? No. I most certainly am not. This place is my livelihood." I cross my arms, mirroring his posture without meaning to. "I can't just shut it down."

"You can, and you will." His tone is final, almost like an order. "You'll come with me to a safe house until Maddox Security can figure out what's going on."

A thousand protests surge to the tip of my tongue—how I need the income, how I can't leave Stuart and my other employees without a job, how I hate the idea of abandoning my business. But that steely determination in his gaze tells me there's no use arguing with him. Even if I do, I suspect he'll just scoop me up and carry me out if he has to.

Well, he'll have to carry me kicking and screaming.

"No. I'll be staying right here," I declare, crossing my arms over my chest as I stand in front of Boone. The smell of tomato sauce and pizza dough still lingers in the air. "Thank you very much," I add, trying not to glare at him. "You can stand guard at the door if you want."

Boone's laugh is a deep rumble that makes the floor feel like it vibrates beneath my feet. "I'm not a bouncer," he says, shaking his head. "This is a serious operation. You're closing your shop."

I plant a hand on my hip, doing my best to keep my voice steady. "Am not," I shoot back. This is my pizza shop—my baby. I can't just shut down and lose sales, possibly more. I still owe rent and have employees to pay.

Before I can argue further, a uniformed police officer steps through the door—carefully, because of the crunch of glass on the tile. His eyes pan across the mess. "Who's in charge here?"

"I am," Boone answers immediately, holding his hand out. "Boone Porter, Maddox Security." His gruff voice and imposing stance say there's no question about it.

"Um, excuse me?" My cheeks heat as I shove past him, refusing to be sidelined in my own shop. "I'm the owner," I announce, taking the officer's hand. "Aubree Ryan. This is my place."

The officer's gaze flicks from me to Boone, then back again. It's obvious he's not quite sure who to address. Finally, he clears his throat and settles on me. "Ma'am, can you tell me what happened here?"

We spend the next twenty minutes explaining how a brick came flying through the window and nearly scared the life out of everyone. Stuart recounts the moment he heard glass shatter and ducked behind the counter. Earl throws in a few comments about how fast it all happened, and about how he could've sworn he saw someone running down the street. Meanwhile, I do my best to stay composed, though my nerves are jangling like crazy.

During that time, Earl slips me his phone number on a scrap of napkin, insisting I call him if I need anything. I catch Boone shooting him a dark look. The second Earl steps away,

Guarding What's Mine

Boone mutters something about "handing that number over," but I shove it in my back pocket instead. Earl's just trying to be nice—and, well, I'm not a big fan of being told what to do, even if Boone does have a commanding presence and gorgeous brown eyes.

When the police officer is done taking statements, he nods at me. "We'll be in touch if we have any updates, Ms. Ryan." Then he heads out, presumably to ask around the neighborhood.

With the help of Boone and Stuart, we manage to cover the gaping hole in the window using some old plywood I found in the storeroom from a previous renovation project. It's not perfect—definitely not the charming vibe I usually aim for—but it'll have to do until I can afford a proper replacement.

Finally, the adrenaline starts to ebb, and I retreat to my little office to breathe. My hands are shaking as I drop into my squeaky chair. The day was already stressful before this whole mess—now, I'm operating on fumes. I press my palms to my eyes, trying to ward off the headache I know is coming.

I glance at my inbox. The email. I click on it and suck in a deep breath. The message is simple: *I'm coming for you.*

I quickly shut the computer down and that's when my phone buzzes in my pocket. I glance at the screen and see my mom's number. Of course. Molly Hancock—the woman who sees everything from her vantage point at the hair salon next door—must have called her first chance she got.

"Mom?" I answer, my voice still shaky.

"Aubree, dear!" Mom's frantic tone crackles over the line. "Molly said the police were at your pizza shop. What's going on? Are you okay?"

"I'm fine, Mom," I say, trying for a reassuring note I don't quite feel. "Someone threw a brick through the window, that's all. We covered it up already. I promise, I'm okay."

She lets out a sharp breath, like she's trying not to panic. "Honey, that's terrible. The man from Maddox Security—did he arrive? I know I paid a pretty penny, but it's worth it if you're safe."

I lean my head back against the wall, already dreading this conversation. "Yes," I huff. "He's here, and he wants me to shut down the shop and go to a 'safe house.' Can you believe that? I can't just close, Mom. I'd lose so much business—"

"I think that's a good idea," she cuts in, her tone leaving no room for argument. "I don't care how much money you lose. Your safety is more important."

I close my eyes, torn between frustration and a sliver of relief. Honestly, part of me wants to hole up somewhere far away from this chaos. But the other part—the one that's poured seven years of sweat and tears into Slice Slice Baby—can't imagine walking away, even for a few days. What if I lose customers? What if employees quit? My mind reels with worst-case scenarios.

But my mother is steadfast. And the image of that brick, plus the hateful note scrawled on it, is still burned into my brain. A cold shiver works its way down my spine.

"I just can't afford it," I finally say, rubbing my forehead. It's not a promise, and I can practically hear Mom gearing up for a lecture.

Yet, with each passing second, the idea of leaving sounds less like a betrayal of my dream and more like survival. Maybe Boone Porter's right—maybe shutting down for a bit and going somewhere safe is the only way to keep this from spiraling out of control.

I hate it. But I'm starting to realize that my life might depend on it. And that's a thought I never expected to have about my little slice of pizza heaven.

"I'll pay your bills. It's worth it to keep you safe."

"Mom, you can't be serious," I say, my voice getting louder with each word, echoing in the tiny office space. The fluorescent light overhead buzzes, and I rub at a sudden tension in my neck.

"I am, Aubree," Mom insists. I can practically hear her pacing around her kitchen, the way she always does when she's worried. "What happens next time if that brick hits you instead of the window?"

A shudder runs through me. I've been trying not to imagine that particular scenario, but her words spark the image in my mind. Still, I straighten my spine and set my jaw. "I can't close the shop. This place is how I pay my bills. You know that."

"I'll pay for it," she says again, matter-of-factly. She's never been one to beat around the bush. And I know she can afford it—my parents aren't hurting financially. But I've spent years proving I could stand on my own two feet. The idea of taking their money feels like a step backwards.

"Mom, I can't ask you for that," I protest softly. My eyes flick to the dented filing cabinet in the corner, stuffed with receipts and paperwork that prove how hard I've worked to get Slice Slice Baby off the ground.

"You're not asking," she replies, her tone as sharp as the glass shards still scattered at the front of my shop. "I'm telling you, Aubree. You go with this security man and you listen to him. Do what he says."

I exhale, my breath coming out shaky. If I keep arguing, I know it'll lead to a full-blown fight, and the last thing I need right now is more stress. "Fine," I manage, even though it feels like I'm choking on the word. My cheeks burn at the thought of walking out there and telling Boone he was right. There goes my pride, tossed in the trash along with the shattered window shards.

"Thank you, sweetie," Mom says, relief evident in her voice. "Call me as soon as you're settled, okay?"

"Sure," I mumble. We exchange our goodbyes, and once she hangs up, I stare at the phone for a moment, my heart racing. This is really happening. I'm about to abandon my shop—even if it's just for a little while.

I drag a hand through my hair and grab a few essentials from the office: my laptop, some paperwork, and a small duffel I keep hidden under the desk for emergencies. I never thought the emergency would be a legitimate threat on my life, but here we are.

A few moments later, I steel my shoulders and head out to the front of the shop. The dining area looks eerily deserted: chairs stacked on tables, the lingering aroma of pizza sauce.

"Thank you so much, Stuart," I say softly. My gaze travels around the mess. "We're going to be closed for a few days while they fix the window and figure out who's behind all of this."

Stuart's brow furrows, but he nods. "Right, okay. Let me know when you need me back. I can come in any time—school's almost out for the summer, so my schedule's wide open." He picks up his worn-out backpack from behind the counter. "Stay safe, Aubree."

I give him a grateful smile as he leaves, watching him unlock his bike from the rack outside. When I turn back, Boone is setting the hammer down on the counter, wiping a bit of sweat from his brow. Even with tension running high, I can't help but notice the easy strength in his broad shoulders, and the way his dark beard shifts when he breathes.

"Do you have everything you need to close for a while?" he asks, his brown eyes scanning me from head to toe as though he's making sure I'm still in one piece.

My chest tightens. I've had my business threatened, my window smashed, and my entire life turned upside down in the span of a few hours. "I need to know one thing," I say, my voice trying for calm but wavering slightly. "How long is 'a while'? I can't expect my mother to pay my bills indefinitely."

Boone pauses, slipping his hands into his jeans pockets. "Uhh… shouldn't be more than a week, give or take. The guys at Maddox Security are good at what they do. They'll figure this out."

"I can't close longer than a week," I say firmly, swallowing the lump in my throat. The mere idea of losing more than seven days of income makes me feel a little ill.

He arches a brow, the muscle in his jaw ticking. "Well, that's not exactly how this works. Security threats don't usually come with deadlines."

"It's how I work," I counter, lifting my chin in defiance. "I can't close for longer than a week, Boone. Deal?" I thrust my hand out, the gesture as much of a challenge as it is a request.

He stares at me, and for a second, I worry he'll flat-out refuse. But finally, he takes my hand in his large, calloused one. When his rough skin meets mine, a jolt of awareness shoots up my arm, startling me.

"Deal," he says, his voice low.

We linger there, hand in hand. The air between us crackles with an unexpected tension I can't quite name. This is the same man who strolled in here with a no-nonsense attitude and an order for me to shut everything down. Yet beneath that stern exterior, I sense something protective—maybe even kind. And I hate to admit it, but that tiny kernel of comfort is enough to make me suck in a shaky breath and hold steady.

"Let's get out of here, then," he says gently, releasing my hand. "I'll fill you in on the rest of the plan once we're on the road."

I nod, though part of me wants to burst into tears at the idea of leaving my pizzeria behind, even if it's just temporary. Still, I manage a small smile. Deep down, I know it's the smart choice. Because if there's one thing I've learned in the last twenty-four hours, it's that someone out there is serious about scaring me—or worse.

Walking away from Slice Slice Baby feels like leaving a piece of my heart behind. But with the chaos swirling around us, I'd rather take the risk of shutting down for a few days than risk my life—especially if it means I'll be protected by a man who, despite his growling demeanor, might just be the shield I need right now.

Chapter 3

Boone

I start the engine of my truck, the rumble of the motor filling the silence as I pull away from the parking lot of Aubree's pizza shop. Her shop. Her livelihood. The place she poured her heart into for years. I get it. I've seen too many people lose their businesses to crime and the stress of it all. But I'm not here to be a therapist. I'm here to keep her alive, to make sure nothing worse happens.

"You good there?" I ask, glancing the perimeter of the parking lot to make sure we're not being followed.

She pulls her hoodie tighter around her, her fingers playing with the hem of it nervously. "Yeah," she mutters, but I can tell she's not.

I nod, focusing on the road ahead, trying to clear my mind of the things I'll need to do once we're out of town. Checking in with Dean, getting the security setup in place, ensuring that we're ready for anything.

Once we get on the highway, I pull out my phone and dial Dean's number. The call rings for a second before he picks up, his voice gravelly with that ever-present authority.

"Porter."

"Hey, it's me," I say, keeping my voice low. "I've got her with me. We're heading to the cabin now."

"Good. Keep her safe. You know the drill." Dean's voice shifts, becoming more businesslike. "Check the perimeter of the cabin as soon as you arrive. Cameras, security system, the works. Don't take any chances."

"I won't. Anything else?" I check the mirrors again, my hands tight on the steering wheel.

"We're running background checks on everyone who works for her. Everyone and anyone. I'll send over everything I find. Keep your eyes open. You're there to protect her, and that's it. Keep things professional."

Aubree's quiet beside me, her profile lit up by the glow of the dashboard. I wonder if she knows how much danger she's actually in. Probably not. Hell, I wish I could tell her it's all going to be okay, but I can't lie to her. I just have to make sure she stays alive, and that's all I can promise.

"Got it," I say to Dean, but he's already hung up. I drop my phone into the cupholder, my mind racing with possibilities, all of them bad.

Aubree looks at me, catching my gaze for a moment before looking away. She's still upset. I can tell by the way her jaw's clenched, by the way her shoulders are tense. I can't blame her. This isn't how anyone wants to spend their evening.

"So... this cabin," she says, her voice soft, breaking through the silence between us. "What's it like? Is it... comfortable?"

I glance over at her, trying to figure out how to put her at ease. "Yeah, it's fine. Nothing fancy, but it'll do. I've got everything set up for a couple of days. It's a place to relax. At least, until we figure out who's doing this to you."

She nods slowly, but I can see the hesitation in her eyes. "And... you're just taking me to your cabin? Like, no questions asked?"

Her voice is cautious now, like she's testing the waters to see what I'll say.

"Look, I'm not here to make things complicated," I reply, my eyes back on the road. "I'm just doing my job. Protecting you. Nothing more. I don't expect you to trust me right away, but you'll be safe there. I'll make sure of it."

"Okay," she says quietly, and I feel the weight of her gaze on me again. It's almost like she's trying to figure me out, and I can't say I blame her.

The drive is long, and the silence between us stretches. The headlights cut through the night, illuminating the winding road ahead, the trees casting long shadows in the dark.

Aubree doesn't speak again until we're pulling into the gravel driveway of the cabin. It's a little run-down but functional, tucked away from prying eyes, just like I need it to be. The isolation is key.

I park the truck, kill the engine. "Here we are," I say, opening my door and stepping out, walking around to the passenger side to open the door for her. She hesitates for a moment, then gets out, her feet crunching on the gravel beneath her.

"I don't need you to open the door for me," she says, glancing up at the cabin. I'm not sure if she's being sarcastic or not, but I don't really care.

I give her a half-smile. "I didn't do it because I'm a gentleman, sweetheart. I did it to keep you safe."

She glances around quickly, her cheeks blushing pink. "Oh, right."

I lead her up the porch steps, unlocking the front door and holding it open for her. Once we're inside, I move immediately to check the security system, making sure everything's armed and set up the way I want it.

Aubree watches me quietly from the doorway. "Do you mind if I take a minute?" she asks, her voice softer than it's been all day.

I glance at her, meeting her gaze for just a second before nodding. "Yeah, take your time. I'll be right here if you need anything."

She steps further into the cabin, and I hear her sigh as she walks around. I don't know what she's thinking, but I'm pretty sure she's feeling the weight of everything that's happened. I can't blame her. I'm feeling it too.

Chapter 4

Aubree

The air smells different here—fresher, cleaner. Maybe it's the mountains, the distance from the city. The cabin is rustic, cozy, and quiet, and I realize I've been holding my breath ever since we arrived. It's like I've been holding on to some tension that's finally starting to settle, but it's not going anywhere fast. I glance around, taking in the wooden beams of the ceiling, the soft glow of the overhead lights, the mismatched furniture that gives the place a lived-in, homey feel.

I pace around the cabin, feeling a little bit lost in the space. The windows are huge, looking out into the trees, the darkness pressing in from all sides. Everything feels so... still, and I'm not sure if that's comforting or unsettling.

I run my fingers over the old wooden table near the fireplace, tracing the smooth grain of it. I can't stop thinking about my shop. Who would want to hurt it? Why? Who's doing this to me? What do they want?

My mind races, spinning with questions I can't answer. The brick through the window, the note, the endless emails. It wasn't just a random act of violence—it's personal. That much is clear. And I can't figure out who would have any reason to target *me*. I don't have enemies. I'm just a pizza shop owner.

I shake my head, trying to push the dark thoughts away. I'm so tired—physically, emotionally, all of it. I feel like I've been running on fumes for days, barely keeping my head above water.

The sound of boots on the wooden steps pulls me from my thoughts. Boone appears in the doorway, his face set in that unreadable expression, eyes scanning the space behind me.

"All secure," he says, his voice rough like it's been carved from stone.

I nod, trying to hide my unease. "Good. Thanks for... well, everything."

He shrugs, not the kind of guy who accepts praise too easily. "It's my job." He crosses the room, his steps heavy and deliberate, like everything he does has a purpose. His presence is larger than the room itself, and the tension in my chest tightens a little more just being near him.

"Hungry?" Boone's voice breaks the silence, his eyes scanning the space before landing on me. His tone is casual, but there's something behind it—something that tells me he's trying to make things feel normal. Or maybe he's trying to give me a distraction. Either way, I appreciate it.

"I guess... a little," I say, shrugging. "You got something quick?"

Boone gives me a small grin, the first one I've seen since I met him, and it's almost enough to make me forget about everything else for a second. "I'll figure something out. You just sit tight."

I sit down on the couch, trying to get comfortable in the quiet. Trying to understand why this is all happening to me. I wish I could call my mother. However, Boone took my phone for 'safety purposes.'

Why is this happening to me? The shop was my place, my pride, my hard work. And now I'm stuck in a cabin with a bodyguard, waiting for whoever is out there to make their next move.

I look up to find Boone standing in the kitchen, pulling out some cans from the pantry, looking like he could survive on just whatever was in this cabin for weeks. He moves with purpose, unbothered by the idea of making a meal out of whatever he can scrounge up. However, I see fresh bread on the counter, so I'm sure he's stocked this place up before we arrived.

He glances at me, catching my eye. "You sure you're all right?" His voice is softer now, but it still carries that undercurrent of seriousness. I wonder if he's asking because he feels obligated or because he actually cares, and I don't know which answer scares me more.

"I'm fine," I lie, offering him a small smile. "Just... not really sure what's going on. But I'm fine."

Boone doesn't respond, just nods like he's heard this before and moves on to the next task. The sound of the can opener cutting through the air is oddly comforting. I lean back, letting myself close my eyes for just a second. But the second turns into minutes, and the minutes stretch on, dragging me into the exhaustion I've been avoiding all day.

"Food's almost ready," Boone calls over his shoulder.

"Thanks," I reply, my voice heavy with fatigue. My eyes flutter open, and I catch a glimpse of Boone working in the kitchen, his back turned to me. There's a kind of quiet assurance in the way he moves. Like he's not worried about much.

And maybe I should take a note from that.

I rise from the couch, stretching my sore muscles. "How did you get into security work?" I ask, wanting something—anything—to break the tension.

He glances at me, his lips twitching just slightly. "I grew up in a rough neighborhood. Figured it was better to protect people than get hurt trying to protect myself."

I nod slowly, trying to picture it. "That sounds... intense."

"It was. But it's what I know. Then I joined the Marines, and learned how to really protect people. So, it's what I'm good at."

I watch him for a moment, his eyes focused on the stove as he stirs something in a pan. There's a vulnerability there, hidden beneath his tough exterior, and it catches me off guard.

"So, what about you?" He turns slightly. "How'd you end up running a pizza place in the middle of nowhere?"

I laugh softly, shaking my head. "It's not *nowhere*, it's Tennessee. And, well, my mom had the idea. I just made it happen."

"Your mom," he repeats thoughtfully. "She must be proud of you."

I smile, though it feels a little forced. "She's proud... and worried. And a little overbearing."

Boone chuckles under his breath, the sound surprising me. I didn't think he'd be the type to laugh. "Sounds like she cares a lot."

"She does," I agree, feeling the warmth of the moment for a brief second. "She just doesn't get how important this shop is to me. It's more than a business... it's my life."

His brown eyes soften as he looks at me, and then he turns back to the stove. "I get it. Everyone's gotta have something they're willing to fight for."

It's quiet again, but this time, it feels... easier. Maybe it's because we're both talking, really talking, and not just doing our jobs. I almost want to ask him if he has something worth fighting for, but I keep my mouth snapped shut.

For the first time tonight, I think maybe I'll be okay.

Chapter 5

Boone

Dinner is simple—canned soup, crackers, and whatever else I could scrounge together from the pantry. It's not much, but I'm not about to win any culinary awards. Aubree picks at her food, eating just enough to keep from being rude, but I can tell she's not exactly hungry. She's got too much on her mind, and I get it. I've been doing this long enough to recognize the signs of someone pretending they're fine when they're really not.

She's pretty, though. That's the first thing I notice. I'd be lying if I said I didn't think it when I first saw her. But sitting across from her now, watching her auburn hair fall around her face in soft waves, the way her eyes flicker with everything she's thinking—well, I can't help but take it in. She's got this natural beauty about her, the kind that doesn't scream for attention, but demands it all the same.

Her eyes are dark, maybe brown, but there's something else in them too. Something guarded. Maybe it's because of everything she's been through today. Or maybe it's just who she is. Her lips are full, soft, and the way she bites the edge of them when she's nervous is enough to make me forget that I'm supposed to be her protector and not... whatever else.

But I can't afford to think like that.

I force myself to focus on the task at hand. She's my responsibility right now. Nothing more.

"So, what's the plan tomorrow?" she asks, leaning back slightly in her chair, her voice soft but inquisitive.

I think about the security measures I'll need to put in place, making sure she's safe, but I don't go into the details with her. I don't want to worry her any more than she already is. "We'll keep things low-key for now. Stay here. I'll make sure the perimeter's tight, and we'll go from there."

She nods, then looks down at her bowl, like she's processing what that might mean for her future. She probably never thought her life would go from pizza shop owner to running from threats and hiding in a cabin with a bodyguard. It's a hell of a transition, and I wish I could tell her it's going to be over soon. But I don't know that.

After dinner, I clear the dishes and place them in the sink, watching her quietly as she picks at the last few pieces of food. She's exhausted, I can see that much.

I pause for a second, then decide to keep it simple. "I'll show you to your room. It's right down the hall."

She looks up at me, a hint of relief in her eyes. "Thanks."

I lead her down the short hallway, opening the door to a modest guest room. A single bed, a small dresser, a few landscaping photos on the wall. Nothing fancy, but it's comfortable.

"The bathroom's right across the hall," I say, pointing to the door at the end of the hallway. "If you need anything, just yell. I'm right down the hall."

She smiles weakly, her shoulders sagging. "Thanks, Boone." Her voice is quieter now, like she's trying to reassure herself as much as me.

I give her a small nod, then back out of the room. "I'll leave you to it. Get some rest."

I close the door behind me, my footsteps echoing softly down the hallway as I return to my own room. I need sleep too, and it's been a long day.

I get ready for bed, my mind racing. It's hard to ignore the way she looked at me earlier, that quiet vulnerability in her eyes. It's hard to ignore the way I felt when I saw her sitting there at dinner, looking so damn beautiful despite the chaos around her. But I push all that aside, reminding myself that my job isn't to get involved. It's to protect her.

I lie down on the bed, my eyes closing as I try to drift off, but the quiet of the cabin is louder than I expect. My thoughts circle around, replaying every moment from the past few hours. I tell myself I'm just doing my job. Nothing more.

But somewhere in the middle of the night, I'm pulled from sleep by the softest sound—a creak of the floorboards, a faint rustling. I sit up quickly, instincts kicking in, but then I hear it. Her voice, low and almost hesitant.

"Boone?"

I freeze, my heart hammering in my chest. The door to my room slowly creaks open, and there she is. Aubree. Standing there, her expression torn, unsure. She's dressed in a loose T-shirt and sweatpants, her hair falling in messy waves around her shoulders.

Guarding What's Mine

"I... I'm sorry," she whispers, biting her lip. "I just... I don't know why, but I couldn't sleep. I feel safer here. With you."

She looks vulnerable—smaller, more fragile than she did earlier in the evening. The soft glow of moonlight coming through the window catches the curve of her cheek, and I realize I've been holding my breath.

I don't know what to say at first. There's a part of me that wants to tell her everything will be okay, but I'm not sure that's the truth. I'm not sure about anything right now.

"Come here," I finally say, my voice softer than I intend. "It's all right."

She steps into the room, hesitating only for a second before sitting on the edge of my bed, her hands clutching the hem of her T-shirt. I move over, making space for her, trying to keep it casual. But even I know that nothing about this is casual. Nothing about this is easy.

She's just scared. That's all this is.

I'm just here to protect her.

She shifts a little, inching closer, until she's lying next to me, her head resting on the pillow. I can feel her warmth next to me, her breathing steady and even. I try not to think about how she smells—how soft her skin looks in the dim light.

For a moment, everything's still. I can hear the wind rustling outside, the distant sounds of the night. And for the first time in hours, I finally feel like I can breathe.

She shifts again, pulling the covers up around her, her hand brushing against mine.

"Thanks," she murmurs, the words barely audible, and I nod in the dark, my heart still racing. "I feel better."

I don't know how to respond. So I don't. Instead, I stay as still as I can, trying to ignore the fact that she's lying next to me, trusting me in a way that feels... wrong. But at the same time, it feels right.

The air is thick with tension, and I can feel her warmth seeping into me. I'm here to do my job, and that's all. But for now, I'll let her sleep. Let her feel safe, at least for one night.

Tomorrow is another day.

Chapter 6

Aubree

I wake up with a jolt, disoriented for a moment, not sure where I am. The softness of the sheets beneath me is the first thing I notice, the warmth of the bed, the faint smell of wood and pine in the air. I blink a few times, trying to clear the sleep from my eyes, and then it hits me—I'm in Boone's bed. I sit up slowly, the sheets rustling around me as I take in my surroundings. The room is quiet, still. The sunlight streams through the window, casting long shadows across the floor. The silence feels peaceful, but also oddly heavy, like something's about to shift.

Boone. He's not here.

My heart beats a little faster at the thought of him. But I shake it off. I don't know why I should care about where he is. He's just my bodyguard, here to do a job. Nothing more.

I pull myself out of bed, stretching my limbs, and head to the bathroom. The cold tile beneath my feet is a sharp contrast to the warm bed, and I welcome the brief shiver. I wash my face quickly, then run my fingers through my hair, trying to make myself presentable. My reflection stares back at me—eyes still a little puffy, face flushed from sleeping.

I take a deep breath. Time to face the day.

I step back into the bedroom, pulling on my hoodie and some sweatpants. I don't feel like being glamorous today. I just need to get through the next few hours without completely falling apart.

I open the door to the hallway and step into the living room, but the house is quiet. Too quiet. I glance around, but Boone's not inside. I walk toward the front door, the sound of the wind rustling through the trees outside drifting through the cracks of the cabin.

And then I hear it.

The rhythmic sound of an axe chopping into wood. The noise is sharp, steady, the impact of each swing echoing against the trees. Curiosity pulls me forward, and before I even realize it, I'm stepping outside, the cold air hitting me immediately.

I stop short when I see him.

Boone's standing out there, by the woodpile, chopping firewood. But it's not just the chopping that catches my attention—it's the way he looks while doing it. His broad shoulders flex with each swing, the muscles in his back rippling beneath his skin. His shirt is gone, his tanned bare skin glistening in the morning light as beads of sweat dot his skin despite the cool air. The sun hits him just right, outlining the defined lines of his body. His chest is broad and sculpted, the tattoo on his arm and neck taking center stage. *Wow.*

Guarding What's Mine

I can't help but stare.

I watch him work, my breath caught in my throat. I've been out of the dating game for a long time, not that I ever had much of a chance to date. My ex, Dustin, was... well, he was nothing like Boone. Dustin was scrawny, quiet, and predictable. Nothing about him made my heart race, nothing about him made me feel like my whole body was alive. But Boone? Everything about him is different. From the way he stands to the way he moves. Even the way he holds the axe seems like it's effortlessly masculine.

I swallow, my heart pounding in my chest. *What am I doing?*

I remind myself to look away, but my gaze flicks back to him again. It's almost like I can't stop myself. His movements are so fluid, so purposeful, and I feel something stir inside me that I haven't felt in... well, forever.

I can't remember the last time I felt attracted to someone. Really attracted. Dustin didn't stir anything in me like this, and after everything, I never thought I'd feel that kind of pull again.

But with Boone, it's different.

I'm still standing here, rooted to the spot, when he looks up and catches me watching. His eyes meet mine across the distance, and for a second, everything freezes. I feel the heat rush to my cheeks, and I know I'm blushing.

Great. Just great.

But instead of looking away or giving me a hard time, Boone's lips curl into a smile. That smile. It's subtle but genuine, and for some reason, it feels like it melts all the resolve I had left.

"Morning," he calls out, his voice low and warm, carrying across the distance between us. "You need something?"

I force myself to move, walking toward him, trying to act like I'm not affected by what I just saw. "Uh... no, I was just... you know, enjoying the view."

Boone chuckles, a rich, deep sound that makes my pulse quicken. "You want breakfast?"

Breakfast. Right.

I look at him, still trying to regain my bearings. "I guess. But, uh, only if you're making it."

His smile widens as he leans on the axe, his eyes gleaming with something playful. "Well, now I'm obligated. I'm a pretty damn good cook."

I laugh, though it's a little shaky. "We'll see about that."

His grin doesn't fade, and I catch myself smiling back before I can stop it. There's something about him that feels... easy, even though everything inside me is anything but. The tension I've been carrying with me starts to loosen just a little bit.

"Come on inside then, I'll get something together," he says, nodding toward the door behind me.

I follow him back inside, and as I walk past him, I can't help but notice how his muscles shift under his skin, how his presence fills the space. He's breathtaking.

As we step into the warmth of the cabin, I remind myself again: he's my bodyguard. Nothing more.

But that doesn't stop my heart from racing just a little faster.

Chapter 7

Boone

I get to work on breakfast while Aubree sits at the kitchen table, her hands wrapped around a mug of coffee, staring out the window. The silence between us is comfortable, but there's something a little too quiet about it. I've learned over the years that sometimes it's best to let the quiet linger, to let the tension settle before you break it.

I pull a few eggs from the fridge, crack them into a bowl, and start whisking. It's nothing fancy, just scrambled eggs and toast, but it's enough to get the day started right. I move with precision, my mind wandering a little. I'm used to solitude, but there's something about having Aubree here that's different. It's not uncomfortable—far from it—but it's unfamiliar, and I can't quite shake the feeling that she's watching me, even though I'm focused on the stove.

"You know," I say as I season the eggs, "I've cooked for myself a thousand times, but never like this. Never for someone else."

She looks up from her coffee, her eyes meeting mine for a brief moment before she quickly looks back down. "I don't expect you to be some kind of gourmet chef or anything. I'm just happy you're feeding me."

I chuckle at that, a grin tugging at the corner of my mouth. "Gourmet, huh? That's setting the bar pretty high."

"Well, knowing my mother she'd hire a bodyguard with high standards," she teases, her voice light and easy. It's the first time I've heard her sound genuinely relaxed since I met her. It's nice to see her like this, even if just for a moment.

I slide the eggs onto a plate and toast the bread, flipping the toast with a quick flick of my wrist. I pour two glasses of orange juice, setting them on the table beside her. "Here you go, gourmet breakfast." I place the plate in front of her, taking a seat across from her as I grab my own plate.

She picks up a fork and takes a bite of the eggs, chewing thoughtfully. "Okay, I'll admit. Not bad. I mean, considering you're a security guy and not a professional cook."

I laugh, the sound coming out easier than I expect. "I guess I have a few hidden talents."

She raises an eyebrow. "I'm sure. You seem like the type who can handle anything."

I shrug, not one to brag. "Just doing my job. That's what matters."

For a while, we eat in silence, the clink of our forks on the plates the only sound. The food is simple, but it's the most relaxed I've felt in days. There's something about her, something easy and real. It's different from the usual tension that comes with guarding someone, but I can't put my finger on why.

"So, tell me something about you," she says after a while, breaking the silence. She looks at me over her cup of coffee, her eyes wide with curiosity. "Where are you from? You don't strike me as a small-town kind of guy."

I set my fork down, leaning back in my chair. I know she's just making small talk, but it's a fair question. "I'm from a place called Pine Ridge. Small town, just like this one, actually. But I left when I was eighteen, joined the Marines. Spent a lot of time overseas."

Her eyes widen slightly, and I can tell she's interested. "Tell me more about the Marines."

"Yeah?" I ask, pushing my plate aside. "I was a Marine Raider for a few years. That was... well, it was intense. A lot of traveling, a lot of danger. But it shaped me. Taught me what I wanted to do with my life. I left when I got tired of fighting, you know? But being a Marine gave me the skills I use now. The discipline, the focus. It's all part of it."

She's quiet for a moment, processing that, before she asks, "What was it like?"

"Hard. Really hard," I say, my voice quieting slightly as I think back to those days. "But it was worth it. It taught me how to handle pressure, how to think on my feet. I've been through some shit, but I wouldn't change it."

She nods slowly, her gaze thoughtful. "I bet. Sounds like it was life-changing."

"It was," I admit. "And that's why I do what I do now. I protect people. Make sure they stay safe. It's what I'm good at."

She's quiet for a long time, her fingers tracing the rim of her coffee cup. "I can see that," she says softly. Then, after a pause, she adds, "I don't know if I'm cut out for something like that. My life's... simpler."

"Sometimes simple's all you need," I reply, keeping my tone easy, though a part of me wonders what she means by that. What's her life been like?

She seems to sense my curiosity. "I don't have a lot of friends," she says, looking down at her hands. "My mom's really the only person I can count on. She's kind of my best friend. I've always been kind of a loner."

I can't help but raise an eyebrow. "Your mom?"

She looks up, a small smile on her lips. "Yeah. She's been there for me through everything. She's the one who convinced me to open the pizza shop. I guess that's part of why it means so much to me. I don't know... I don't really let other people in."

I lean back in my chair, the weight of her words hitting me harder than I expected. "That's not a bad thing. You don't have to let everyone in."

She looks at me, the faintest hint of a smile tugging at her lips. "You don't let anyone in either, do you?"

I smile, but there's no humor in it. "Guess you could say that. I'm not really the sharing type."

She laughs softly. "I can tell."

I look down at my watch and check the time, realizing it's getting late. "We should head to town. We're running low on supplies. Let's get you some things for the cabin."

She nods and stands up, stretching. "You're right. I need to pick up a few things myself."

I walk to the door, holding it open for her as she heads out. "All right, let's go then."

The drive to the store is quiet, but it's not uncomfortable. She's sitting beside me, her presence a calm, steady force in the truck. I steal a quick glance at her as I drive, noticing how she's humming along to the radio, the smallest hint of a smile on her face. It's a good look on her.

We get to the store, and as we walk inside, I'm acutely aware of her beside me. There's something about her that's easy to be around, and I'm not sure what to do with that. But for now, it's enough.

Chapter 8

Aubree

The air smells fresh as we walk into the store, the crisp scent of pine trees and the faint whiff of something sugary from the bakery section. I can't help but feel a little out of place, like I'm a world away from my pizza shop in Nashville, surrounded by the calm and stillness of Boone's cabin. But here I am, wandering the aisles with Boone in tow, looking for whatever supplies we'll need to get through the next few days. It's a strange feeling, this mix of tension and peace, and I'm not sure how to process it all.

We're standing in the canned goods aisle when I spot him—a familiar face I didn't expect to see here. Hank.

I freeze for a moment, staring at him as he pushes his cart down the aisle. He's one of the regulars at the pizza shop—always orders the same thing: a large meat lover's pizza, extra cheese. He's the kind of guy who doesn't say much but likes to linger at the counter, always asking me how the shop is doing, offering unsolicited advice about how I should "run the place better." He's a handyman from town, a big guy with a thick beard and arms that look like they could lift anything. But there's something about seeing him here, so far from Nashville, that makes the hairs on the back of my neck stand up.

"Hank?" I call out hesitantly, stepping toward him.

He looks up, his eyes lighting up with recognition. "Well, if it isn't the famous pizza lady. What're you doing all the way out here, Aubree?"

I try to smile, but there's an odd feeling in my chest. Something feels... off. Boone's right beside me, puffing his chest out with one glance at Hank. "Just picking up some supplies."

Hank's face softens with that knowing look. "I heard you closed the shop for a few weeks. You doin' okay?"

I nod, though I'm not entirely sure if I should be telling him anything about what happened. It's not like we're close, and I don't need the whole town buzzing about me being followed around by security. "I'm fine. Just... need a break, I guess."

He gives me a slow nod, looking me over like he's not convinced. "Well, if you need anything fixed, you know where to find me. I'm always around, even if you don't see me much. Got a lot of projects I'm working on."

I'm about to answer when I feel a shift in the air beside me. Boone's body is tense, and his eyes are scanning Hank like he's trying to figure out what exactly Hank is doing here. I can see Boone's hand inching toward his jacket, the subtle shift of his posture telling me he's on high alert.

"Who's he?" Hank asks, turning his attention to Boone for the first time. He doesn't seem to notice the way Boone's eyes narrow.

I glance at Boone, and he shoots me a quick look. "I'm her boyfriend." His voice is casual, but there's something in the way he says it that makes Hank straighten up, just a little.

Hank chuckles, clearly unaware of the underlying tension. "I didn't realize Aubree had a man. That's cool. I'm just picking up a few things for the house. You know, I live a couple miles outside of Nashville, but I come in here when I need to grab supplies. You know how it is."

I nod, though I can't shake the feeling that something about this is... strange. Hank is a regular at the pizza shop, so it's not like I haven't seen him before. It's weird to think of him being this far out, but maybe he likes this place.

"Well, it was nice to run into you, Hank," I say, my voice sounding a little too high-pitched even to me. "I should get going."

Boone steps forward, just a little too close, and places a hand lightly on my shoulder, his body shielding mine from Hank's gaze. "We're in a bit of a hurry," he says, his tone not quite friendly. "Have a good day."

Hank raises his eyebrows, but he doesn't press. "Sure thing. Take care, Aubree."

We make our way out of the aisle quickly, Boone walking just a touch ahead of me, the tension rolling off him in waves. I feel the sudden urge to ask him what's going on, but I hold my tongue. We reach the checkout counter, and as we start loading up the items, I glance at Boone, his jaw tight, his eyes cold. He doesn't look at me, but I can tell he's deep in thought.

He told Hank he was my boyfriend, and honestly, I'm not mad about that. In fact, I give myself permission to imagine what it would be like to really be his. I can't stop the goofy smile on my face, and once we're outside, I bring myself back to reality.

When we're loading the bags into the truck, Boone finally speaks. His voice is low, deliberate. "You know him well?"

I nod, unsure how to answer. "Hank's a regular at the pizza shop. He's done some work for some of the other places in town. I don't really know him all that well, though. He's just a local handyman."

Boone doesn't look convinced. "Something's off. What's he doing this far from Nashville?"

I swallow, feeling the knot tighten in my stomach. "I don't know. Maybe he just likes shopping at this place." I gesture to the store that's a good hour from Nashville.

Boone's eyes narrow, and I can see the wheels turning in his head. "I'll have Dean run a check on him. Got a last name for Mr. Handyman?"

I nod, unsure what to think of the situation. "Arnold."

"I didn't like the way he was looking at you," Boone says, his tone firm. "Stay alert, Aubree. I don't trust anyone right now."

His words settle in my chest like a stone. The uneasy feeling I had when I first saw Hank resurfaces, and I can't shake it. Something isn't right, and I don't know how to make sense of it. But I'll keep my eyes open, just like Boone says. Maybe it's nothing. Maybe it's everything. Either way, I'm not taking any chances.

As we drive back to the cabin, the weight of Boone's words lingers in the air, thick with unspoken concern. I don't know who to trust anymore, but I know one thing for sure: I'm not going to ignore anything that feels wrong.

Chapter 9

Boone

I step outside onto the porch, taking a deep breath of the cool mountain air, feeling it fill my lungs. The silence around me is heavy, the only sound being the rustling of the trees. I pull my phone from my jacket pocket, swiping the screen and calling Dean. As I wait for him to pick up, I glance back at the cabin, noticing how peaceful it looks in the early afternoon light. I should be focused on keeping her safe, but there's something about the quiet here that makes my mind drift.

"Porter," Dean's voice crackles through the phone, cutting through my thoughts.

"Hey, it's me. I need you to run a background check on someone." My tone is steady, but there's a slight edge to it. Something doesn't sit right with me about today's encounter with Hank.

"Who's the target?" Dean asks, and I can almost hear him tapping away on his computer, already pulling up the information.

"Hank Arnold. Local handyman in Nashville. I ran into him earlier today at the store. He's a local at Aubree's shop. Just something about him didn't sit right."

Dean's voice shifts, the usual professionalism giving way to curiosity. "All right, I'll check him out. Give me a minute."

I hang up and stare out at the trees, thinking back to the tension I felt when Hank approached us in the store. There was something in the way he spoke, like he was too comfortable with Aubree, too familiar. Maybe I'm overthinking it, but I don't trust people easily. Especially not with her.

I stay outside for a while, giving Dean the time to pull up the report. The wind rustles through the pine trees, carrying the scent of the forest and something faintly sharp, like fresh mountain air. My mind drifts back to Aubree. It's hard to not think about her when she's always just a few steps away. She's a lot more than I expected—smarter, sharper, and definitely tougher. But there's this vulnerability about her, something raw that she doesn't let many people see. I know, because I've caught glimpses of it.

The phone vibrates in my pocket, and I pull it out, seeing Dean's name pop up.

"All right, here's what I've got," Dean says. "Hank Arnold—he's clean on the surface. No criminal record. Works in Nashville, been doing handyman stuff for years. But I dug a little deeper on your other guy."

I frown, wondering who Dean means. "What other guy?"

"Stuart, the kid who works at her pizza shop. He's got a couple of priors—petty theft, shoplifting, nothing major, but enough to be flagged. Just thought you should know."

My frown deepens. Stuart never struck me as the type, but it doesn't surprise me. People aren't always who they appear to be. "Thanks, Dean. Keep me posted on anything else with Hank."

"Will do."

I hang up and put my phone back in my pocket, my gaze flicking back toward the cabin. I'm not sure what to make of Stuart's past. It's not a huge deal, but it's something to keep in mind. Dean will have to keep an eye on him while we're here. As for Hank, I still don't like the guy. There's something off about him. But for now, I've got to focus on what's in front of me.

I head back inside, pushing open the door and stepping into the warm, cozy cabin. The quiet is welcoming, the familiar smell of pine and wood filling the air. My eyes immediately find her.

Aubree's standing at the counter, an old radio propped up on the edge. The music is blaring, and her hips sway in time with the beat, a carefree rhythm that makes my chest tighten in a way I don't expect. She's smiling as she hums along, her voice soft and off-key, but it's... charming. She's laughing at something, probably her own ridiculousness, and I can't help but watch.

I lean against the doorframe, just taking her in. She's dancing like she doesn't have a care in the world, like the weight of the threats and the unknowns doesn't matter. I catch a glimpse of her eyes, sparkling as she spins around, and for a brief second, it's like the whole world stops moving. I shouldn't be standing

Guarding What's Mine

here, shouldn't be letting myself feel this way, but there's something magnetic about her. She's magnetic.

I think back to earlier, when I casually called myself her "boyfriend." The word slipped out before I could stop it, and I couldn't help the strange satisfaction I felt when I said it. And even now, watching her dance, I realize there's something else behind it. Maybe it was the way she looked at me, like I was something more than just a hired gun. Maybe it was the way she made me feel like I was actually *doing* something—like I wasn't just standing on the sidelines, watching life happen.

I never thought I'd care about pretending to be someone's boyfriend. Hell, I never thought I'd want to be anyone's boyfriend. But being hers, even if it's just for the sake of keeping her safe... well, it didn't feel bad. It felt right. And as I stand here, watching her, a laugh escaping her lips, I realize I like it more than I should.

She twirls in place, her hair flowing around her face like something out of a movie. The movement catches me off guard, and for a second, I'm lost in the way she moves, the way she holds herself. There's a grace to her, even in the small things. Her hands are quick and sure as she puts groceries away, but there's an ease about it all, like she's comfortable in her own skin.

Her eyes flicker toward me, and our gazes lock. She falters for just a moment, her smile fading as she realizes I'm watching. But then she recovers, offering me a sheepish grin.

"Caught me, huh?" she says, holding up a jar of pickles as if it's a microphone.

I chuckle, pushing myself off the doorframe. "I didn't realize I was interrupting a performance."

She laughs, shaking her head, and I can't help but smile at how carefree she looks, how unburdened, even with everything going on. It's like watching someone forget their worries for just a moment, and I can't help but wish I could do the same.

"Well, thank you, Mr. Bodyguard. I didn't know you were such a fan," she teases, her eyes twinkling with amusement.

"I'm a fan of a lot of things," I say, my voice low, trying to keep it casual, even though I'm not sure I'm succeeding. "You just haven't seen the half of it yet."

She raises an eyebrow, clearly amused. "You've got moves, huh?"

I laugh. "I've got a few. But you... you've definitely got something I didn't expect."

She gives me a quick wink before spinning around, moving like she owns the space. There's a natural confidence to her that I didn't expect. Aubree isn't just tough, she's got a warmth to her that I didn't know I needed until I saw it. And now, it's hard not to want more of it.

She pauses, looking back at me with a playful grin. "All right, all right. Enough dancing. I'm sure you're tired of watching me make a fool of myself."

"Not a chance," I reply, moving toward her. "You keep going. I'm enjoying the show."

She rolls her eyes but doesn't stop moving. For the first time in a while, I feel like I'm exactly where I'm supposed to be.

Chapter 10

Aubree

The day has been quieter than I expected. After running errands and dealing with the tension I felt after seeing Hank, Boone and I settled into an unexpected rhythm. He's been more laid-back than usual, the occasional joke escaping his lips when I least expect it. And for the first time in hours, I feel like I can breathe.

But there's something I want to do. Something normal. I want to make him a pizza.

I glance over at Boone, who's lounging on the couch, flipping through a magazine—probably trying to figure out the best way to keep an eye on me without making it too obvious. I have a feeling he's not the type to just kick back and relax. He's the kind of guy who thrives on action, which makes me even more determined to do something fun, something that has nothing to do with threats or bodyguard duties.

"You know," I say, looking over at him with a grin, "I think it's time you learned how to make a pizza."

Boone raises an eyebrow, his lips quirking up slightly as he sets the magazine down. "I'm sorry, what? You want me to *make* a pizza?"

I cross my arms and lean against the counter, trying to keep a straight face. "Yes. You're going to learn the art of pizza-making. Trust me, you won't regret it."

He stands up slowly, his hands on his hips as he gives me an incredulous look. "Are you telling me that *I*—the guy who can bench press a truck—am supposed to learn how to make pizza from you?"

I can't help but laugh. "Yes, exactly. You've got muscles, but you've got to have pizza skills too. It's a balanced diet."

Boone looks at me for a long second before shrugging dramatically. "Well, if it means I get to eat it, I'm in."

"Great!" I say, pulling out the ingredients from the fridge. "First things first. The dough. You have to get the right kind. You can't just slap a frozen pizza crust on a pan and call it a day."

He chuckles. "I'm pretty sure that's what my mom did every Friday when I was a kid."

"See? That's where you went wrong," I tease. "That's why I'm here. We're doing this the right way."

Boone watches as I start to roll out the dough, trying to keep it even, though I'm admittedly not the best at it. It's definitely a bit thicker than I want it to be, but he doesn't seem to mind. He leans over the counter, eyeing me as I work.

"You look like you're trying to create a pizza masterpiece," he says with a grin. "If this goes wrong, I'm going to hold you responsible."

"Oh, it won't go wrong," I assure him. "Trust me, I've been making pizza for years. This is my thing. I know pizza like the back of my hand."

He raises his eyebrows, clearly impressed. "So you're saying you're a pizza expert?"

I tilt my head, smiling. "Well, I wouldn't call it 'expert,' but I'm pretty good at it. My mother always said I had the best pizza-making skills in the family."

Boone looks at me skeptically. "I think your mom might be biased."

I laugh. "Maybe. But you'll see. I'm about to blow your mind with this pie."

I start spreading sauce onto the dough, carefully smoothing it out with the back of a spoon. I grab some shredded cheese and pile it on, then hand him a piece of pepperoni.

"Alright, Boone, now you're in charge of topping the pizza. Don't get crazy with it, just... use your instincts."

He picks up a slice of pepperoni and holds it up like it's a piece of fine art. "Is this how it's done? With *artistic flair?*" He places one slice of pepperoni delicately in the center of the dough, giving me a look of pride.

I can't help but laugh. "Okay, not *that* artistic. Maybe just a little less... minimalistic."

He shrugs, his grin widening. "I'm just trying to make a statement with my art."

"Well, your art is a little too avant-garde for me," I joke. "Try spreading the pepperoni out a little. Maybe add some mushrooms, olives, whatever you like."

"Okay, okay," he mutters, rearranging his masterpiece like it's a crime scene. "I'll stick to the classics. But you have to promise me one thing."

"What's that?"

"When this pizza is done, we're not just eating it. We're going to pretend it's the best pizza in the world, like we're in a pizza commercial."

I burst out laughing. "Deal. But if you start dramatically holding a slice up to the camera and staring at it like it's a piece of art, I'll lose it."

He smirks and adjusts the pizza, nodding like it's a serious task. "I'm serious, Aubree. This pizza has to be memorable."

"I'm with you," I agree, my voice full of mock seriousness. "Memorable pizza is the only kind."

Once the pizza is assembled, we slide it into the oven. The smell starts to fill the cabin, and I watch as Boone leans against the counter, his arms folded.

"Where did you get your love of pizza from?" he asks, breaking the comfortable silence between us.

I think for a second, the memory hitting me like a wave. "Well, when I was younger, pizza was the go-to treat for anything. Birthdays, celebrations, lazy Sundays. My mom would order pizza whenever we had something to celebrate or just wanted to feel like we were 'doing something special.' Pizza was our thing. And it stuck."

Boone watches me, his eyes softening slightly. "Sounds like it was a big deal for you."

"Yeah, it was. It was always a moment to look forward to. Something that made everything feel normal, even when life wasn't."

He nods thoughtfully. "I get it. I used to have my own thing. When I was younger, pizza was the reward after every hard training session. It was like a tradition."

"See? Pizza is a universal language," I joke, and he chuckles, shaking his head.

The oven dings, and I pull the pizza out, setting it down on the counter. I slide a knife through the cheesy goodness and cut a slice, handing it to Boone.

"Well, you might not have been lying about your pizza skills," Boone admits, taking a bite. "This is actually really good."

I beam. "Told you."

We eat in comfortable silence for a few minutes, the pizza disappearing faster than I expected. Then Boone clears his throat, setting his slice down. He looks at me seriously, his brow furrowing slightly.

"So, when did all the attacks at your shop start?" he asks, his tone more somber than I expected.

I glance down at my plate, the smile fading from my lips. It feels like a weight on my chest now, but I take a deep breath. "It started about six months ago. At first, it was small stuff. A few things went missing. Then it escalated. Broken windows. That brick through the window yesterday was just the worst of it."

Boone's eyes narrow, his protective instinct kicking in. "And you haven't had any leads? No idea who's behind it?"

I shake my head. "Nothing. We've checked the cameras, but there's never anything conclusive. It's always just... random enough to make it hard to pin down."

He's quiet for a moment, taking another bite of pizza before asking, "How long has Stuart worked there?"

I think for a second, then respond. "Seven months. He started right after I had to let go of a couple of other guys. I figured he'd be a good fit. He's quick, and he seems like a hard worker."

I pause, suddenly feeling uneasy under Boone's watchful eyes. I look at him, furrowing my brow. "Why? Do you think Stuart could be the one doing this?"

Boone's gaze hardens for just a second before he looks back down at his plate. "I don't know. But I'll keep an eye on him. Anyone with a record—even a small one—deserves to be watched."

I swallow, feeling the weight of his words. "Okay. But I'm telling you, Stuart isn't the type. He's just... a kid. I trust him."

Boone doesn't respond, but I can tell he's still processing everything. The air feels thick now, like everything is about to change. The pizza no longer tastes as sweet.

Chapter 11

Boone

The night falls quietly over the cabin, and the soft crackle of the fire in the hearth is the only sound filling the room. Aubree and I have spent the evening in easy conversation, the tension from earlier in the day fading into something more relaxed. But as we move toward bedtime, the weight of my thoughts grows heavier.

I can't get the image of her out of my head. Her laughter, her smile, the way she looks at me when she thinks I'm not paying attention. I try to shove all of that aside, reminding myself that I'm here to do a job, and nothing more. She's my responsibility—nothing more, nothing less.

But that thought doesn't stop the way my chest tightens when I glance over at her, standing near the bathroom door, her hair falling loosely around her shoulders. There's something about the way she moves, the way she carries herself, that's slowly worming its way into my mind. It's messing with my focus, and I don't like it.

"I'm heading to bed," I say, trying to sound casual, as I head toward the bedroom.

She looks up from where she's standing and gives me a small smile, her eyes soft in the dim light. "Okay. Goodnight, Boone."

The way she says my name makes my chest feel tight. Something about it. Her voice. Her smile. It hits me in a way I didn't expect.

I swallow, forcing my thoughts away. "Goodnight, Aubree."

I start to turn, but then something unexpected happens. She hesitates, her fingers twitching nervously at her sides. My heart pounds in my chest as I watch her, wondering what she's about to say.

"Boone?" she says softly, her voice quiet in the stillness of the night. "Can I... sleep in your bed again tonight?"

My breath catches in my throat. My mind races, every part of me screaming not to say yes, not to make this any more complicated than it already is. But her shy tone, the way her eyes drop to the floor as if she's embarrassed to ask, does something to me.

"Are you sure?" I ask, even though I already know the answer. I can hear the stupid question as soon as it leaves my lips. What am I even asking? I want her to sleep in my bed. I want her close. I just... can't admit it. Not yet.

She looks up at me, a tiny blush staining her cheeks. "Yeah. I just... I feel better when I'm near you."

God, that hits me harder than it should. My chest tightens again, a foreign feeling spreading through me. It's something I can't quite name, but it's making it hard to breathe. I don't want her to feel vulnerable. I don't want her to be scared. I want to be the one who makes everything better, even if I'm just here for protection.

"Of course," I say before I can second-guess myself. "Come on."

I step aside to let her enter, my heart pounding as I watch her walk past me. She pauses at the edge of the bed, glancing at me before sitting down on the edge, her hands smoothing out the blanket. She's acting shy again, like she's not entirely sure if it's okay to be here.

I swallow hard, trying to ignore the growing ache in my chest. I strip off my shirt and throw it into a chair, turning off the lamp beside the bed. The room is dark, save for the faint moonlight spilling through the window.

She climbs into the bed beside me, her movements slow, cautious. The air between us is thick with unspoken things, things I'm not ready to acknowledge. She's lying there, her back facing me, and I can't help but notice the way the curve of her shoulders looks in the low light, the way her hair falls just perfectly over her back.

I don't want to overthink it. But I can't help it.

The bed is small enough that there's no way we're not touching, not with the way the space is designed. I can feel the warmth of her body, the heat radiating from her skin, and I try my best to keep my distance. I lie on my back, my hands pressed against the mattress as if I'm trying to hold myself together.

She shifts a little, and for a moment, I think she's going to say something. But instead, she just sighs, settling into the bed, the tension in her body slowly dissipating.

I close my eyes, my mind racing as I try to ignore the way my heart is pounding in my chest, how I'm acutely aware of her presence next to me.

"I'm glad you're here," she whispers into the darkness, her voice soft and vulnerable.

The words hit me harder than I expect. My heart clenches, and I find myself turning toward her without thinking, just needing to feel closer to her. She doesn't say anything more, but when I turn to face her, I see the faintest trace of a smile on her lips.

For a second, everything feels perfectly still. And then, before I can stop myself, I move closer, just enough to feel the warmth of her body next to mine. The bed creaks as I shift, but she doesn't pull away. Instead, she edges a little closer, until we're lying side by side, barely inches between us.

I reach out instinctively, my hand brushing against hers. My breath catches, and I can feel my pulse beating hard in my chest. This is too much. It's too much too soon. I'm supposed to be keeping her safe, nothing more. But here I am, lying next to her, my body betraying me.

"Aubree," I whisper, my voice strained. "I don't want to make you feel uncomfortable. You don't have to—"

She interrupts me with a soft sigh, turning her head just enough so that our faces are inches apart. "I'm not uncomfortable, Boone. I'm just... I feel better when you're close."

The air between us shifts, crackling with something I can't deny. I should pull away. I should be the professional here. But I don't. I can't.

Before I can stop myself, I lean in, just a little, and brush my lips against hers. It's soft, just a quick touch, but it sends a shock of heat through my body, and I feel everything inside me stir. She doesn't pull away. In fact, she inches closer, and that's when I lose it.

I kiss her again, deeper this time, my hand reaching for her waist, pulling her closer, feeling the warmth of her body pressed against mine. It's like an avalanche, this rush of desire that I'm not prepared for.

She kisses me back, her lips soft, hesitant at first, but then she relaxes into it, her hand coming to rest on my chest. Her touch is gentle, but it sparks something inside me that I've been trying to suppress.

I break the kiss, my breathing heavy, my chest rising and falling with every beat of my heart. I pull back slightly, resting my forehead against hers. I can feel the heat between us, the pull that's impossible to ignore.

"Aubree," I whisper, my voice hoarse. "I need to keep you safe. That's all I'm here for."

"I know," she replies softly, her voice barely a whisper. "But I think I'm starting to want more than that."

The words hang in the air, and for a moment, everything stops. I don't know what to say. I don't know what's happening between us, but I know one thing for sure—I can't stop it.

The bed feels smaller now, and I'm not sure how we're going to get through the night without breaking every rule I've set for myself.

Chapter 12

Aubree

I can't believe this is happening. The warmth of Boone's body against mine, the softness of his lips on mine, feels like a dream. But when he pulls away, the reality of the situation crashes down on me like a bucket of cold water.

"Aubree," Boone's voice is low, serious, and it makes my chest tighten. "We can't do this."

His words hit me harder than I expected. I blink a few times, trying to process what he's saying. "What do you mean?"

"This... kissing. Making out. It's a bad idea. We both know it."

The words sting, even though I know he's right. He's here to protect me, not to get involved with me. I can't believe I let myself think there could be anything more between us. He's a bodyguard, my bodyguard. I should have never allowed myself to go there.

I pull away from him, rolling over to my side of the bed, the space between us suddenly feeling like miles. "Right. Yeah, sorry. I shouldn't have—" I pause, taking a shaky breath. "It's just... you're right. I guess I got carried away."

He doesn't respond right away, but I can feel his presence, solid and warm next to me. But he doesn't say anything else, just lies there in the quiet with me. I'm not sure what I expected, but it certainly wasn't this... awkward silence. I'm mortified, honestly. Why did I think I could start something with him? He's here to keep me safe, nothing more.

I close my eyes, forcing the thoughts to quiet down. I can't dwell on this now. I just need to sleep. And I do, even though my mind is still spinning.

THE MORNING LIGHT is soft when I wake up, and the first thing I feel is the distance. I can't stop thinking about what happened last night. I roll over and see Boone still asleep beside me. His face is relaxed, his breathing steady. But I can't look at him the same way now. I'm embarrassed, and I hate myself for thinking there could be anything more than this. I should've known better.

I quietly slip out of bed, careful not to wake him. The cold air of the room brushes against my skin, and I grab my sweatshirt, pulling it over my head. I tie my shoes quickly, feeling the weight of the awkwardness settle around me.

When Boone stirs behind me, I head for the door without saying a word, heading for the porch. I need to clear my head. I need to get out of here, even if it's just for a short run.

I step outside, the crisp morning air biting at my skin, and I start jogging down the gravel road. My feet hit the ground in rhythm, each step pushing me further away from the mess of last night. I'm moving faster now, the cold wind against my face helping to clear my mind, but my thoughts keep swirling back to Boone.

Suddenly, I hear the sound of footsteps behind me. I glance over my shoulder, and there he is—Boone, moving quickly, chasing after me. I speed up, trying to put distance between us, but he's not slowing down.

"Aubree!" he calls out, his voice carrying over the wind. "Where are you going?"

I don't want to stop. I don't want to talk to him, especially not now. I push myself harder, my legs burning as I run faster, trying to outpace him. I know I can't keep this up forever, but right now, I just want some space. I need to clear my head.

He catches up to me quickly, his longer legs eating up the distance, and soon enough, he's beside me. He's not even breathing hard, like he's done this a million times.

"You planning on running me into the ground?" he asks, his voice teasing but with that edge of concern I can never seem to shake.

I don't look at him, just focus on the road ahead. "I'm fine," I mutter, pushing myself harder.

"Aubree," he says again, his voice softer this time. "What's going on? We need to talk about last night."

I don't want to talk about last night. I don't want to deal with the embarrassment of it. "I don't want to talk about it, Boone," I snap, my frustration building. "I just need some space."

He slows down a bit, but his presence is still there, right beside me. "I just want to make sure you're okay."

Guarding What's Mine

I bite my lip, the anger and embarrassment mixing into a strange knot in my stomach. I can't look at him right now. I can't even think straight.

"I'm fine," I say again, my voice barely above a whisper. "I just need to be alone for a little while. Okay?"

He looks at me for a second, his jaw tightening like he's about to argue, but then he just nods. "Alright. But I'm not going anywhere. I'm right here if you need me."

I keep running, not slowing down. I don't want him to follow me, but I know he will. I'm not sure how I feel about it, but right now, I just need the distance. I need to run. To think.

I push harder, faster, trying to outrun the feelings I can't seem to shake.

Chapter 13

Boone

I sit on the couch in the cabin, the weight of the silence pressing in on me. Aubree's run this morning has thrown me off more than I'd like to admit. I can't stop thinking about her, about last night, about how everything is starting to feel... complicated. It was supposed to be simple. I was supposed to protect her, keep her safe. That was it. No emotions. No attachments.

But the more time I spend with her, the harder it becomes to follow that rule.

I pull my phone out, needing to focus on something else. I dial Dean's number, trying to push away the thoughts of Aubree and last night's kiss. I need to check in, see where the investigation stands.

"Porter," Dean answers, his voice low and steady.

"How's the investigation going?" I ask, trying to keep my voice casual, even though I'm itching to hear something useful.

"Nothing concrete yet," Dean replies. "Everyone's turning up clean. No criminal records, no shady connections, except for what I found on Stuart. We've looked into the usual suspects and then some, but so far, there's nothing that leads us anywhere. The guy you asked about—Hank—he's clean too, but it's not like we didn't expect that."

I lean back against the couch, rubbing a hand over my jaw. "Yeah, I figured as much. But you still need to check out every angle. Just because someone doesn't have a record doesn't mean they're not involved."

"I hear you," Dean says. "We're following up on a couple of things, but right now, nothing's connecting."

I'm quiet for a moment, processing the information. Nothing. Nothing at all. It's frustrating. But I know how these things go. Sometimes it takes time, and sometimes the right lead doesn't show up until you least expect it.

"Yeah, well, keep digging," I finally say. "By the way, I did a little more digging on Aubree. She fired a few guys at the shop before Stuart was hired. Says she didn't feel like they were the right fit, but it could be relevant. I'll keep an eye on Stuart for now. Just be aware of the timing."

Dean's voice softens a little. "Understood. You're doing good, Boone. Keep me posted on anything new."

"Will do," I mutter, hanging up the phone.

I sit there for a moment, lost in thought. I can't shake the feeling that there's something we're missing. Aubree's been through so much, and every time I think we're getting closer to figuring this out, I hit another dead end. But it's not just the case that's been consuming my mind lately. It's her. It's always been her, even if I refuse to admit it.

The sound of the water turning off in the bathroom pulls me from my thoughts, and my heart skips a beat. I glance toward the bathroom door, my mind immediately racing with the idea of her stepping out, fresh from the shower.

I stand up, walking toward the window to distract myself, but it's no use. I can still hear the faint sound of her movements, the soft rustling of the towel, the sound of her steps.

The door opens, and then she steps out.

I freeze. My breath catches in my throat. Aubree's standing there, a towel wrapped around her body, droplets of water still clinging to her skin. Her hair is damp, curling slightly around her shoulders, and I can't stop myself from staring at the way the towel hugs her curves.

I swallow hard, trying to force the thoughts away. My body reacts instantly—every inch of me aching to pull her close, to touch her, to feel her skin against mine again. But I stay still, fighting every instinct telling me to move.

She doesn't seem to notice me standing there at first, focused on drying her hair with another towel. I stand in the doorway, my hands clenched into fists at my sides, trying to keep control of the thoughts that are flooding my mind.

"Boone?" Aubree's voice breaks through the haze of my thoughts, and I quickly snap my gaze back to her face.

"Yeah?" I force the word out, my voice rougher than I intended.

She raises an eyebrow, giving me a curious look. "You okay?"

I nod, quickly turning away, trying to calm the storm that's building inside me. "Yeah, just—just checking in. Everything okay?"

She smirks slightly, tossing the towel over her shoulder. "Fine. Just taking a shower."

I nod again, but my body is still tense, every nerve on edge as I move toward the kitchen. I can feel the weight of her gaze on me, even though I'm not looking at her. I know she can feel the shift in the air, the sudden tension that's thicker than it's ever been.

"You hungry?" I ask, trying to keep my voice steady, but it comes out a little too clipped.

She's quiet for a moment, and then I hear her move behind me. I feel her step closer, just a few inches from my back, and I can barely breathe.

"Yeah," she says softly. "I could eat something."

I turn, my body close enough to hers that I can feel the heat radiating off her. She's so close, I can almost taste the electricity in the air. The way her towel clings to her body drives me to the edge, and I have to take a step back, forcing myself to breathe evenly.

But when I do, she moves with me, her eyes meeting mine with an unreadable expression. The moment hangs between us like a thread ready to snap.

"Aubree," I murmur, my voice barely a whisper. "You don't know what you're doing to me."

She doesn't say anything, but I can see it in her eyes—she's feeling it too. The pull. The desire.

She takes a small step back, the moment breaking, but not completely. We're still standing there, a hair's breadth apart. I want to reach for her, to close the distance between us, but I know I can't. Not like this. Not when she's confused.

"I should... go get dressed," she says, her voice quieter now, like she's trying to steady herself, just like I am.

I nod, swallowing the lump in my throat. "Yeah. I'll...I'll make us some lunch."

But as she walks away, I know I'm not getting out of this feeling. It's only getting stronger. And the worst part? I have no idea how to stop it.

Chapter 14

Aubree

I walk quickly toward the bedroom, my heart still racing from the way Boone looked at me. The way he stared at me, his eyes heavy with something I couldn't name but definitely felt. It was like he wanted me. And that thought makes my stomach flip in a way I'm not sure I can handle.

I shut the door behind me once I get inside, leaning against it for a moment, just trying to catch my breath. What's going on with me? I don't normally get like this, especially not with someone who's here to do a job. He's my bodyguard, and I'm supposed to keep my distance, but everything about him makes it hard.

I shake my head, trying to clear it, and I move toward the dresser. I need to get dressed, to focus on something other than Boone's gaze and the way my pulse raced when he looked at me like that.

I grab a pair of leggings and a loose sweatshirt, pulling them on quickly. I don't want to dwell on what happened. I can't. The kiss, the touch, the tension between us—it all feels like too much.

After taking a few steadying breaths, I leave the room and head toward the kitchen. The air feels thick between me and Boone, and I know it's because of everything that happened last night, and this morning, and honestly, everything that's been building up since I got here. I try to shake it off, but it's hard when he's in the room, standing there looking... like he's still trying to figure me out, just like I'm trying to figure him out.

"Hey," I say as I step into the kitchen, my voice sounding way too casual. "What's for lunch?"

Boone glances up from the stove, where he's plating something that smells way better than I expected. "Just a simple grilled cheese sandwich. Hope that's okay."

I force a smile. "It's fine. Thanks."

He sets the plates on the table, and I sit down across from him. The food looks delicious, but the atmosphere feels strained, like we're both unsure of how to act now. I can feel the awkwardness thick in the air, like a tangible thing I can reach out and touch.

Boone picks up his sandwich and takes a bite, clearly trying to break the silence. "I can make you something else."

"It's fine." I take a bite of my sandwich, but the tension doesn't fade. Every bite feels mechanical, like I'm just going through the motions. My mind keeps drifting back to the way Boone looked at me earlier—how I could feel the heat in his gaze, how badly I wanted him to kiss me again.

"I should've never... I mean, last night was a mistake," I say, the words spilling out before I can stop them. I feel foolish, but I have to say something.

Boone's eyes meet mine, and for a moment, I see the flicker of something—regret? Frustration?—before his face goes unreadable again. "It's not your fault, Aubree. I just... we can't let things get complicated."

I nod, even though it feels like the wind has been knocked out of me. I try to smile, but it feels forced. "Right. I get it. No complications."

We both fall quiet again, and I focus on my food, not looking at him, not knowing what to say. I'm sure he feels it too—the awkwardness, the tension—but neither of us seems to know how to break the ice. I just want to get through this meal without making it worse.

"So," he finally says, his voice a little rough, "what do you want to do for the rest of the day? We can keep things low-key, or I can keep monitoring the area."

I pause, thinking for a moment, then shake my head. "I don't know. I think I just need some time to myself. Maybe a walk or something. Get out of my head for a bit."

He nods. "I'll stay close. But yeah, I get it."

I nod, trying to offer a smile, but it doesn't quite reach my eyes. I feel like a mess, trying to act like everything's fine when it's not. The words are there, but they feel like a heavy weight I can't lift.

The rest of the meal goes by in silence, the awkwardness hanging between us like a cloud. It's almost unbearable, and I can't wait for it to end. When I finally finish my food, I push the plate away, sitting back in my chair.

"Thanks for making lunch," I say softly. "I think I'm just gonna head out for that walk now. Maybe some fresh air will help clear my head."

Boone stands up and looks at me, his expression unreadable. "You sure you're okay?"

I feel the sting of frustration rise in my chest. "I'm fine, Boone," I say quickly, more sharply than I intend. "I just need some time alone."

His brow furrows, and I see the flicker of concern in his eyes, but he doesn't push. "All right. But I'm still here if you need anything."

I nod, grabbing my jacket and heading for the door without another word.

I step outside and feel the cool air hit my skin. The quiet of the woods surrounds me, and for the first time today, I feel like I can breathe again. But even with the fresh air, I can't shake the feeling that I'm running away from something I don't fully understand.

Chapter 15

Boone

The night has been quiet, but that quiet is the kind of silence that makes me uneasy. Aubree and I haven't spoken much since lunch. She's been distant, and I get it. I've been keeping my distance too, trying to respect the space she clearly needs. But it's hard. It's hard when all I want to do is be close to her. To protect her, but also... to be something more. I can't let myself feel that way. Not when I'm supposed to be the one keeping her safe.

I make my way to my room, mentally preparing myself for the same restless sleep I've been getting. But then I hear it.

A faint sound—something like a twig snapping, too soft to be the wind. Instantly, my senses sharpen. Every muscle in my body tightens as the weight of my training hits me. I'm up in an instant, grabbing my gun from the nightstand and slipping quietly out of my room.

I move fast, slipping out of the door and into the cool night. My boots barely make a sound as I move toward the trees, the shadows of the property stretching long in the moonlight. There's no breeze to mask the sound of someone moving around, and I'm immediately on edge. The feeling in my gut tells me something's wrong. I can feel the hairs on the back of my neck rise, and every step I take, every noise I hear, sends a spike of adrenaline straight to my bloodstream.

I don't hear Aubree follow me at first, but then I do. The soft rustling of footsteps behind me. I spin around quickly, my gun still raised, but it's only her.

"Aubree, go back inside," I order, my voice low but sharp.

Her face is pale, the moonlight catching the worry in her eyes. "What's going on?" she asks, her voice trembling, but her resolve is strong.

"There's someone on the property. You need to stay inside. Go back in the cabin now."

I don't wait for her response. She doesn't need to be anywhere near this. I turn back toward the trees, moving quietly, my gun held firmly, scanning every inch of the yard. Every shadow, every rustling noise feels like it could be the person I'm looking for. My heart pounds in my chest, my senses firing. I know that someone's here. They're close. I can feel it.

I see him.

A figure steps into the open for just a second, barely visible in the shadows near the fence. It's a man. He doesn't see me, but I see him. I'm too far away to make out his features, but I know he doesn't belong here. The instant I spot him, I move faster, stepping silently through the trees, closing the distance between us. My heart hammers in my chest as I make my way through the underbrush. I'm almost there.

But then I hear the unmistakable sound of a car door opening—quiet but distinct. My instincts scream at me to go after him, but when I break through the last line of trees, I see him slipping into an SUV parked at the edge of the property.

The engine starts with a low hum, and before I can react, the vehicle is already speeding away, the taillights glowing red before disappearing into the night.

I stand there, frozen for a moment, my gun still raised, my chest heaving. I don't move right away, too stunned by how quickly it all happened. Whoever that guy was, he was prepared. And it's not over. I know it. I can feel it in my gut.

I stay in place for a few more seconds, listening for any other sounds, but the night is still again.

"Aubree," I call out, lowering my gun. "You can come out now."

She steps from behind the door, looking relieved but still clearly shaken. "What happened? Did you catch him?"

I shake my head. "No. He got away. Slipped into a car and drove off before I could get close enough."

She stands there for a long moment, processing what I've just said. "Do you think he was the one—" She stops herself, looking at me with uncertainty in her eyes.

I don't say anything, not sure how to explain that I don't have all the answers. All I know is he was here, and now I'm more certain than ever that something's not right.

"We'll figure it out," I say, my voice low, trying to reassure her, though I'm not sure I believe it myself. "But for now, you need to stay inside. I'm not letting anyone get close to you."

She nods, her eyes still wide. "What do we do now?"

"Now, we wait. I'm going to check the perimeter one more time. Make sure everything's locked up." I start to walk away, but when I look over my shoulder, I catch her watching me, the worry still etched on her face.

"Aubree," I add, my voice softening. "Stay inside, alright? I mean it. It's not safe."

She doesn't argue, just nods again before heading back toward the door. I watch her go, my chest tight with a mixture of frustration and something else—something I can't place. I want to protect her, to keep her safe, but I know I can't do that if I don't figure out what's going on.

I wait until she's inside before I start my perimeter check, walking the boundaries of the property, every sense still on high alert.

It's quiet now. Too quiet.

But I know this feeling. The calm before the storm. Something's coming, and I'm not going to be caught off guard again. Not when it comes to her. Not when I'm starting to feel like she's more than just someone I'm protecting.

Chapter 16

Aubree

I'd never admit this to anyone ever, but I'm afraid. I'm terrified. However, having Boone go into this all protective alpha hero is kind of a turn on. I'm loving it, and I feel so guilty about it.

The cabin is quiet, the kind of stillness that's too heavy, too suffocating. I'm sitting on the couch, my knees pulled up to my chest, staring at the empty space in front of me. I'm not sure if it's the events of the day or just the weight of everything I've been through lately, but I'm too scared to go to bed.

I keep replaying what happened earlier. I know Boone was right—he couldn't catch him, and I know he's trying to keep me calm, but my mind keeps racing. I can't shake the feeling that whoever was watching us, whoever was lurking out there, knows more than they should. They know *too much*.

I stand up to pace, needing to move, to do something to distract myself from the fear building in my chest. But the sound of Boone's boots on the porch pulls me from my thoughts. He's back. I feel a strange relief at hearing him, but also a sense of tension that hasn't eased.

When he steps inside, his face is hard, his posture tense, but his eyes soften when they meet mine.

"Everything okay?" I ask, my voice sounding small in the vast quiet of the cabin.

"Yeah. I checked the perimeter again. Everything's locked up tight." He shrugs off his jacket, but I can see it's not just the cabin he's worried about. His gaze flicks to me, and I know he's trying to gauge if I'm okay.

I sit back down on the couch, trying to calm my nerves. "I just... I couldn't sleep. It feels too... off, you know?"

Boone nods, his eyes still assessing me like he's searching for any sign of distress. Then, he hesitates before speaking again, his voice a little too formal. "Who paid for your pizza shop?"

I blink, not expecting that question. "My mother. She used the money she got from my father's death."

His eyebrows furrow, and he tilts his head slightly. "What about your stepfather? What does he do?"

I hesitate. There's always been tension between me and my stepfather. He's not around much, hasn't been for years. He's always been a businessman, more concerned with his career than his family. "He's... he's in real estate. He doesn't really talk to me much."

Boone seems to process that, and I can see the wheels turning in his head. I don't know what he's thinking, and it's making me uneasy. "What are you thinking?" I ask, my voice more abrupt than I intend.

Boone's eyes lock with mine, and for a moment, I swear I can feel the weight of everything in his gaze. He's quiet for a long time, his jaw clenched like he's battling with something he's not sure he wants to say. "I'm not sure yet," he says finally, his tone low.

I feel my stomach tighten at his response. It's not the reassurance I was hoping for. He's still trying to figure me out, trying to connect the dots, and I can't help but feel like I'm a part of something bigger than I understand.

"Do you think it's safe to stay here?" I ask, the words escaping before I can stop them.

Boone exhales slowly, running a hand through his hair. "I was wondering how they found you," he mutters, almost to himself. His eyes flick toward me, sharp. "How they found us."

"Boone, what's going on?" I ask, my voice almost desperate.

After a long moment, Boone finally speaks. "I'm calling Dean," he says, his voice clipped, the tone one I've come to associate with urgency.

He uses his phone to call Dean and waits for the line to connect, his eyes never leaving mine. "Dean," he says as soon as the call picks up, his voice calm but with an edge to it. "We've got a situation. I'm going to need you to check something for me."

He pauses, listening intently to whatever Dean is saying on the other end of the line.

Boone launches into the details of the night, making my skin crawl with panic. As soon as he's done, he listens to Dean for a while.

"I need to know who all has this location." Boone nods. "Right. Yes." Boone moves toward his room in the back. "Got it. We're leaving now."

My eyes widen because things have gone from safe to not safe in a matter of seconds. Who is doing this to me? I'm starting to fear I'll never find out.

Chapter 17

Boone

The night feels endless. It's late, and both of us are exhausted, the weight of the day and everything that's happened settling heavily over us. The silence in the cabin is thick, broken only by the soft crackle of the fire.

I hang up with Dean. And Aubree's afraid. I hate this for her, but this place is no longer safe for us.

"What's going on?" she asks.

"We're leaving," I answer, though the word tastes bitter on my tongue. "I'm not comfortable staying here tonight."

She starts to say something, but I shake my head. "Aubree, it's not worth the risk. I'm not taking any chances."

Her gaze flicks to the gun in my hand, and I see the flash of fear in her eyes. Not fear of me, but fear of the entire situation she's been forced into. I can't blame her. This is her life on the line, and I just about forgot that because I couldn't keep my hands off her.

She swallows, then nods. "Okay. Let me just…" Her voice cracks, and she takes a moment to steady herself. "Let me pack what I need."

"Do it fast," I say, moving to the bedroom. I slide my gun back into the holster at my hip, snatch up my boots from near the door, and jam my feet into them without bothering with socks.

Aubree throws her duffel on the bed and hastily shoves in clothes, toiletries, and a few other personal items. My chest tightens at the sight—she's barely holding it together, but she's doing her best. As she zips the bag, her hands shake, and my instincts shout at me to reach out, to pull her into my arms and promise it'll be okay.

But I don't. I can't. Not when I've just reminded myself how easily I can be distracted. Instead, I stand by the bedroom window, scanning the yard outside like a hawk. The pale moonlight shows the battered old pickup in the driveway and the faint silhouette of trees. Still, no movement.

Once she's ready, we swap places. She stands at the window, on guard, while I gather my own minimal gear—clothes, my phone, a first-aid kit I keep for emergencies. In under two minutes, we're both set. The tension is so thick, I feel like I could slice through it with a knife.

"Ready?" I ask.

She nods. "As I'll ever be." Her voice trembles. She glances at me, and for a moment, I see the echo of what we were doing before the noise. There's longing there, but also fear.

I push away the guilt. We don't have time for that now. "Let's go."

We move through the cabin carefully, lights off, so as not to advertise our departure. I keep my gun in hand, unlocking the front door just long enough for us to slip out. The night air envelops us. The sound of crickets once again assaults my ears, a thousand insects singing in the darkness.

I gesture for Aubree to stay close behind me. She does, pressing near enough that I feel the warmth of her body. Each step we take crunches on the gravel, and I'm painfully aware of how loud we seem. But there's no use tiptoeing; if someone's out there, they already know we're leaving.

We reach the truck—a black, older model Chevy, big tires and reinforced suspension. I pop the passenger door open. "Get in," I whisper.

Her eyes dart around, scanning the yard before she climbs into the seat, clutching her duffel bag. I shut the door gently behind her, run around to the driver's side, and haul myself in. As soon as I lock the doors, a rush of relief hits me. Not total relief, but enough to know we're marginally safer inside than we were out in the open.

The engine growls to life, and the headlights slice through the darkness. For a few seconds, I aim them at the trees, hoping to catch a glimpse of any intruder. Nothing. Still, I don't doubt that someone could be hiding just out of view. Without hesitation, I slam the truck into gear and peel out of the driveway, gravel kicking up behind us.

Aubree rests her forehead against the window, gazing back at the cabin. "I was just starting to think I could sleep there," she mutters, more to herself than to me. I catch a note of sadness in her voice, and it twists at my insides. This woman deserves peace, not constant fleeing from threats.

I roll my shoulders, trying to release some of the tension that's built up. "We'll find a hotel," I say, my voice low. "It's late, but we'll find something soon enough. I won't stop until we're somewhere safe."

She nods, but she doesn't take her eyes off the dark outline of the cabin until it vanishes behind a bend in the road. "Safe," she echoes. "Right."

I grip the steering wheel tight, focusing on the road ahead. My headlights illuminate old country roads lined by trees. The nearest real town is a half-hour drive, at least. We have no guarantee we'll find a vacancy, but I'm not taking any chances by staying in a remote spot tonight. Whoever's threatening Aubree is bold enough to show up in the dead of night, at a cabin in the woods. They're not messing around.

As we head away from the cabin, the highway stretches out like a long, empty corridor. There are few cars at this hour, just a passing eighteen-wheeler here, a silent sedan there. Aubree stays quiet, her breath hitching every so often, like she's still too keyed up to relax. I flick a glance at her from time to time, and my chest tightens at how small she looks, curled against the door, her bag clutched in her lap.

We pass a closed gas station, neon sign off for the night. Up ahead, there's a battered old motel, but it looks deserted and poorly lit. I slow down, eyeing it. Paint is peeling from the sign, the parking lot cracked and sparse. It might be our only choice.

I glance at Aubree. She meets my eyes, biting her lip. "I don't like the look of that place," she admits.

I give the motel another once-over. My instincts scream to keep going. It's too isolated, no security cameras that I can see, only a flickering lamp in the office window. "Me neither."

I press the gas, speeding past it. She exhales, relieved. I can almost feel her tension ebbing a fraction. "Thank you," she whispers, turning back to stare at the road.

"I'll keep driving until we find something better," I promise.

It takes another twenty minutes of winding roads and the occasional streetlight before we see a bigger cluster of lights—signs for fast-food joints and a truck stop. The first chain hotel sign glows in the distance, a Motel 6. I flick on my turn signal and veer into the parking lot, which looks halfway decent and well-lit. That's enough for me. I triple check to make sure we haven't been followed.

Aubree shifts, sitting up straighter. Her eyelids droop, fatigue etched into her face, but she tries to stay alert. I park near the lobby entrance, leaving the truck running for a moment while I scan the area. No suspicious vehicles, no shady figures in the corners. Just a handful of cars belonging to tired travelers.

"Okay," I murmur, shutting off the engine. "Looks good enough. You ready?"

Aubree nods, though she still looks a bit dazed. "As I'll ever be."

We step out, locking the doors behind us. The fluorescent glow of the parking lot lights stings my eyes. I keep my head on a swivel, my hand hovering near my holstered gun. Once we're inside, I find the lobby empty except for a bored-looking clerk behind the desk.

After some polite conversation and an exchange of cash, I secure us a room on the second floor.

The clerk hands over a key card with a small yawn. "Elevator's around the corner, have a nice night."

"We'll try," I mutter under my breath. Aubree doesn't say a word, just clutches her bag and waits.

In the elevator, she finally breaks the silence. "I'm sorry I dragged you into all this. I know it's your job, but—"

I hold up a hand. "Stop. You didn't drag me anywhere. This is exactly what I signed up for when I joined Maddox Security—protecting people who need it."

Her eyes shimmer with unshed tears, but she nods. The elevator dings, and we find our room at the end of the hall. I insert the key card and push the door open, scanning the interior. It's a standard hotel room, with only one bed. Not that it catches me by surprise, because after everything I'm sure Aubree will be asking to stay in my bed.

Where she belongs. It's crazy how possessive I've become over her, and I've only known her for a few short days.

I check the closet, the bathroom, even glance under the beds. Old habits die hard. Then I lock the door behind us, flipping the deadbolt and setting the chain.

Aubree sets her bag down, looking exhausted but unable to relax. She hovers near the edge of the bed, shoulders hunched, arms wrapped around herself. "Boone…" she says softly. "What if—what if that person follows us here?"

I swallow hard, remembering the moment at the cabin, how close we came to crossing a line that could've jeopardized her safety. If I had been a second slower, if I'd been too distracted… "We'll handle it," I say firmly. "Nobody's getting through me to you."

The vow in my voice seems to calm her a bit. She nods, then sinks down on the mattress, her eyes heavy. She's still wearing her hoodie and jeans, and I realize she's too spent to change or even fuss about the bed. Carefully, I step forward, kneel down, and tug her shoes off. Her eyes flutter closed, and a moment later, she's drifting in that space between awake and asleep.

I stand, moving to the other side of the bed. My heart thumps as I remember how her body felt beneath me, the softness of her lips, the taste of her breath. It's crazy, wanting her in the middle of all this chaos. But I do. I want her fiercely, more than I've wanted anything in a long while.

Yet the memory of that quiet noise outside the cabin, the jolt of realizing we were vulnerable, keeps replaying in my mind. If someone had ambushed us while I was tangled up with her... the outcome could've been disastrous. I clench my fists, anger sparking at the unknown threat. My entire body coils with tension at the idea of failing her, letting her get hurt on my watch.

No. Her safety is my top priority, no matter how badly I crave the feel of her. If I can't stay focused on that, I have no business calling myself a protector.

Drawing in a steadying breath, I turn off the overhead light, leaving only a small lamp on. The hotel room is cast in shadows, but it's enough to see if something happens. I set my gun within arm's reach on the nightstand. Tomorrow, I'll call my contacts at Maddox Security, update them, see if we can get more intel on whoever's tailing Aubree. Tonight, though, we're just two exhausted souls in a cheap motel, hoping for a few hours of peace.

I glance over at Aubree again. She's already asleep, her breathing slow and even. In slumber, the lines of worry smoothed from her face, she looks so vulnerable. A fresh bolt of protectiveness surges through me.

I check my phone—one message from Ranger asking for a status update, another from the Maddox office. I shoot back a quick text: "We've relocated to a safe location for the night. Will advise in the morning." Then I silence my phone, because the last thing I need is a ringtone waking Aubree and sending her heart skittering all over again.

Finally, I ease back against the pillows on the bed. My body is wired, my mind spinning with scenarios: vantage points, escape routes, possible suspects. But the strongest thread weaving through it all is the memory of her trembling mouth beneath mine, the way she clung to me with such trust.

God fucking help me, I'm in trouble here—caught between my duty and a desire that could jeopardize everything. But there's no turning back. If protecting Aubree means locking down every last one of my own urges, that's exactly what I'll do. Because the only thing worse than not having her... would be losing her altogether.

Outside, a car rumbles into the parking lot, headlights illuminating our curtains for a split second before fading away. I force my eyes to stay open a moment longer, scanning the corners of the room out of habit. Slowly, exhaustion seeps in. My muscles ache, my mind is heavy with worry.

Still, I remind myself I don't get to truly rest. Not until we're sure she's out of harm's way. Until I know for a fact that we're no longer the hunted in this twisted game.

My gaze drifts to Aubree one last time. She's quiet, her chest rising and falling in the steady rhythm of sleep. It's a small comfort in the midst of the storm. A silent vow echoes in my head—tomorrow, I'll find answers. Tomorrow, I will track down whoever is behind this, and I will make them regret ever putting her life in danger.

And I'll do it without letting my guard down again. Because the taste of almost losing control tonight is enough to remind me just how quickly everything could slip through my fingers.

Guarding What's Mine

Her safety is paramount, and I will not fail her. Not now, not ever.

With that final thought circling in my mind, I keep one hand on my gun and let the lull of her quiet breathing pull me into a restless half-sleep, ready to snap awake at the slightest hint of danger.

Chapter 18

Aubree

Sunlight filters through the thin curtains, casting a hazy glow across the hotel room's worn carpet. I blink a few times, my eyes adjusting to the morning light, and slowly become aware of the steady low rumble of Boone's voice. He's standing by the window, phone pressed to his ear, his posture stiff and alert. A chill creeps across my arms when I remember why we're here.

My body feels heavy, like I haven't slept in a year. I push myself upright against the headboard, noticing Boone is fully dressed: jeans, boots, and that dark T-shirt that clings to his broad shoulders. He's speaking quietly, but I catch words like "safe house," "security detail," and "timeline." It's the kind of conversation that, just a week ago, would've felt like something out of a movie. Now, it's my reality.

I run a hand through my tangled hair, wishing I'd had the energy to shower last night. Everything happened so fast—one moment we were alone at that cabin, dangerously close to something I've never experienced before, and the next, we were bolting out of there because of a potential threat outside.

I rub the sleep from my eyes and glance around for my phone. My first instinct is to check Slice Slice Baby's social media, or my texts from Stuart, but my phone isn't on the bedside table where I usually keep it. I slide out of bed, rummage through my duffel bag, and remember Boone took it.

My gaze drifts back to Boone. His voice is low and firm, the kind of tone that brooks no argument. He's pacing a little now, hand on his hip, brow furrowed in concentration.

I let out a sigh and decide to get ready. My clothes from yesterday feel stale, and I grab my duffel looking for a new outfit. I grab the toiletry bag from my duffel as well, and head into the bathroom. The yellowish light flickers for a second before turning on, revealing the speckled counter and a chipped mirror that's seen better days.

The water runs warm, which is a small mercy. I splash my face a few times and brush my teeth, taking a moment to stare at my reflection. My eyes have dark smudges beneath them—no surprise there. I can practically hear my mother's voice chiding me for not getting enough rest, though under the circumstances, who can blame me?

I think about Boone's kiss, how I melted into him like it was the most natural thing in the world. A flush creeps up my neck. It's beyond crazy—I've only known him for a few days. He's my bodyguard, for crying out loud. But every time I even glance his way, it's like my brain short-circuits. And the memory of how his mouth felt on mine… yeah, that's impossible to erase.

I towel my face dry and change into some new clothes. I reenter the room to see Boone ending his call. He slips the phone into his back pocket, exhaling sharply. There's a tension in his features, but when his gaze flicks toward me, something in his expression softens.

"Morning," he says quietly, eyes flicking over me as if assessing whether I slept okay.

"Morning," I reply, my voice still scratchy from sleep. I look away, not wanting him to see all the mixed-up feelings etched on my face. This man has seen me at my most vulnerable, and I can't decide if that terrifies me or comforts me.

Anxious energy buzzes under my skin. I spot a small pad of paper and a pen on the table near the coffee maker. It's one of those free hotel stationery sets with the logo stamped at the top. On impulse, I grab them and drop into the chair. "I need to figure out who's behind all this," I say, more to myself than to Boone. "I can't just sit around and wait to be attacked again."

Boone crosses the room, leaning against the wall opposite me. "What're you doing?"

I start scribbling names: Stuart, Earl, Mitch—an older employee who left last month to move closer to his grandkids. Next, I add Vicki, my part-time employee who's sweet as pie, and Hayley, a high school junior who works a few days a week after school. The pen scratches across the paper with each name, and a lump forms in my throat as I realize how bizarre this is—drawing up a suspect list of people I actually know.

"I'm making a list." I glance up at him. "Just… people I can think of who might have a motive. Or who might just seem a little off. I don't know," I admit, sighing. "I'm not a detective. But it's a start."

Boone steps closer, surveying the names. "That's smart," he murmurs. "Getting it all down where we can see it."

I chew on my lip, tapping the pen against the pad. "It might be someone I never even considered, you know? We get all kinds of customers, but the ones I see regularly—like Earl, or even that new guy, Harvey—" I shake my head. "I don't know. Should I write every single customer's name?"

His gaze flicks up to mine. "We'll work through your list systematically. Then we'll see if Maddox Security can cross-reference names with any known troublemakers or suspects in the area. Don't forget to add Hank on there."

"Right." My shoulders slump slightly. "Thank you," I whisper. "I just... I feel so helpless."

He sets a warm hand on my shoulder, making me jump slightly. The contact is brief but comforting. "You're not helpless, Aubree," he says, voice soft. "You're just dealing with a situation that most people never have to face."

I meet his eyes, swallowing hard. "What about your phone call? You mentioned a safe house?"

"Yeah," he replies, stepping back and crossing his arms over his chest. "I was checking in with my contacts, seeing if there's a closer location we can move to. Our last spot was compromised, obviously. Now we need somewhere more secure."

I nod, hugging the notepad to my chest. "So, any luck?"

"Possibly," he says, rubbing the back of his neck. "There's a property about two hours north of here—friend of a friend who's out of the country. It's not official Maddox property, but it's off the grid enough that no one would suspect we're there."

"Two hours north." I bite my lip, thinking about my shop. "I guess there's no point in heading back to Slice Slice Baby yet, right?"

His eyes darken. "Not unless you want to walk into a situation where we're unprepared. Whoever's harassing you is getting bolder."

I nod, grimacing as I glance down at the list of names I've jotted on the paper. It looks so short—Stuart, Earl, Mitch, Hank, Vicki, Hayley, plus a few other past employees whose names I'm not even sure I can remember. Hard to imagine any of them wanting to harm me, but I can't afford to overlook anyone.

"There's no telling who might've hired someone else to do their dirty work," Boone continues. "Maddox Security has resources to dig deeper, but I'm gonna need your cooperation. That means you telling me everything, even the smallest detail, that might seem suspicious or out of place."

I swallow. "I can do that." I force a smile, though it wobbles at the corners of my mouth. "I'm just… not sure what else I'm missing. I mean, who hates pizza enough to break a window and send threats?"

Boone's lips twitch, almost like he wants to smile but can't quite manage it. "Not exactly about hating pizza, I'd guess. But we'll figure it out. In the meantime, I need you to trust me."

His words linger in the air, and I think about how I trusted him the other night—how I let him get so close. My cheeks flush at the memory, but I push it aside. There's something else swirling in my mind: a realization that maybe I do trust him, more than I should after only a few days. More than I've trusted most people in a long time.

"All right," I say, tapping the pen absently on the corner of the notepad. "I'll trust you. Just… promise you won't let me down."

Guarding What's Mine

His gaze locks onto mine, and for a second I feel that heat again, the magnetism that drew us together the other night. "I promise," he replies, voice low and certain.

I exhale slowly, smoothing out the page of names with my hand. It's not a solution, not yet, but it's a start. Between Boone's connections and my local knowledge of who might have a grudge against me, maybe we'll unravel this mystery before anyone else gets hurt—or before I have to abandon my life for good.

And as I sit there, pen in hand, mind racing with questions, I can't stop thinking about him. About how safe I felt when he was near me, how his kiss made the whole world fade away for just a moment. It scares me as much as the threats do—because if I let myself feel that way again, what happens if he can't protect me next time?

I push that thought aside. One crisis at a time. Right now, we need to regroup, find a better hiding spot, and keep me alive. Everything else—my growing feelings for the man who's supposed to keep me safe—will have to wait.

Chapter 19

Boone

I'm sitting in a booth at a little roadside diner, watching Aubree pick at the corner of her napkin, and the tension coiled in my chest hasn't loosened an inch since I woke up this morning. My back is to the wall, so I can keep an eye on the entrance and the windows. It's a habit I picked up in the military and never really lost. I've got a direct line of sight on the door and on everyone else in this place.

The diner is one of those small, unassuming joints with red vinyl booths, a checkered floor, and a faint smell of bacon grease that seems permanent. The waitress who seated us gave me a look like she expected me to cause trouble—I guess my scowl isn't exactly subtle. But with everything that's happened, I can't afford to relax.

Aubree notices me tense up and offers a small smile. "You okay?" she asks, her voice barely audible over the low hum of conversation around us.

"Yeah," I mutter, scanning the patrons again. The lunch counter is occupied by two older men eating pancakes, and a couple in their twenties hovers over a shared plate of waffles. Nothing looks threatening, but I'm on edge anyway.

She wets her lips, then glances at the menu again. We've already ordered, but I see her hand tremble slightly as she tries to act like she's just browsing. Guilt knots in my gut. She shouldn't have to live like this—scared, on the run, trusting a guy she barely knows to keep her safe.

A moment later, one of the men at the counter stands, dropping some bills onto the table. As he leaves, he passes our booth and flicks a glance in Aubree's direction—probably just giving her a once-over because she's pretty, but it's enough to send my adrenaline spiking. I shoot out a hand, nearly grabbing the guy by his collar.

"Hey!" His startled yelp makes the entire diner pause.

The man stumbles back, eyes wide. He's wearing a ratty jacket and jeans, and something about him reminds me of an old farmer just looking for a hearty meal. Definitely not a threat. But for a split second, the fear and tension in my body override logic. I'm halfway out of my seat, my fingers curled, ready to slam him against the wall if needed.

"Boone," Aubree whispers sharply, her hand on my forearm. Her touch is gentle, but the urgency in her voice snaps me out of it.

"Sorry," I grunt, sitting back down with my heart still pounding like a jackhammer. The man mutters something under his breath and hurries out the door, the bell above it jingling in his wake. A hush lingers before the other diners go back to their meals, though they shoot me the occasional wary glance.

Aubree stares at me, eyes a little wide. "He was just…looking. Like, curious. It's not like he attacked me."

I drag a hand down my face. "I know," I say, my voice rougher than I intend. "I'm on edge. Sorry."

Her lips part, and I can see her searching for the right thing to say. She ends up just nodding, her expression a mix of worry and understanding. The tension between us is thick—equal parts fear, adrenaline, and something else I can't quite name. Maybe it's the memory of the two of us in that hotel room last night, or the cabin before that, how close we came to crossing a line. But I try to shut that thought out. Right now, I need to keep my focus on keeping her alive.

The waitress arrives at our table with two plates. She sets a plate of scrambled eggs, bacon, and toast in front of me, and a stack of pancakes in front of Aubree. "Here you go, hon," she says, clearly directing her kindness at Aubree instead of me. Then she flicks her gaze my way, eyes narrowing. "Anything else I can get for you two?"

Aubree offers a tight smile. "We're good, thanks."

I dig into my eggs, though they taste like nothing. My appetite's shot, but I force the food down because I don't know when we'll get another decent meal. I'm about to check my phone for messages when I remember I turned off Aubree's phone earlier. My phone's still on, vibrating occasionally with texts from Dean, but hers is a dead brick in my jacket pocket —just another precaution. If the person threatening her somehow tracked her phone's signal, that's a risk I won't take.

She only manages a couple bites of pancake before pushing the plate away. "I'm sorry," she says, fingers fidgeting with the napkin. "I just… I'm not hungry."

"I get it," I say. My voice is softer now. "We'll get it to go if you want."

She shakes her head. "I think I'm done."

I wave the waitress over to get a box for Aubree's leftover pancakes. She hustles behind the counter, and while we wait, Aubree leans forward. Her voice is low when she speaks. "How was that phone call earlier? Find out anything?"

I glance at my phone. A single new text from Dean reads: "Still digging, talk soon." That's all. "He's still working through your list," I say, keeping my tone neutral. What I don't mention is that I asked him to look into her step-father, too. It's just a hunch. But I'm not going to tell Aubree that yet, not until I have something concrete.

"Right," she murmurs. "He told you he's scanning their names, seeing if any of them have records or something?"

"Exactly." I hold her gaze, trying to project confidence. "Between Dean and the rest of the Maddox crew, they'll figure out if any of those folks pop up on a background check."

Aubree exhales a shaky breath. The waitress returns with a small foam box, and I slip the pancakes into it, handing it back to Aubree. We pay the bill quickly—cash, another precaution—and walk out to the parking lot. The morning sun is bright, making us squint as we cross the cracked asphalt. My truck is parked in a corner space, away from most of the other vehicles, but I still check around it like I'm expecting an ambush.

I open the passenger door, and Aubree climbs in, hugging the to-go box to her chest. She leans her head back against the seat, looking pale. I round the front of the truck, scanning the lot one last time before getting in. The engine rumbles to life as I pull out onto the main road.

We drive for a few minutes in silence. The diner fades into the rearview mirror, replaced by farmland and stretches of highway. I'm waiting for her to speak, but she just stares out the window, lost in thought. Finally, I clear my throat. "We've got a two-hour drive, give or take, to the safe house. Might be more with traffic."

"Right," she says absently.

I grip the steering wheel, letting the hum of the tires on the asphalt calm me down a little. Once we're on the highway, I figure it's a good time to pick her brain. We need details—every single threat, every weird email, every suspicious look. That's how we solve this. "Aubree," I say, my voice cutting into the quiet. "Tell me everything about the past few months. Start from when the threats began."

She twists in the seat to face me, pulling her knees up under her. "Everything?" she asks, sounding uncertain.

I glance over briefly, then back to the road. "Yeah. Don't leave anything out. The more I know, the better I can protect you."

She nods, inhaling deeply. "Okay, so… it started about three months ago. It began with these weird emails to my work account—Slice Slice Baby has an email address for catering orders and stuff. The first one just said, 'I'm watching you.' No context, no signature. I thought it was a prank, you know? The place is near a high school, so I figured some bored teenager was messing with me."

I keep my eyes on the road, letting her words wash over me. "When did you realize it wasn't just a prank?"

She shifts, fiddling with the hem of her shirt. "The second or third email. It said something like, 'We don't want you here.

Leave now before something bad happens.' Or something along those lines. It was more direct, personal. It used the word 'we,' like there was more than one person. I started to get nervous, but I still didn't call the police or anything. I told my mom, and she was the one who freaked out, telling me to hire security. I thought she was overreacting."

I grunt. "Sounds like your mom has good instincts."

She snorts softly. "Or just a lot of money and an overprotective streak. But yeah, maybe she was right." She stares out the window for a moment, watching the farmland blur by. "Anyway, the emails kept coming, about once a week. Always from different addresses—like whoever it was knew how to mask their IP or something. They'd say stuff like, 'You don't belong here, get out,' or 'You'll be sorry you stayed.' I tried to ignore them, but then we started finding weird things."

"Weird things?" I prompt, my muscles tensing.

She nods. "Notes on the door of the shop. Sometimes they were taped to the glass, sometimes shoved under the mat. They were basically the same message: 'Leave. You're not wanted.' But then it escalated more—like the brick."

My jaw tightens at the memory of that shattered window, the note scrawled in black marker. "And in between the brick and the emails, there was nothing else?"

She blows out a breath. "There were phone calls. A few times I answered, and no one would speak. Just heavy breathing. I changed the shop's number after that, which is why I didn't think about it anymore. I guess I thought it'd go away."

I'm quiet for a minute, letting the new information sink in. A heavy breather on the phone, menacing emails, a thrown brick—this is more than casual harassment. It's personal.

"You mentioned you fired someone around the same time all this started," I say, recalling our conversation in the hotel.

She bites her lip, nodding. "Mitch. He was an older guy—late fifties, maybe? He worked for me for about four months, but then things got weird. He would show up late or not at all, and he had this attitude whenever I tried to talk to him about it. I warned him a few times, but he never improved, so I let him go. He stormed out, cursing me out. Called me all sorts of names, said I'd regret it."

I frown, turning that over in my head. "Sounds like a prime suspect to me. Did he ever come back? Ask for a second chance?"

"No," Aubree says, hugging the foam box tighter. "But I heard from Stuart that Mitch was spotted hanging around the high school a couple times after that. Not sure if he was messing with Slice Slice Baby or just being a creep. Stuart confronted him once, I think, and Mitch said something along the lines of, 'This place is going down, sooner or later.'" She exhales, her breath shaky. "I just wrote it off as him being bitter."

My jaw clenches. "Bitter enough to threaten you, apparently. Did you ever file a police report about Mitch?"

She shakes her head. "No. I guess I should have, but I didn't want to escalate things. I was naive."

I can hear the self-blame in her voice and resist the urge to reach over and place a hand on her thigh. I can't afford that kind of contact right now, not when I need to stay objective. "We'll see what Dean digs up on him," I say firmly. "If he has a record, we'll know soon."

She nods, falling silent again. I let the conversation lapse for a few miles, focusing on the road. The scenery is changing—rolling hills, thick clusters of trees. We'll be heading up into more remote terrain soon, away from main highways. That's exactly what I want: somewhere off the grid, difficult to track.

Eventually, she speaks up, her voice small. "Hey, Boone?"

"Yeah?" I keep my gaze forward, scanning the horizon.

"Can we... can we call my mom?" She shifts, as though she's about to reach for her pocket, forgetting that her phone isn't there. "Just to let her know I'm okay. She's probably worried sick."

My grip on the steering wheel tightens. I remember the conversation I had with Dean this morning, the details he dug up on Aubree's step-father. I don't have definitive proof he's involved, but something about the financial records—transfers, odd payments—makes me suspicious as hell. I don't like the idea of telling Aubree, not until I'm certain. I also don't like the idea of calling her mom, who might pass along our location to her husband.

"Not a good idea right now," I say carefully, trying not to sound too harsh.

She frowns. "Why not?"

"Because if your phone's traceable—and it might be, if these people are determined enough—calling your mom could give away our general area. Even if they can't pinpoint our exact location, they'll know which cell towers we're using." It's not a lie, but it's not the full truth either. I decide to push the technical side, so I don't have to mention her step-father yet. "I'm not willing to risk that."

She inhales sharply, her frustration palpable. "My mom's going to freak out, though."

I glance over and see tears gathering at the corners of her eyes. My resolve wavers. But then I steel myself. Her safety is more important than her mother's peace of mind, at least for now. "Aubree, I get that. But this is about survival. We can't contact anyone until I'm sure it's safe."

She bites her lip, tears threatening to fall. "Fine," she whispers, turning her head to stare out the window again.

I know she's hurting. I don't like doing this to her, but it's the only way. For all I know, her step-father could be the one pulling the strings—some messed-up plot to scare her out of town. The possibility seems wild, but stranger things have happened. Until I have answers, I'm not taking any risks.

The highway narrows, and soon I take an exit onto a smaller state route. The trees loom taller, the land more isolated. We pass a scattering of houses, most set far back from the road. Time slips by, the monotony of the drive broken only by the occasional passing vehicle.

Aubree leans her head against the window, and I can practically feel her disappointment rolling off her in waves. I want to reach over, rub her shoulder, something—anything—to comfort her. But I don't. I just keep driving.

After a while, she starts talking again, filling in more details about the threats. How she got an email with a crudely photoshopped image of a broken pizza sign, her shop's sign, made to look like it was burning. "That's when my mom hired Maddox Security," she says. "I guess she was right. I should've done it sooner."

"You did the best you could at the time," I reply, my voice quiet. "Nobody expects something like this until it happens."

She nods, tears gathering again, but this time she blinks them back. "I can't believe I might lose my shop," she says, voice trembling. "I've worked so hard for it. Seven years, Boone."

My throat tightens. "We'll do everything we can to make sure that doesn't happen. And in the meantime, just focus on staying safe. I can't help you rebuild if you end up hurt—or worse."

She swallows, glancing my way. There's gratitude and sadness in her expression, and maybe a flicker of something else. Something that reminds me how she felt in my arms the other night, how I almost lost my damned head over her. I shove the thought away and focus on the road.

The trees grow thicker as we climb a gentle slope, the road twisting and turning. The safe house is a friend-of-a-friend's cabin near a lake, if I recall correctly. I've never been there in person, but I have a rough idea of where we're going. Supposedly, it's secure, out of the way, and rarely visited. Dean said the owners are traveling abroad, which suits our situation perfectly.

I keep my eyes peeled for the turnoff. The sunlight filters through the foliage, creating patches of shade and light across the asphalt. Another ten minutes or so, and we'll arrive.

I glance at Aubree again, her features drawn in exhaustion. She's been through hell—anyone can see that. The guilt pricks at me once more, reminding me I'm the reason she can't even call her mother. But the moment she's in a truly safe spot, I'll figure out a way to get a message to her mom discreetly—assuming Dean can clear the step-father of suspicion. If not, well… we'll cross that bridge when we come to it.

Finally, I spot the unmarked dirt road that leads down to the lake. I slow the truck, turning onto the path, branches scraping the sides of the vehicle. The further we go, the quieter it becomes. No passing cars, no houses in sight—just dense woods and the occasional chirp of birds.

Aubree sits up straighter, peering through the windshield. "Where are we?"

"Just about there," I answer, scanning for the right fork in the road. "The place is tucked away, so we might have to do some searching to find it."

After a few hundred yards, the path branches. I take the right fork, which slopes downward toward a distant gleam of water. The truck bounces over rocks and ruts, the tires kicking up dust. Eventually, we come to a clearing. A small, single-story cabin stands at the edge of a lake, framed by towering pines. The water sparkles in the midday sun, and for a moment, it's almost picturesque—like a painting.

I park the truck near a weathered wooden porch. Cutting the engine, I wait, scanning the surroundings. Everything looks deserted—no other vehicles, no sign of recent activity. My phone vibrates in my pocket, and I fish it out. Dean's name appears on the screen, but I ignore it for now. First, I need to secure the property.

"Stay here," I tell Aubree firmly, though I already know what she'll say.

"But—"

"Stay," I repeat, fixing her with a stare. "I'm just gonna scout the place, make sure nobody's around."

She folds her arms, but I see the worry in her eyes. "Fine," she mumbles, sinking back into her seat.

Gun in hand, I step out of the truck, the door creaking. The air here is cooler, carrying the scent of pine and lake water. My boots crunch on gravel as I move around the cabin, checking windows and doors. No signs of forced entry, no footprints in the dirt except for animal tracks. Once I'm satisfied, I unlock the front door with a code given to me by Dean.

Guarding What's Mine

The interior is small, just a living room, a kitchen, one bedroom, and a bathroom. Minimal furniture—a couch, a table, a couple of chairs, a bed. Dust motes float in the beams of sunlight from the windows, suggesting it's been empty for a while. Perfect. This is exactly what I need: a secure, out-of-the-way location nobody would think to check.

I do a final sweep, then head back outside. Aubree's perched on the edge of the truck's seat. I open her door, and she steps out, glancing around like she expects someone to jump from behind a tree. "All clear," I say, tucking the gun away. "Let's get your stuff inside."

She exhales, looking momentarily relieved. "This is... remote. Really remote."

"That's the point," I say with a shrug, grabbing her duffel from the back. "Nobody should find us here."

She nods, following me up the porch steps. The old boards creak beneath our weight, and I can tell she's still uneasy. So am I, if I'm honest, but I try to project calm confidence for her sake. Once we step inside, I lock the door behind us, sliding the deadbolt into place. Then I draw the curtains, dimming the midday light.

"It's not much, but it's safe," I tell her.

She sets her foam takeout box on the small table, eyes scanning the cabin. Her gaze lands on me. "So... what now?"

I run a hand over my short hair, considering. "Now we wait. Dean and the team at Maddox will let us know if they get a lead on who's behind the threats. In the meantime, we lay low, keep off the radar. No phone calls, no leaving the property unless absolutely necessary."

She sighs, sinking into one of the chairs. "So basically, I'm a prisoner here."

The hurt in her voice stings more than I expect. "No, you're not a prisoner," I say, pushing back the flicker of guilt. "But you are a target. Until we handle that, we can't afford to let our guard down."

She looks up at me, and for a second, the tension eases. "Thank you," she says softly. "For all of this. I know you're… giving up a lot to keep me safe."

"I'm just doing my job," I answer, but the words feel inadequate. Because the truth is, it's more than a job now. The way my heart clenches when she's scared, the way I can't stop thinking about that kiss—it's not just business. And that terrifies me almost as much as the threats themselves.

She nods, then stands, crossing over to the dusty couch. With a thoughtful glance at me, she says, "Guess I'll unpack."

"Good idea," I reply, though my mind is already racing with next steps—like how to secure the perimeter so nobody can sneak up on us again.

As she unzips her duffel and starts rummaging for clean clothes, I take a moment to check my phone. Dean's text simply reads: "Got a partial lead on Mitch. Will call soon." My gut tightens. A partial lead is better than nothing. Maybe we're finally getting somewhere.

I slip the phone into my pocket, letting out a slow breath. One step at a time. First, secure this place, make sure nobody can ambush us. Then wait for Dean's call, see if Mitch or someone else stands out as a prime suspect. If so, we move. We get the proof we need, or we confront them directly, whichever method is safer.

And as for Aubree's step-father… well, I'll keep that suspicion to myself until I have more to go on. I'm not going to break her heart with half-baked theories.

Before I fully set my attention on my next task, I allow myself one quick moment to appreciate the sight of her. She glances back at me, meeting my eyes, and a flicker of a smile crosses her lips. Despite everything, she's still got that spark. And I realize that spark is what's going to keep us both going—until we've put a stop to whoever's behind these threats, once and for all.

Chapter 20

Aubree

I wake up to the soft golden light creeping through the thin curtains, illuminating the dust motes floating around the bedroom. It's been about three days since Boone and I arrived at this off-the-grid cabin, and somehow, I've managed to settle into a pattern of existence that feels both strangely peaceful and unbearably suffocating at the same time.

The first morning, I barely slept, terrified of every creak and rustle in the woods. I spent half the night replaying the threats in my mind, thinking of how everything in my life had been turned upside down. But Boone insisted that a routine would help, that structure can stave off the anxiety. In some ways, he's right. Every day has been almost identical. It's a little after six in the morning, and I already know how most of the day will unfold.

I push back the covers, slide out of bed, and stretch. The small cabin bedroom is modest—just a narrow closet, a dresser, and a bed. I can hear Boone in the living room; he's a morning person, or at least, he's up at dawn out of habit. I shuffle into the adjoining bathroom, do a quick wash, tie my hair back in a loose ponytail, and change into some leggings and a hoodie. The air in the cabin has a permanent chill to it this early, and the old wooden floors don't help.

When I emerge into the living area, Boone is perched by the window, sipping a mug of coffee. He's wearing sweatpants and a T-shirt, his hair still slightly damp from his shower. The rays of sunlight catch the angles of his face, highlighting that strong jaw and the subtle thickness of his beard. Even though he's only been here a few days, the cabin life already looks good on him. Then again, I suspect Boone could adapt to almost any environment. There's a contained energy in him that reminds me of a coiled spring.

He glances over as I step in. "Morning," he says in that deep voice.

"Morning," I reply, stifling a yawn.

I gather what I need for coffee, mindful of how limited our supplies are. We haven't exactly ventured out much. Aside from the small run Boone did to a grocery store two towns over, we've been living off a combination of what was already stocked here—canned goods and some dry staples—and the fresh ingredients he managed to grab. Yesterday, I taught him how to cook a simple pasta dish. It was adorable how focused he became, like he was on a secret mission. I'd have teased him more if I wasn't so grateful for the distraction.

He stands when he sees me fiddling with the coffee maker. "I got it," he says, coming over to take the kettle from my hands.

I let him step in, thankful of the way he takes care of me. Boone keeps everything in the cabin meticulously organized. He calls it 'operational efficiency.' I guess when your job is security, the concept of leaving anything to chance doesn't exist.

We don't talk much as we finish our coffee. Mornings are quiet—our unspoken agreement to let each other wake up before diving into heavier topics like who might be trying to kill me. Or how we're going to keep my pizza shop afloat when I'm here in the middle of nowhere.

Eventually, he sets his mug down with a soft thud. "Ready for the jog?"

I force a small smile. "As ready as I'll ever be."

Jogging is Boone's idea, of course, a leftover from his military days. The first time he suggested it, I nearly laughed in his face—running hasn't ever been my favorite activity. But he insisted it'd help me blow off steam, and to my surprise, it kind of does. There's something about the repetitive pounding of my feet on the dirt path, the crisp morning air filling my lungs, that momentarily clears my mind.

We head outside, the grass still wet with dew. I wait while Boone locks the cabin door behind us. Then we set off at a light pace around the property. The route is basically a big loop circling the lake, passing through a patch of forest, and finally curving back to the cabin's gravel driveway.

We run in silence, just the sound of our breaths mingling with the crunch of gravel underfoot. Sometimes, I catch myself glancing at Boone's profile. Strong shoulders, steady stride. He's always scanning the perimeter, even as we jog, eyes shifting left and right, searching for threats. It reminds me how seriously he takes his job—and how thoroughly he's put distance between us on a personal level.

Over the last few days, we've shared the same small space, cooked together, laughed a few times, and yet...he hasn't made another move. No more kisses, no more lingering touches. Part of me wants to blame the tension we're under, but the truth is, I can see it in his eyes—he's purposefully holding back. And that stings more than I care to admit.

By the time we finish our circuit, my legs are burning and I'm gasping for air. Boone hardly seems winded, which is borderline hot as hell. He offers me a bottle of water from the porch, and I take it, murmuring thanks as I gulp it down.

We head inside, and Boone immediately checks his phone, scanning for any updates from Maddox Security. Most of the time, there's nothing new. I can tell he's frustrated by the lack of progress—though he tries to hide it from me, I've learned to read him at least a little.

I linger near the kitchen counter, feeling uncertain. "I'm going to do some meal prep," I say, my voice sounding oddly loud in the silent cabin. "We've still got those chicken breasts to use up."

"Sure," Boone replies, sounding distracted. His gaze is on the phone screen, brow furrowed.

I try not to let his distance bother me, but it does. I tell myself it's for the best—he's supposed to be protecting me, not falling into bed with me. But I can't deny the ache of disappointment. There's a gnawing sense of loneliness, like I'm stuck in limbo, waiting for my life to begin again.

By the time evening rolls around, I can't stand being inside another moment. The weather's lovely—clear skies, mild temperature, and a faint breeze that ruffles the tall pines surrounding the lake. An idea strikes me, and I spring into action.

I rummage through the kitchen cupboards until I find some pasta, a can of tomato sauce, and a hunk of mozzarella I'd been saving. And chicken. I'll make a nice chicken parmigiana. Perfect. I busy myself boiling water, chopping onions, and adding spices. The smell of garlic and tomatoes fills the small space, lending it a cozy warmth that momentarily makes me forget all the ugliness that drove me here.

Boone looks up from where he's checking the locks on the windows. "You cooking dinner?"

I offer him a playful smile, something I haven't felt in a while. "Yeah. But we're not eating in here tonight."

He arches a brow. "We're not?"

"Uh-uh." I glance out the window. "I thought maybe we could, I don't know, eat under the stars. Since it's such a nice evening."

His gaze flits to the window, and for a second, I catch a flash of longing in his eyes. Maybe he needs to break the cabin monotony too, but he won't say it. He just nods. "All right. But keep it close to the cabin. I can't protect you if we wander too far."

"Deal," I say quietly, turning back to stir the pasta.

I set the table just enough to gather two plates, utensils, and some napkins. I find an old quilt folded in the closet—faded blue and white squares, smelling faintly of mothballs. With a wrinkle of my nose, I spritz it with a little fabric spray I find in one of the drawers. Good enough.

The pasta sauce simmers for a while, filling the cabin with a mouthwatering aroma. I tear up the mozzarella into small bits and stir them in, letting them get all melty and gooey. My stomach rumbles in anticipation, and I can't help but think about how this is the closest I've been to my old life in days—cooking for someone else, conjuring up a sense of normalcy through food.

Once everything's ready, I load up two plates with chicken, steaming pasta, sauce, and cheese, set them on a tray along with two glasses of water (wine would be nice, but we're fresh out), and carry it all outside. Boone follows me, carrying the folded quilt over his arm.

We pick a spot in the yard not too far from the cabin, a patch of soft grass under a wide expanse of sky. The sun is setting, painting the horizon in bright pinks and blood oranges, and the first stars are just beginning to glimmer. Boone spreads the quilt out, and I place the tray in the center.

He takes one last look around, like he's scouting for threats. Then he sits down beside me, crossing his long legs. Even in the dimming light, I can see the weariness etched into his features—shadows under his eyes, a tightness around his mouth. Yet, when he looks at me, there's a warmth too, a kindness I crave more than I want to admit.

"Smells good," he says, picking up his fork.

"Thanks," I reply, a small bubble of pride swelling in my chest. "It's nothing fancy, just something quick I used to make at the shop. But I used to put pepperoni on it to make it pizza-esque."

He laughs softly, and for a moment, I bask in the sound of his quiet laughter. We start eating, and I'm amazed at how just being outdoors, under the open sky, makes everything feel lighter. The lake is a dark mirror reflecting the twilight, and a gentle breeze rustles the pines.

We eat in companionable silence for a while, until the stars fully emerge overhead—tiny pinpricks of light in a vast indigo canvas. I can't help but tilt my head back and gaze at them. The hush of the night is mesmerizing, and for a few seconds, I almost forget the danger that brought us here.

Boone sets his plate aside. "You grew up around here, didn't you?" he asks softly.

"Sort of," I say, drawing my legs up under me. "I was born in Nashville. My mom moved us to Saint Pierce for a while so she could be closer to my grandparents. But I always loved Tennessee. Couldn't stay away for long. Plus, I was obsessed with pizza from, like, middle school onward, so I guess it was destiny to open my own place."

He smiles in the faint light. "Obsessed with pizza, huh?"

"Completely." A little chuckle escapes me. "You have no idea. In high school, my friends used to call me 'Brie-cheese.' Like Aubree, Bree, and well…"

He arches an eyebrow. "Brie-cheese?"

I groan, but I can't help smiling at the memory. "Yeah. They said it was because I would literally put cheese on anything—sandwiches, salads, even scrambled eggs. Mozzarella was my favorite, but I wasn't picky. If it was cheese, I wanted it."

Boone rubs his chin, the scratch of his beard just audible. "So wait, how exactly did that translate to them calling you Brie-cheese?"

"I guess because whenever we ordered pizza, I'd always demand extra cheese," I explain, rolling my eyes at my younger self. "It became a running joke. At some point, one of them said, 'We don't even need to ask what Aubree wants—just slap on the extra cheese. Brie-cheese. And it stuck."

He chuckles, a low rumble that warms me from the inside. "All right, Brie-cheese, that's pretty adorable."

I bump his shoulder lightly with mine. "Hey, don't get any ideas. I outgrew that nickname."

He laughs softly. "I'll keep that in mind. And also, thank you for doing this," he says, gesturing to the quilt, the plates. "I needed it."

I tuck a strand of hair behind my ear. "Me too. I've been going stir-crazy. There's only so many games of cards I can play before I start feeling like a prisoner."

He nods, a hint of regret clouding his expression. "I know. I'm sorry. I wish I could tell you we'll be out of here soon, but…"

"It's okay," I cut in. "I get it. We're waiting on leads from Dean and the rest. I just…" I trail off, not sure how to articulate the frustration lodged in my chest.

He clears his throat. "We are. And trust me, they're working around the clock. Dean sent me a text earlier. Said they've narrowed down a few suspects. Doesn't mean they have proof, but they're getting closer."

My heart picks up at that. "So maybe in a few more days we'll have answers?"

"Maybe," he says, noncommittal but not discouraging. "We can hope."

We both turn our eyes back to the night sky. My shoulders relax a little, comforted by the idea that maybe the end of this nightmare is in sight. Though I can't deny a small pang of sadness at the thought of leaving Boone behind when it's over. Or maybe he'll be the one to vanish from my life, duty done. The idea sends an unexpected jolt of loneliness through me.

I shove the feeling down and force a smile instead. "Hey," I say, nodding at the darkness around us. "You sure no bears are going to come snatch us up?"

He barks a quiet laugh. "Pretty sure. But if they do, I'll wrestle them. No big deal."

I grin, imagining him wrestling a bear. "Now that's something I'd pay to see."

He shakes his head, a rare, genuine smile tugging at his lips. In the dim light, he looks softer somehow, not quite so guarded. My heart flutters in a way that catches me off guard. It's been days since he so much as brushed my hand without business in mind. I'd almost convinced myself that night at the cabin was a fluke. A moment of weakness on his part.

A breeze rustles the trees, carrying a faint whisper of pine needles. The temperature drops a notch, and I shiver. Boone notices immediately and slides his arm around my shoulders, pulling me closer. The warmth of his body is instant, and my eyes drift shut for a moment, relishing the contact.

My heart starts pounding at the memory of him. It's so easy to imagine letting myself sink back into those feelings—except I know Boone's made a conscious choice to keep distance. I feel it in the way he holds me, protective yet cautious.

"Thanks," I whisper.

He hums in acknowledgment, but doesn't let go. And for a little while, we just sit there, side by side, watching the sky. Our half-eaten plates rest on the quilt, and I'm sure the pasta's gone cold by now, but I don't care. This moment feels almost dreamlike.

I'm not sure how much time passes before he shifts, easing me upright. "C'mon," he murmurs. "Let's get you inside before you freeze."

I don't want this moment to end. I blink up at him, my heart roaring in my ears and whisper, "Please kiss me."

Chapter 21

Boone

"Please kiss me."

I have to pretend she didn't just ask that. I shake my head, trying not to stare at her mouth, but it's getting harder by the second. Aubree leans against me, head resting on my shoulder, and I swear her lips are just inches from my line of sight—taunting me. The night sky sprawls overhead, stars sprinkled across the darkness, and the moon casts a silver glow on the quilt we're sitting on. The air is crisp, smelling of pine and lake water, but the only thing I'm really aware of is her warmth against my side.

I tell myself I shouldn't be thinking about kissing her. Not now, not when she's depending on me to keep her alive. But that familiar jolt of desire shoots through my veins, the same one I've been denying since the first time I laid eyes on her. My grip on her shoulder tightens a fraction, and my pulse pounds like I'm sprinting up a hill in full gear.

We've been talking quietly—about nothing, really. The day, the weather, the same comfortable routine we've built over the last few days. But with every minute that passes, I'm more keenly aware of how close she is, how my arm drapes casually around her shoulders, and how tempting her skin looks in the moonlight.

"Aubree..." I begin, my voice low and gravelly. Her brown eyes are bright, lips parted just enough to make it impossible to ignore the ache in my chest.

She arches a brow, a hint of a smile tugging at her mouth. "Yeah?"

I swallow, trying to rein in the tension thrumming through me. "We should probably head inside," I say, though the words taste like regret.

She doesn't move. Instead, she fixes me with a look that steals whatever coherent thought I had left in my head. Slowly, she rises on her knees, close enough that I can feel her breath against my cheek. "Boone," she whispers, her voice trembling just a bit. "Please kiss me."

Her plea knocks the air from my lungs. In that instant, all my carefully erected barriers, all the reasons I've been telling myself we should keep our distance, crumble. I can't resist anymore. Not with her eyes so earnest, not with the way she leans into me, fingertips grazing my chest as though she's afraid I might disappear.

I shift, turning so I can cup her cheek in one hand. My palm tingles at the warmth of her skin, and for a moment, we both pause—like we're standing on the edge of a cliff, deciding whether to jump. Then I tilt her face up and lower my head, pressing my lips to hers.

Guarding What's Mine

The kiss sparks through me like lightning. Her lips are soft, a perfect fit against mine, and I lose myself in the sensation. My fingers slide into her hair, drawing her closer as I deepen the kiss. I'd intended this to be gentle, cautious. But the weeks of tension, the days of pretending we're just two people sharing space, erupt into something hotter, more desperate.

Aubree lets out a soft sound of approval and tangles her fingers in my shirt, pulling me closer. My heart jackhammers against my ribs, and I angle my body so I can wrap my other arm around her waist, holding her securely. Every breath feels stolen, every second charged with a new urgency.

The moonlight casts shifting shadows over us as we move, her hands sliding up my arms, over my shoulders. I feel the goosebumps rise on her skin when I trail my knuckles along her forearm. I tug her gently onto my lap, and she comes willingly, her knees bracketing my hips. The press of her body against mine sends a fresh surge of heat coursing through my veins.

My mind flashes with warning signals—this is dangerous, we're vulnerable, we should be inside—but right now, the only thing I care about is the taste of her lips and the feel of her body against me. Every sense is overloaded: the night air cooling our exposed skin, the scent of pine and faint woodsmoke from the cabin's fireplace. It all merges into a heady rush as we kiss and kiss, like we've been starved for this connection.

She breaks away for a moment, panting softly, her eyes searching mine. "We...should..." she tries to say, but I pull her back in, capturing her mouth before she can finish the thought. My tongue grazes hers, and she shivers against me, a soft moan escaping her lips.

My hand slides down to the small of her back, anchoring her to me. Her nails dig gently into my shoulders, not enough to hurt but enough to make me feel how much she wants this too. I groan low in my throat, the sound swallowed by our kiss.

Eventually, the need for air forces us apart. We stay there, foreheads touching, both of us breathing hard. My chest rises and falls in time with hers. She's trembling, and I realize my own hands are shaking too—from adrenaline, from need, from everything.

"You have no idea," I manage, voice rough, "how long I've been trying not to do that."

Her lips curve into a wobbly smile. "I might have an idea," she says, placing a hand over my racing heart. "Because I feel the same way."

I exhale, pressing a kiss to her temple. Warmth floods my chest, mingling with a potent cocktail of desire and relief. For the first time in what feels like ages, I let go of the rigid rules I've set for myself. We both deserve this moment—deserve to feel something other than fear.

"We should probably still move this inside," I whisper, taking a quick glance around. There's no immediate threat, but the open yard isn't exactly the safest spot for letting our guards down.

Aubree nods, her breathing still uneven. "Let's go," she agrees, though her fingers linger in my hair as though she's reluctant to break away.

I help her up, and for a second, we wobble on unsteady legs. She tugs me back in for one more quick kiss, and I indulge her gladly, savoring the taste of her lips in the moonlight. Then, hand in hand, we gather our belongings and head toward the cabin, the night air cool against our flushed skin.

And as we cross the threshold, my arm around her waist, I swear I can still feel the imprint of her kiss, the echo of her heartbeat against mine. I fucking want her.

We head inside, and the moment I shut and lock the door, I've got her in my arms. My lips crash down against hers as I push her against the thick wood of the door.

"I need you, Aubree. I've been fighting with myself for days. Since I met you. I've been fighting, trying to tell myself this isn't a good idea." I smooth a hand down her hair. "But I'm tired of fighting this feeling."

She nods. "Me too."

I kiss her, more gently this time as my hands roam through her long tresses. I fist a hand in her hair, tugging her, angling her face so I can deepen the kiss. I love the way she tastes. Like candy and sunshine all rolled into one. I keep kissing her, swallowing down each of her tiny moans.

Together we work quickly to remove all of our clothing. Once I get her to the bedroom, I shut the door, and gaze at her. She's breathtaking.

"I've wanted you since the moment I first laid eyes on you. Since I first saw the photo of you."

She sucks in a breath as she moves to the edge of the bed. "Really?" she whispers.

I nod. "Really," I say as I stalk closer, fisting my hard length in my hand. "Look at what you do to me." I squeeze the tip of my cock, showing her exactly how hot she makes me.

"You turn me on too."

My eyes nearly glaze over as I stare at her. "Show me."

She blinks. "Umm…"

"On the bed. Legs spread. I want to see how wet you are."

Her cheeks blush at my dirty way of talking to her, and it turns me on even more. I'm beginning to realize everything she does turns me on.

"Legs spread," I say again when she hesitates.

Her cheeks are flaming red, and the look is absolutely adorable. I love it. "I, uh…" her words fall away as she scoots up further on the bed. "I'm shy."

I climb on the bed with purpose, grabbing her ankle toward me. "Don't be. There's never any reason you need to be shy around me."

She falls back as I tug at her ankle. "Boone," she says with a laugh. "No, I can't do this."

I squeeze her ankle, locking eyes with her. "Yes, you can."

Chapter 22

Aubree

I can't believe I'm really going through with this—letting Boone see me like this. I've always been the type who prefers sex under the covers, lights off, insecurities tucked away. It's not that I hate my body, but everyone's got their trouble spots, right? I definitely do. But when Boone looks at me—really looks at me, like I'm the most exquisite thing he's ever seen—every stray thought about late-night pizza binges or so-called imperfections just disappears.

He makes me feel beautiful. There's this hunger in his eyes, as though he's studying a masterpiece, and I'm suddenly not afraid to be on full display. It's thrilling, being the object of that intense focus. Sure, Boone could have anyone—he's downright gorgeous—but in this moment, the way he watches me makes it feel like I'm the only one in the world, and that is a heady, electric feeling I never want to end.

I spread my legs for him, letting him see the desire first hand. He draws in a ragged breath, his eyes fixated solely on me. My cheeks flame red-hot as he positions himself between my legs. He leans down—*and oh my god*. He swipes his tongue through my wetness and I nearly bound off the bed.

"I've never…" my words fall away as I try to articulate a complete thought.

His eyes gaze up at me. "Never what?"

"I've never really enjoyed this," I tell him truthfully. "No man has ever made me orgasm by doing this, so it's okay. We can just have sex." I feel almost embarrassed at my lack of being able to come multiple times in one sexual session.

He grips my inner thighs with both hands and drags his tongue over my pussy, his eyes never leaving mine. "I just don't think you've ever been eaten properly."

My eyes widen as I gaze into the depths of his dark brown eyes. "Well…I…" am speechless. I don't even know what to say to him in this moment, so I do the only thing I can. I close my eyes, lay my head back and let him continue.

And…once again, *oh my god*. This man has a tongue made of magic, and before I can even tell what's happening, or which way is up…I feel my body, ready to break free. I'm ready to come undone, and all I can do is grip onto his thick hair and hold on as I buck against his face. I can't believe this is happening to me.

I can't believe I'm feeling this free. *This alive*. It's like somebody's set off a firework deep in my soul and I'm barely trying to hang on.

Wow. "Oh, Boone," I call out into the emptiness of the room. My body lets loose, the past few months of anguish unleashes, and I topple down. "I'm coming," I shout, and Boone grips harder onto my thighs as he uses the pad of his tongue on my clit, applying the right amount of pressure to keep my orgasm spiraling out of control. "Oh, Boone. Boone, I'm so…" I don't even know how to finish this sentence. Because in this moment I don't know what I am.

I feel like a leaf caught in free fall, drifting helplessly through the air. Each gust of wind seizes me, carrying me across the lawn while I remain powerless in my own body. Boone keeps a grip on me, not letting me go as he continues to work his tongue over my heated skin.

The sensations are too much to handle, and I cry out that I can't handle it, but he doesn't let up. He keeps going, causing something in my body to happen that has *never* happened before. I feel that initial climb once again. The start of another orgasm. This can't be happening. Can it?

I mean…

"Oh my fuck, Boone," I scream out, my body betraying me. This second orgasm rips through me like a violent storm, overwhelming every sense and leaving me trembling in its wake. "I can't believe this." I keep grinding myself against his face as I squeeze my eyes shut. "This can't be real…*fuck, oh my*…Boone."

He doesn't let up as he keeps going. "I need inside you, Aubree."

Right now, it's the only thing I crave. I nod, my heart pounding wildly in my chest. Boone rushes up my body as I try to get my breathing under control. He kisses me, passionately.

"You're so fucking pretty when you come all over me."

I'm so far past blushing at this point, but still, his words do something to me. My body's spent, yet I still crave him. Still want him. More than I've ever wanted anything in my entire life.

"I've never had two back-to-back orgasms like that before."

He smiles, pride swelling in his chest. "You're not done yet."

I don't want to argue with him, but three orgasms in one night is unheard of. I've never had three orgasms in a week, let alone one night. "Oh," is all I manage to say, and Boone lifts a brow.

"Don't believe me?"

I laugh lightly as he positions himself between my legs, hovering over me. "Well, it's highly unlikely. Listen, two orgasms while going down on me is a huge feat. You should be proud."

He chuckles lightly. "Aubree, when I'm done with you tonight you'll be begging me to take it easy. Because it's now my mission to make you come as many times as possible tonight. And you know my mission success rate?"

"No."

He whispers, "It's a hundred percent. I never fail," and the confidence in his voice sets my heart racing. Then he leans in again, capturing my mouth in a slow, intoxicating kiss that seems to suspend time. The heat of his lips against mine sends a tremor through my entire body, and with each gentle sweep of his tongue, he makes every other kiss I've ever experienced vanish from memory. In this moment, I feel desired, cherished —like I'm the only person in the world he wants to touch.

His hands roam over my body, like he's memorizing every curve. His hand grips his dick between us, and I glance down. The engorged tip pushes at my entrance. "Are you on the pill?" he rushes out.

"I, umm…yes. I'm on the pill."

He appears relieved and pushes the head of his cock inside me. Inch by glorious inch. He's so big, a part of me wonders if it'll even fit, or if we'll be working this thing inside me all night long. "You're just a tight thing, aren't you?"

I blink up at him as he watches the spot where our two bodies are joined.

"So fucking tight." He punches his hips forward once more, causing his dick to push further into me.

"Ah, Boone." I grip onto his back, my nails digging in slightly to his heated skin. The feel of his muscles working beneath his skin is a major turn on. His body is made by the Gods. Each muscle etched in stone.

It's like a masterpiece, and I can't stop marveling at him.

He smooths a hand over my hair, his mouth close to my ear. "Your pussy was made for my dick, do you know that? It's a perfect fit." He pushes all the way inside me, and my body acclimates to him quickly.

It's like what he's saying is true. Like our bodies were made for one another. He gazes at me as both of us stop moving. Our breaths mingle together as his eyes meet mine.

"You're gorgeous, Bree. Seriously, I can't stop staring at you."

"I feel the exact same way," I tell him, honestly. "I haven't been able to stop staring at you since you barged into my pizza shop."

He smiles slowly, his hips thrusting forward slightly. "I didn't barge. I thought you were hurt. I rushed in to make sure you were okay."

I grip his face, feeling his bushy beard under my hands. "I appreciate how you always put my safety first. I mean, I know it's just your job…"

He cuts in, "No, it's not just my job, Aubree. I care way too much about you. I'll always keep you safe. Or die trying."

I close my eyes, not liking the sound of him dying out there in the world. The next thing I know we're lost in the art of making love. Or fucking. It's rough, and gentle all at the same time. He holds me close as he pounds away inside me. He kisses me tenderly as he pulls my hair. He thrusts deep, almost at a punishing pace as he caresses my soft skin.

"You're like an enigma," he tells me. "So fucking pretty. I can't figure you out."

"There's not much to figure out."

He gazes at me as he moves his dick in and out of me. "I can't understand why anyone would ever want to hurt you." He peppers kisses along my temple, moving down my cheek, crossing my jawline. He continues placing kisses along my neck, down the column of my throat, and across my collarbone. "I'll never let the fuckers after you get close enough to hurt you. They'll have to go through me first."

He grips my hair, as he repositions our bodies. "I need deeper inside you." He tosses one of my legs over his shoulder. This causes him to slide even deeper inside me.

"Oh, Boone," I call out. My body's like a livewire, and I'm unable to control the next orgasm that rips right through me. "I'm coming." That's orgasm number three.

Wow.

Boone keeps screwing me, pounding, thrusting, diving into me so deep all I can feel is only him. He turns me on in a way I've

Guarding What's Mine

never experienced before. Like he's never had anything so amazing in his life.

He's feeling this too, right? This crazy connection? It's not just a one-time thing, right?

No, I refuse to believe Boone is anything but genuine with me. I trust him. He's been the one thing that has kept me feeling safe in a time when I feel anything but. It's all him. I don't want to start getting thoughts of happily ever after, because who knows what happens when all this is said and done. I don't even know if he lives in Tennessee full time.

"The way your pussy grips my hard cock is enough to make me never want to stop doing this." He groans against me. "You're so fucking needy for me."

And I am. I *so* am.

"Oh, Boone." My body tightens as he keeps pounding away inside me. He moves his hand between our bodies and toys with my clit, but there's seriously no way there's another orgasm left in me.

I'm spent.

"Give me another," he whispers close to my ear. "Just one more."

"Will you fail your mission if I don't?"

He chuckles, his warm breath fanning across my cheek. "I never fail. I'll get you off one more time." He props up, and gazes down at me. "This time."

"What do you mean this time?"

He smirks. "I'm nowhere near done with you tonight."

He thrums my clit between his fingers, and ...*wow*... I'm coming again. For the fourth time.

"God, you fucking turn me on so damn much. Your pussy feels way too perfect wrapped around me." He groans and grunts a few curses. "I'm gonna come so deep inside you, Bree. Fuck. *Too tight.* Jesus." His body picks up speed as he grips onto me tighter. "Too damn good... *fuck.*"

His body crumbles in my arms as his orgasm completely annihilates him. He's cursing and calling out my name as he comes, and I am here for it. Watching this man lose control is a major turn on.

I'm not gonna lie, but it makes my chest crack wide open. I could easily fall in love with this man, but I need to remember this is only temporary.

Once we catch whoever's after me, life will return back to normal. Whatever that may be.

Chapter 23

Boone

I'm still reeling from her taste—hell, the way she felt wrapped around me—when we finally pull ourselves apart and decide we should eat something. It's early, like maybe five in the morning. My heart's thumping an irregular beat in my chest, and my skin still hums in all the places she touched me. It's crazy how fast this escalated from carefully tiptoeing around each other to full-on fucking. But I'm not complaining.

We toss on some clothes and head into the kitchen. I hang back, still catching my breath. "I'll cook something for us," I offer, running a hand over my hair, which feels a little wild after her fingers were tangled in it. "You already did the heavy lifting with dinner last night."

She sidles closer, and just the heat of her presence sends a pulse of awareness through my body. She must notice my hungry expression and giggles. "Let me cook for you."

I blink at her. "But you cooked last night."

She shrugs. "I enjoy cooking. It relaxes me."

"I can't argue with that." I pull eggs out of the fridge, and she gets to work on making an omelet. "I'm starving." I smile.

Aubree smirks, flipping the omelet expertly. "Yeah, we really worked up an appetite."

Warmth blooms in my chest at the memory. "That was… unexpected."

"Good unexpected, I hope," she says, her voice quieting.

"Definitely," I murmur, stepping closer to rest a hand on her lower back. She leans into the touch, her body language telling me she's as affected as I am.

Our moment is cut short by the chime of my phone on the counter. I sigh, letting go of Aubree to check the screen. It's a text from Dean, and judging by the urgency in his message—"Need to talk. Info on stepfather"—I know it's not gonna be good. I unlock the phone and scan the details.

Aubree's brow furrows. "What's up?"

I glance over at her, torn between telling her outright and trying to soften the blow. But I promised to keep her in the loop, and she deserves that. "Dean says your stepfather, Charles, has had a few large transactions in his bank account recently. They're suspicious because nobody knows where the money's coming from, and one of the transactions happened the night before your pizza shop was attacked."

Her spatula slows as she processes my words. "The night before the brick?" she echoes, eyes widening. "That can't be a coincidence."

"Dean doesn't know for sure if it's connected," I add, watching the flicker of anxiety in her expression. "But he wants to dig deeper. See if Charles is funneling money for something shady."

Aubree turns off the stove and slides the finished omelet onto a plate. I reach out, steadying the plate before it falls from her trembling hand. She busies herself by grabbing a second plate from the cupboard and dividing the omelet, but I can tell her mind's a million miles away.

Finally, she sets the plates on the small table and gestures for me to sit. "Well," she says, exhaling sharply, "I can't say I'm surprised. I've always suspected Charles was after money."

I lower myself into a chair across from her, tension gathering in my shoulders. "You did?"

She nods, looking down at her plate instead of at me. "Yeah. My mom's... she's well-off. My father left her a big inheritance when he died, plus she's got a successful real estate business of her own. Charles came into the picture about a year ago, all smiles and charm. But I never fully trusted him. I don't think he married her because he loves her."

I watch her push the omelet around with her fork, appetite seemingly forgotten. "So, you think Charles might be in financial trouble, or something like that?"

"That's exactly what I think," she says, glancing up with a bitter twist of her lips. "He supposedly runs a real estate office, but my mom mentioned it was bleeding money. He's a smooth talker, though, so she wrote it off as temporary problems. He's always going on about how 'the next big deal' is right around the corner."

I'm quiet for a moment, absorbing what she's saying. If Charles has money problems, it's not a huge leap to wonder if he's capable of something worse—like hiring someone to scare Aubree out of town to get control of her mom's assets. It's a stretch, but I've seen worse motivations in my line of work.

Aubree sighs, finally forcing a bite of her omelet into her mouth. She chews slowly, her gaze distant. "I just hate thinking my mom could be so easily manipulated. She's smart, but she always wants to see the best in people."

"It's not her fault," I say gently, crossing an arm over my chest. "Some people are experts at deception. If Charles is one of them, I'm sure he's very convincing."

She nods in reluctant agreement, then sets her fork down, apparently giving up on eating. "You think he's behind it, don't you?" she asks softly, folding her hands together in her lap.

"I don't know," I admit. "Dean wouldn't have mentioned those transactions if he didn't think it was worth looking into. It could be a coincidence, or it could be that Charles is funneling money to someone who's threatening you. We don't have evidence yet."

She exhales, leaning back in her chair. "You realize what that means, right? If my stepfather is behind this… It's not just about me. It's about my mom too."

A pang of worry stabs through me at the thought of Aubree's mother being at risk. If Charles is that desperate for cash, who knows what else he's capable of? "I know," I say firmly. "But let's not jump to conclusions until we have proof. Dean's good at digging up information. If there's something to be found, he'll find it."

Her eyes flick to the phone. "Could we at least let my mom know I'm okay? Without mentioning any suspicions, I mean."

The urge to protect her is as strong as ever, but I also need to protect her mother. I chew on my lip, weighing the risks. "I still think we should wait," I say gently. "At least until Dean finishes looking into Charles. If we contact your mom and he's monitoring her phone or her messages, it could give away our location. I can't let that happen."

Her face falls, and guilt claws at me. But she nods, accepting the logic. "I just hate that she's in the dark. She's probably worried sick."

I reach across the table and cover her hand with mine. "I know. As soon as it's safe, we'll figure out a way to let her know you're okay. But we can't risk Charles intercepting that call." My thumb strokes the back of her hand, trying to offer some reassurance. "Trust me. We'll do this the right way."

She squeezes my fingers in return, her eyes glistening. "Okay," she whispers, sounding a little defeated. "Thank you, Boone. For...everything."

I want to say more, but the words get tangled in my throat. Instead, I give her hand another reassuring squeeze and then clear my throat, turning my attention back to the food. "We should eat before it gets cold. You worked hard on that omelet."

A flicker of a smile crosses her lips. "Yeah, I did." She picks up her fork again, taking a small bite.

We lapse into a heavy silence as we eat. The omelet is actually really good—she wasn't bragging when she said she's a great cook. But neither of us seems to have much appetite now. Every forkful is forced, the tension pressing in on us like a weight.

Eventually, I push my plate away, half-finished. "I guess we just wait to hear more from Dean," I say quietly. "In the meantime, we stick to the plan: stay here, stay hidden, stay safe."

She nods, her eyes dropping to the table. "Yeah. Stay safe," she echoes, like she's trying to convince herself it's possible.

I stand up and start gathering the dishes. A feeling of helplessness swamps me. I hate that we're stuck in this limbo, depending on other people to uncover the truth. But if Charles is behind this, we need real proof to confront him—or to protect Aubree's mom from a dangerously desperate man.

As I rinse the plates in the small sink, I hear Aubree move behind me. She slides her arms around my waist, pressing her cheek to my back. The quiet gesture surprises me, but I relax into it, letting the moment soothe some of the tension.

"Thank you," she repeats, voice muffled against my shirt.

I turn in her arms, resting my hands on her hips. "I promised to keep you safe," I remind her. "That doesn't stop at just physical threats. If Charles is involved, I'll make sure he doesn't hurt you or your mom. One way or another."

She looks up at me, eyes brimming with gratitude—and a lingering sadness. "I believe you," she says.

I nod, wishing I could do more than offer hollow promises. We stand there, locked in a wordless embrace, the faint sound of wind rattling the windows. No matter how chaotic things get, I'm determined to protect her. Even if that means tearing down her stepfather's schemes to do it.

Eventually, we pull apart, and I give her a small smile, trying to ease the knot in my chest. With every new piece of information, the puzzle gets darker. But one thing's certain: we won't get blindsided by Charles or anyone else. Not on my watch.

I glance at her one last time before flipping off the kitchen light. She meets my gaze, and I pull her closer. "I don't want you to think about any of this right now, okay?"

She nods, her beautiful, big eyes meeting mine. "Okay." She smiles softly, and I have to fucking kiss her or I'll die right here.

I lean in, capturing her lips with mine. "I'm going to take your mind off everything." Together we move into the bedroom and I lean in to press my body against hers. She smells incredible. Good enough to eat… again.

She smiles up at me, gazing at me from under her long lashes. "I'm ready for my dessert," she whispers in the sultriest voice I've ever heard.

My cock goes from semi to full on hard as steel. "I was kidding when I said that. I'd never…" my words die on my lips once she sinks to her knees.

Fuck me.

"Bree, baby. You don't need…"

She shushes me as she lowers my gray sweatpants. My cock's already hard as a rock, and she licks her lips. "I'll never get used to the size of you." She blinks up at me, and she looks so good down there, about to suck my dick into her mouth.

The way she says she'll never get used to the size of me has me picturing a life with her. The sentence was probably just something spoken in the moment, but the implications are life-altering. I want her to get used to me. I want to be around long enough.

She darts out her pink tongue, swiping it across the tip of my dick. I groan as soon as her tongue comes into contact with me. *It feels so good.*

"You keep looking at me like that and this'll be over a lot quicker than I intend for it to be."

She smiles wide, and I immediately fall head over heels for this woman. She's gorgeous. "Noted," she says, her breath fanning across the heated skin of my balls. She licks her lips once more, blinking up at me.

She opens her mouth and sucks my length in between her lips. *Fuck.* And then she starts sucking like a porn star, cradling my balls with one hand. With her other hand she wraps it around the base of my cock.

I sink my fingers into her long tresses as she continues to suck me into her mouth, deep down her throat. I fuck her mouth, my groans echoing throughout the room. "You're so sexy. So fucking sexy sucking on my thick cock."

My dirty words egg her on, and she works faster...*harder*...as she bobs her head up and down, working my dick perfectly. Stars explode behind my eyelids, a white-hot heat I can't ignore.

She massages my balls in one hand, and I'm so close to coming it's insane. I don't want to come down her throat. Not tonight. Not right now.

No, I need to be all the way inside her when I unleash. I pull out of her mouth, and turn her around so I can slam into her from behind. I smack her ass as I push deep inside her.

"Take my cock, you dirty girl," I say, fisting my hand in her hair, tugging her back so I can kiss her swollen lips. "You handle me so well," I say as I break the kiss.

Then I kiss her again, our tongues desperately tangling together, our breaths mingling as well. My other hand grips her hip, my fingers digging into her flesh.

"Oh, Boone," she calls out, and I keep pounding into her.

Her pussy grips my cock so perfectly.

"You were made for me." I keep fucking her, my mind focused on getting her off before me. However, I'm so fucking close. I slide my hand off her hip, moving up her body to fondle her tits.

I pinch one nipple and then the other as she moans. She's on all fours, pushing her backside up against me as I bottom out inside her. "Fuck, baby. You feel so fucking good." I could get used to a woman like this in my bed every night. I kiss her again, letting my feelings for her pour into the kiss.

Once I'm done with her nipples, I sink my hand lower, toying with her clit so I can get her off. I'm so fucking close.

"I'm coming," she yells, and it's like music to my ears.

My orgasm chases after hers, and once we're done we fall apart. Out of breath, and completely spent we lay together, trying to calm our bodies in unison.

"That was… amazing." I roll closer to her, wanting to hold her in my arms.

She rises from the bed before I can grab her. "I need to clean up."

I take that as an invitation and follow her into the bathroom, turning the shower on. "Care to join me?"

She nods, a sultry smile gracing her face. "Sure." She giggles lightly, the soft sound filling the emptiness of the bathroom.

Once the water is hot enough, she climbs into the shower. I climb in after her, and shut the glass door. First thing I do is wash her hair. It feels so good to sink my fingers into her thick, auburn hair.

"This feels so good," she moans.

After the shampoo, I use conditioner on her hair, letting it sit a while as I soap up her body. This is the best part. She does the same thing to me, lathering me up as she raises up on tiptoe to kiss me.

The kiss lingers, both of us taking our time with each other. After we wash ourselves clean, I pin her against the tiled wall, letting my cock sink into her welcoming heat. Fuck this woman feels so fucking good wrapped around me.

Her fingernails sink into my skin as the hot water rushes over us. I push deep inside her, needing to claim her tight body once more. I don't think I'll ever get enough of her.

She clings to me as I sink my teeth into the soft skin of her shoulder. My hands dig into her ass as I keep her body in place. "Oh, Boone," she cries out.

The hot water rains over us as our orgasms crash down around us at the same time. As soon as our bodies have calmed, I lower her back to the shower floor, and we wash up again.

I lather the soap over her body once more, getting turned on all over again. "If I keep washing you I'll never get out of this shower."

She laughs lightly, tugging her hands into my hair. "I don't mind."

I lean down, kissing her completely. There's something about this woman that has me thinking of things like forever.

Chapter 24

Aubree

It's been a little over a week since Boone and I arrived at this new safe house—another remote cabin, this one tucked near a secluded lake, ringed with tall pines that create a fortress of green. Somehow, despite the circumstances, we've managed to fall into a daily routine that almost feels normal, if I squint my eyes and forget we're essentially in hiding.

The days start early. Sometimes Boone is up before the first hint of sunrise, doing perimeter checks or pacing around with that gun of his strapped to his hip. When I wake up—usually around six—he's already brewed coffee, the rich scent drifting through the cabin like a silent good morning. We don't say much first thing, preferring the quiet warmth of each other's presence, sipping coffee in companionable silence.

We run together, and then we break for our respective chores. He busies himself with endless security measures—testing the locks on the doors, checking in with Dean for updates—and I find solace in the kitchen.

Temporary. The word sticks in my brain sometimes, reminding me that this—the easy laughter, the morning coffees, the teasing about who does the dishes—is all borrowed time. I keep catching myself wishing it wasn't so, that maybe somehow we can stretch this out after the danger is gone. But then reality sets in: this is only happening because someone is threatening my life, and Boone's assigned to protect me. Would any of this still exist when the threat is gone?

I hate that I'm falling for him, but I can't stop it. Every time he smiles in that slow, careful way—like he's not used to smiling often—or when his hand brushes mine, I feel my heart skip a beat. And the nights we've spent curled up on the couch or tangled in each other's arms have only fueled the fire. Sometimes I catch him watching me like he can't decide whether to keep his distance or close it entirely. It's that push-pull that keeps me on edge... and wanting more.

Today, though, we're back to a more subdued vibe. The day started with a run around the perimeter, Boone's suggestion for maintaining our stamina—and probably his way of keeping me from going stir-crazy. It's mid-afternoon now, and I'm in the kitchen testing out a new pizza recipe I've been mulling over. Even without my trusty pizza ovens, I can make do with the cabin's oven and a few modifications. That's what I keep telling myself, at least.

I've got flour dusting my jeans and hands as I knead the dough on the wooden countertop. I hum softly under my breath, trying to drown out the fact that Boone's on the phone in the other room—likely talking to Dean. Every so often, I hear muffled snippets of his low voice—my name, Charles, mother, or other phrases that send a jolt of worry through me.

But I focus on the dough, pressing and folding, adding a bit more water or flour as needed.

My mind drifts to the future. If this all ends well, maybe Boone and I can… what? I try to imagine him in my normal life—me, back at Slice Slice Baby, tossing dough and taking orders while he stands by the register with that vigilant expression, scanning for danger. The thought makes me smile, but also breaks my heart a bit, because deep down I know it might be too much to hope for. There's a chance he'll move on to the next assignment, and I'll be left with only memories of that protective, infuriating, wonderful man who kissed me under the stars.

The dough takes shape into a neat, soft ball, and I set it aside to rest. I've already prepped the sauce—my special blend of tomatoes, garlic, a touch of basil—and it simmers on the stove, filling the kitchen with a mouthwatering scent. I hum again, dipping a spoon into the sauce for a taste. It's tangy with a hint of sweetness, just how I like it.

Boone's voice rises a little in the living area. I catch the words "no, not yet," and "we'll see," which makes my stomach clench. He's definitely being vague, which probably means they haven't made any new breakthroughs. Or maybe they have, and it's not the kind of news he wants to break to me.

A few minutes later, I'm rolling out the dough into a circular shape, sprinkling cornmeal on the counter so it won't stick. That's when I hear his footsteps approach the kitchen. I glance up to find him standing in the doorway, phone in hand, his expression unreadable.

"How's it going?" I ask, trying to sound casual while my heart thumps in my chest.

He slips the phone into his back pocket. "Pretty good," he says, gesturing at my dough. "You, uh… making a new masterpiece there?"

My eyebrows lift. "I hope so. It's a new recipe I've been playing around with—sun-dried tomatoes, caramelized onions, fresh basil, and a sprinkle of goat cheese. Once it's out of the oven, we'll see if it's a masterpiece or a disaster."

He smiles faintly, but there's tension around his eyes. "I'm sure it'll be great. You've got that pizza magic, after all."

I laugh, though I'm sure he's just trying to distract me. I keep my voice light. "Is that what you and Dean were talking about on the phone? My pizza magic?"

Boone's face shutters for a moment, like he's trying to figure out how to dodge the question. "Nah," he says eventually, stepping into the kitchen and leaning against the counter. "We were just going over some intel. Nothing major. So, how much longer on that dough?"

He's deflecting, and I know it. But I also sense he's not ready to share. I think about pushing him on it for a split second, but decide not to. I'd rather not force a confrontation when I'm not sure I'm ready for the answers. So I play along. "It's pretty much done," I say, nodding at the flattened circle of dough. "I'll top it now and let the oven preheat."

Boone nods, relief flickering in his gaze. "Great. I'm starved."

"Then I'll get right to it," I reply, dabbing a bit of sauce onto the dough. I spread it in concentric circles, marveling at how easily I slip into my old habits, the ones I used every day at Slice Slice Baby. I can't help but feel a pang of longing for my little shop, even though it's also tied to memories of fear and threats.

Guarding What's Mine

Boone hovers behind me, and I can practically feel his warmth. "Need help?" he offers.

"Sure," I say, handing him the container of goat cheese. "Sprinkle this on top, but go easy. Goat cheese is strong."

He sets to work, carefully scattering crumbles of cheese over the sauce. I add the onions, the sun-dried tomatoes, and a drizzle of olive oil. The smell is already divine, and I'm not even done yet.

"You're gonna spoil me," he says, a teasing note in his voice. "After this, how am I supposed to go back to normal people's food?"

I grin, flashing him a sidelong glance. "Guess you'll have to keep me around, huh?"

He stills for a moment, then recovers by chuckling softly. "Guess so," he murmurs, a hint of seriousness in his tone.

The moment stretches between us, and I sense it's one we should talk about—what happens when all this is over. But instead, I set my jaw and slide the pizza onto a baking sheet, then slip it into the oven. "All right, that'll take about fifteen, twenty minutes."

"Smells amazing already," he says, his gaze lingering on me rather than the oven. I feel a tingle of awareness run up my spine as our eyes lock.

I clear my throat, drawing my attention back to tidying up. "Let's clean up. Then we can eat."

"Sure."

We work side by side, washing the utensils and wiping down the counters. The conversation stays light—he asks me about how I first started experimenting with recipes at Slice Slice Baby, and I ask him about his favorite meals growing up. He mentions that in his military days, "favorite meals" were often just rations that didn't taste awful, and I snort a laugh.

When the timer beeps, I open the oven, releasing a wave of fragrant heat. The pizza crust is golden brown at the edges, the cheese melted and lightly browned in spots. My mouth waters, and I hear Boone inhale sharply. "Wow," he says, shaking his head. "If that tastes half as good as it looks, I'm gonna be in heaven."

I slide the pizza onto a cutting board, slice it into wedges, and set the pieces on two plates. We carry them into the small dining area—really just a table by the window—and settle in. The first bite is pure bliss. The tang of the goat cheese melds with the sweetness of the caramelized onions and the intensity of the sun-dried tomatoes, all riding on a perfectly crispy crust. I'm almost proud enough to forget the heaviness lingering in the air.

"This is incredible," Boone mumbles around a mouthful of pizza.

I offer a small smile. "Thanks. It's not the same as using the huge ovens at the shop, but it'll do."

He devours his slice quickly, then grabs another. We don't talk much as we eat—both of us too engrossed in the flavors and the relief of a good meal. By the time we're finishing, the earlier tension seeps back in. I can feel it in the set of his shoulders, in the quick glances he casts toward his phone. Whatever Dean told him is still in the back of his mind, nagging at him.

But I decide to let it slide, at least for tonight. It's been days since we truly relaxed—days we've spent in this cocoon of routine, training our bodies not to panic at every twig snap. The threat is always there, looming like a thundercloud on the horizon. I'd rather enjoy whatever solace we can find tonight, and press him for answers tomorrow.

After we clear the dishes, Boone rakes a hand through his short hair, exhaling a long breath. "That was... I needed that. Good food, good company."

I tuck a stray lock of hair behind my ear, warmth flooding my chest. "Me too," I admit. "It almost feels... normal."

A ghost of a smile touches his lips. "Yeah, it does."

He nods toward the living area. "Wanna just... chill for a bit? Maybe watch the fire?" The cabin came with an old stone fireplace, and even though it's not particularly cold tonight, there's something comforting about the crackle of flames.

I nod, grateful for the suggestion. "Sounds perfect."

Within minutes, we're on the couch, the soft glow of the fire flickering across the walls. Boone has one arm draped along the back of the couch, and I'm leaning into his side, my head resting near his shoulder. The wood pops and hisses, sending sparks dancing briefly in the air before they vanish.

For a while, we just talk—about the days we've spent here, the hikes around the lake, the silly card games we've invented to pass the time. He teases me about how I always manage to lose in poker (he's definitely got a better poker face than I do), and I remind him that I made up for it by teaching him how to cook a killer pasta dish.

Eventually, the conversation takes a softer turn. He asks about my childhood, and I tell him about how I used to rollerblade around my neighborhood, imagining I was an explorer charting unknown territory. He laughs, saying he could picture me as a little kid with boundless energy.

I watch the firelight dance in his eyes, and I realize just how comfortable I've become in his presence. The worry that used to claw at my gut is still there, but it's diminished by the confidence I have in him. He's not just my bodyguard or some hired muscle; he's Boone. A man who's shown me compassion, strength, and gentleness all at once.

He shifts slightly, his free hand finding mine. The contact sends a pleasant jolt through my body. It's such a simple thing—his fingers lacing with mine—but it sparks the memory of our kisses, of how he held me under the stars. My pulse quickens, and I look up to find him watching me intently.

"What?" I ask softly.

"Nothing," he says, though the deep timbre of his voice gives him away. He slides his hand along my jaw, his thumb brushing the corner of my mouth. "Just thinking about how I'm going to miss this."

"Miss what?" My voice catches, breath hitching in my throat.

He swallows, and I see the flicker of uncertainty in his gaze. "Miss us…like this. If, you know, we get pulled back into the real world soon."

My heart clenches. I pull my legs under me and shift closer, resting my palm against his chest. His heartbeat thumps strong beneath my fingertips. "Maybe we don't have to miss it," I offer quietly, half-terrified of his answer. "Maybe we can keep it."

He draws a shaky breath, leaning in so our foreheads nearly touch. "Aubree," he murmurs, voice low and intimate. "I want that. But I just don't want to make promises I can't keep."

I lick my lips, reaching up to thread my fingers through his hair. "I'm not asking for promises," I say gently, "just… let's see what happens. Maybe we'll surprise ourselves."

For a moment, he just stares at me, his expression warring between wanting to protect me and wanting me. Then, with a soft groan, he closes the distance, pressing his lips to mine. The kiss is slow at first, exploratory, like we're reminding ourselves how to move in sync. But it doesn't stay gentle for long.

Warmth floods my limbs as he deepens the kiss, parting my lips with a quiet urgency. I make a small sound of approval, sliding my hands up his arms, feeling the corded muscle beneath his shirt. He angles me backward, carefully guiding me to recline against the cushions. The firelight flickers across his face, gilding the sharp planes of his jaw.

His mouth moves to my neck, peppering my skin with soft, heated kisses that leave me trembling in their wake. My breath comes in short gasps, a mixture of anticipation and relief, like I've been waiting all day for this moment. I tangle my fingers in his hair, pulling him closer, wanting more.

"Aubree," he whispers against my skin, voice husky. My name on his lips sends a shiver down my spine. I arch into him, the press of his body a comforting weight.

He slips a hand under my shirt, skimming the bare skin of my waist. Every nerve ending feels like it's sparking to life, and I let out a quiet whimper. The sound seems to embolden him, and he returns to my mouth, claiming it in a series of slow, deliberate kisses.

For a moment, I let the outside world fade—no threats, no stepfather with suspicious transactions, no timeline. Just us, hidden away in a cabin, devouring each other's taste like we can't get enough. His grip tightens slightly, and I feel the tension in his muscles. I know he's still holding back a little, concerned about hurting me or pushing too far, but I nudge him to let go.

"Boone," I whisper, tugging the front of his shirt. "Don't overthink. Just… be here with me."

A soft chuckle escapes him, though his eyes are dark with desire. "Yes, ma'am," he teases, leaning in again.

We lose ourselves in that kiss, in the gentle dance of tongues and lips, the sounds of our own breathing mingling with the crackle of the fire. My heart pounds a frantic rhythm, and I find myself wishing this moment could stretch on forever, free of any looming threats or responsibilities. Just two people, sharing something real.

Eventually, the need for air forces us apart. He presses his forehead to mine, his breath coming in ragged pulls. I brush a hand over his cheek, my chest heaving as I try to steady myself.

"That was…" I begin, but my voice trails off. I'm not sure I have the words to describe what it was.

"Yeah," he agrees, swallowing hard. "Let's see if I can do even better."

I laugh as we tumble together, his mouth covering mine with another mind-numbing kiss. One that I'll never be able to recover from.

Chapter 25

Boone

My phone buzzes on the coffee table, and I tense up the second I see Dean's name flash across the screen. It's late—later than when he usually calls—so right away my guard is up. Aubree's in the bedroom folding laundry, humming a little tune I can't quite place. I stand, running a hand over my hair, and swipe to answer.

"Dean," I say, trying to keep my voice low and even, "what's going on?"

A sigh crackles through the line before Dean speaks. "Finally got some updates. Got Bravo Team watching your girl's stepfather, and so far…nothing. No suspicious meetings, no weird transactions, aside from the ones we already know about. All he does is go to the office, then come home to Aubree's mom," he states with a muttered curse. "It's a damned waiting game. I hate waiting, you know that."

I pace the living room, glancing every so often at the closed bedroom door to make sure Aubree isn't listening. "Yeah, I know. But if there's nothing, there's nothing. At least it means he's not making any new moves."

Dean's quiet for a beat. "Look, Boone, I also talked to her mom. I gave her a rundown—nothing too detailed, just enough so she knows Aubree's safe. She was getting worried."

I feel a knot loosen in my chest. Aubree's been worried sick about her mother, but we didn't want to reach out in case her stepfather was monitoring her calls. "She's all right? The mom, I mean?"

"As far as I can tell, yes," Dean replies. "She's anxious, but that's normal. She wants to see her daughter. I had to convince her that laying low is still the best option. Frankly, she's got doubts about Charles, but nothing concrete. It's a mess."

I exhale slowly, raking a hand over my beard. "All right. Well, thanks for letting me know." My eyes drift to the fireplace, the dying embers casting a faint glow across the cabin's interior. "Any other news?"

Dean makes a low noise of frustration. "Not much else. The police have been slow to release info about the brick incident a while back, the one at the shop. Forensics is tied up. And—"

Suddenly, a shrill beep blasts through the phone, loud enough that I recoil, nearly dropping it. Dean hisses a curse on the other end. "Hold on, something's coming through... Shit. That's—" He breaks off, presumably reading something on his end. "Boone, an alarm just triggered at Slice Slice Baby. Looks like a forced entry. The system we installed is going off."

My stomach twists. "Someone broke in just now?" At least we know the system is working, but that's cold comfort if the place is getting trashed.

"Yeah," Dean confirms. "I'm pulling up the feed from the local PD... They're on their way. Gonna take them a few minutes to get there. I'll get all the info I can—footage, time stamps, maybe a description if the asshole tripped a camera."

"Understood," I say through gritted teeth. "You let me know the second you figure out who it is. Or if there's anything suspicious linking it to the threats."

"You know I will," Dean replies. "I hate sitting on my ass while this goes down. But that's the update for now. Let me see what the cops turn up."

I nod, even though he can't see me. My thoughts reel with images of Aubree's beloved shop—how she's poured her life into it, how she's probably going to take this news like a gut punch. "All right," I murmur, shifting my weight from foot to foot. "Keep me posted, Dean."

He signs off with a clipped "Will do," and the line goes silent.

For a moment, I just stand there, phone still pressed to my ear, staring blankly at the flickering shadows across the wall. My protective instincts surge, telling me to hop in the truck and tear down the highway back to Nashville, but that's not possible. Not unless we want to risk leading whoever's behind all this directly to Aubree. We've done too much to stay hidden.

I have to tell her. The thought sends a pang through my chest, because I know exactly how she'll react—she loves that shop like a child. And right now, with her emotions already wound so tight, I'm not sure how she'll handle another blow.

Forcing myself to take a calming breath, I slip my phone into my pocket and head for the bedroom door. I knock lightly, but there's no answer. Cautiously, I push it open and peek inside.

Aubree's perched on the edge of the bed, folding what looks like one of my T-shirts—it's huge, practically swallowing her up. She glances up, a soft smile at first, then her brow furrows at my expression. "Boone?" she asks, worry creeping into her tone. "What's wrong?"

I take a step inside, shutting the door behind me. My voice feels tight in my throat. "There's, uh…some news," I begin. "From Dean."

She stands, the T-shirt sliding off her lap and onto the floor. "News? About Charles? My mom? Or…?"

I cross the room in two long strides. My hands find her shoulders, and I rub gently, trying to ease the tension that's already knotting her muscles. "Not exactly. Dean says Bravo Team has your stepfather under surveillance, and so far, it's quiet. He also spoke to your mom. She's safe, and she knows you're safe."

Relief flickers in her eyes, but it's quickly replaced by caution. "You said not exactly. So there's something else?"

I nod, swallowing hard. "An alarm was triggered at Slice Slice Baby. Looks like someone broke in tonight."

Her face goes pale. "Broke in?" she repeats, voice trembling. "What— how—? Is there any—"

"Police are on the way," I say quickly, sliding my arms around her waist. "Dean's getting updates in real time. We don't know yet if it's just petty theft or something tied to the threats."

Aubree's mouth opens, but no sound comes out. Her eyes glisten, and I see the tears welling up before she blinks them away.

"Someone's in my shop?" she manages, her voice breaking. "Breaking things, or stealing, or—?"

Unable to watch her anguish silently, I pull her closer, letting her bury her face against my chest. The moment she feels the contact, a sob escapes her. It's a raw, heart-wrenching sound, and I feel my own chest tighten in response. I stroke her hair, murmuring reassuring words even though I can't promise everything's fine.

"It's going to be okay," I say softly, though the words feel inadequate. "Dean and the police will handle it. We'll figure out what happened."

She shudders, her fingers clutching at my shirt. "Why can't this just stop?" she asks in a broken whisper. "What did I do to deserve this?"

I press a hand to the back of her head, smoothing the strands of hair. "You didn't do anything. Someone else—whoever is behind all this—they're the ones who'll answer for it," I promise. "We'll see to that."

For a long while, she just cries quietly, tears soaking through the fabric over my chest. Each muffled sob resonates in my gut. I hate seeing her like this—defeated, helpless. It ignites a blaze of anger deep inside me, fueling the determination to put an end to this madness once and for all.

Eventually, her tears subside, and I lead her over to the bed so we can sit. My arm stays wrapped around her shoulders, her cheek pressed to my collarbone. "I'm sorry," she mumbles, swiping at her wet cheeks. "I know you must think I'm weak, crying like this."

"Never," I reply, my voice firm. "You have every right to be upset. That shop is your life. It's only natural you'd be torn up about someone violating it."

She nods, letting out a shaky breath. "I just… I put everything into Slice Slice Baby. It's not perfect, but it's mine, you know? And now…"

Her voice trails off, and I know she's imagining the worst—broken windows, trashed equipment, stolen cash, or even worse, malicious graffiti or some new threatening note. I grit my teeth at the thought of her walking in there someday to see the damage firsthand.

I brush a hand down her arm, trying to think of some reassurance that isn't empty. "Dean will get the details," I say finally. "We'll know soon exactly what went down. And if it's connected to these threats, that's just another piece of evidence that'll bring us closer to stopping whoever's behind this."

She lifts her head, meeting my gaze. Her eyes are red-rimmed, lashes wet. "And if it's just some random burglar?"

"Then the cops will handle it," I assure her. "Either way, you're still here and still safe. That's what matters most."

She sniffles, nodding slowly. "Yeah. I just… I hate being so helpless. I want to go there. I want to see it for myself, I want to fix whatever's broken."

My heart clenches again at her desperation. "I know," I murmur. "But going back now could expose you. We don't want that. Let me… let Dean… let us take care of it."

She closes her eyes and leans into me, arms looping around my waist. I hold her tightly, feeling the steady beat of her heart against my chest.

After a few minutes, I feel my phone buzz again. My body tenses, and Aubree notices. She pulls back, eyes anxious. "Is that Dean?"

"Probably," I say, fishing it out of my pocket. Sure enough, Dean's name lights up the screen. I glance at Aubree. "You want me to answer here, or…?"

She nods, straightening her posture. "I want to hear it."

I hit the green button, putting the call on speaker. "Dean," I greet, my voice tight. "You've got news?"

Dean's voice crackles through. "Yeah, I do. Cops got there, found the front door busted in. Cash register was pried open. Not sure how much was in it, but they're taking prints. Doesn't look like there's major vandalism, but who knows if anything else is missing. Could be a smash-and-grab."

Aubree closes her eyes, relief and frustration mingling on her face. "So it might just be a burglary?" she asks, her voice shaking.

"Could be," Dean replies. "But I won't rule out it being connected to the threats until we see the footage. A security camera at the corner store across the street might've caught something. I'm on it."

"Thanks, Dean," I say. "Let us know if you find out anything else."

"You got it," he says, then pauses. "How're you doing, Aubree?"

Aubree forces a small smile, though there's no way Dean can see it. "I'm okay," she whispers.

"She's hanging in there," I reply. "Anything else?"

"Just that we keep pressing on. Bravo Team has eyes on Charles, no new developments. If it's random, we'll know soon enough. If it's not…" Dean huffs a breath. "We'll handle it."

"Roger that," I say, acknowledging. "Take care, Dean."

He disconnects, and the line goes silent again. I set my phone aside, turning my focus back to Aubree. She lets out a shaky breath, her hands knotting together in her lap. "So maybe it's just a robbery," she says, like she's trying to convince herself. "People break in all the time looking for easy cash, right? Good thing I left the shop empty. Whoever tried to rob me tonight got nothing."

"Yeah," I answer softly. "Good girl."

She nods, though she doesn't look entirely convinced. Then her gaze flicks to me, eyes full of questions I don't have the answers to. "And if it's not just a robbery?"

I hesitate, hating that I can't offer a firm reassurance. "Then we'll deal with it," I say. "We've come this far, right?"

She clenches her jaw, a spark of fierce determination flickering to life. "Right."

I slide my arm around her again, pulling her close so she can rest her head against my shoulder. She takes a few slow breaths, the tension in her body gradually easing. In the quiet, I can't help but reflect on how insane our situation is—hiding in a cabin, her life's work being ransacked, the constant question mark hanging over her stepfather's involvement.

But for now, I hold her, letting her tears dry on my shirt as the minutes tick by. We're in limbo yet again, waiting for the next piece of information that might change everything. As I press a kiss to the top of her head, one thought resonates clearly: Whatever comes next, I'll face it with her. Because I'm not about to let some lowlife—and whoever's pulling the strings— rob Aubree of the life she's built or the future she deserves.

Chapter 26

Aubree

I can barely sleep at all. Between the fear and anger swirling in my head—someone broke into my shop, the shop I poured my entire heart into—and the guilt that I can't do anything but hide away, my mind won't shut down long enough to rest. Boone holds me while I toss and turn, and eventually, I drift into a fitful doze on his chest, lulled by the steady rise and fall of his breathing.

Morning arrives all too soon. A slice of sunlight slips through the curtains, and I open my eyes with a dull ache in my temples. I blink, momentarily disoriented by the rustic cabin walls before remembering exactly where I am and why. Then it all crashes back: the break-in at Slice Slice Baby, the possibility that it's connected to whoever's threatening me, and the helpless feeling gnawing at my stomach.

Boone's already awake. I can tell by the way he shifts his arm, careful not to jostle me. My cheek's pressed to his shoulder, and for a moment, I pretend like I'm still asleep, soaking up the comfort of having him near. But the weight in my chest is too heavy to ignore for long.

"Morning," Boone says softly, his voice a gentle rumble.

I manage a weak smile, pushing myself upright. "Morning," I reply, brushing hair away from my face. I look at him, and for a second, I see the concern etched in his features, that same guarded look he gets whenever he's about to tell me I can't do something.

It's enough to snap my fragile calm. I swing my legs off the bed and stand, arms crossed, suddenly restless. "I hate this," I mutter, pacing the small bedroom. "Just... waiting. Doing nothing while my shop gets trashed or robbed, or who knows what."

Boone rises to a seated position, the mattress creaking beneath his weight. "I know," he says gently, raking a hand through his short hair. "I hate it too."

I let out a shaky sigh. "Then what are we doing here? Why can't we just go back, talk to the cops, figure it out ourselves?"

"Because it's too big a risk," he reminds me, his tone patient. "Until we know who's behind this, charging back in could expose you. Expose us."

I open my mouth to argue but close it again, biting back the frustration. He's right. Deep down, I know he is. If I just waltzed back into town, I could be walking into a trap. But that logic doesn't make me feel any less powerless.

He stands, crosses the small distance, and places his hands on my shoulders. "I know you're angry," he says quietly. "I'm angry too. But let Dean and his team do their jobs."

My anger softens at the concern in his eyes, and I release a breath I hadn't realized I was holding. "I just... it's my life, you know? Everything I've worked for feels like it's going up in flames."

He nods, thumbs gently stroking the tops of my arms. "We'll salvage it," he promises. "But for now, come on." He tilts his head toward the open door. "Let's do something to keep our minds busy today. I can't stand seeing you so torn up."

I can't help it; a tiny grin tugs at my lips. "Okay," I say, exhaling. "What do you have in mind?"

ABOUT AN HOUR LATER, we're standing on the edge of the lake, the morning sun sparkling across the water's surface. The cabin is tucked just behind a line of tall pines, the gentle breeze rustling their branches. Boone and I walk down a short dirt path that leads to a little sandy area—a makeshift shoreline, I guess. My feet sink into the soft ground, a welcome change from the rough, anxiety-laden floor of the cabin.

"You ever swim this early?" Boone asks, stripping off his T-shirt. I glance over and catch a glimpse of his muscled torso, the defined lines of his shoulders, and my cheeks warm. Even after everything we've shared—kisses, confessions—his body still makes my stomach flutter.

"Not usually," I say, clearing my throat and averting my gaze in a playful attempt at nonchalance. "But I guess there's a first time for everything." With a shrug, I peel off my own T-shirt to reveal a bikini top I found buried in the cabin's random storage closet. It's not the best fit, but it'll do.

Boone's gaze flicks to me, and I catch the slight hitch in his breath before he tears his eyes away, focusing instead on the water. "Yeah," he manages, "there is."

I wade in first, the chilly lake water lapping at my ankles. A shiver ripples up my spine, but it's refreshing compared to the sweltering swirl of my thoughts. Boone steps in next to me, and we inch forward until the water's around our waists.

He whistles softly. "That's cold."

I can't help but grin. "Big tough ex-military man can't handle a little cold?"

He snorts, rolling his eyes. "Watch it, or I'll dunk you."

"You wouldn't dare." My tone is mock-serious, but there's a spark of challenge in my eyes.

"Oh?" He arches an eyebrow. Suddenly, his hands grasp my waist, and before I can protest, he lifts me up and gently throws me into the deeper water. I shriek as I go under, the icy shock stealing my breath.

When I resurface, spluttering, I find him grinning like a mischievous kid. "You jerk!" I exclaim, wiping droplets from my face.

He swims closer, a contrite smile tugging at his lips. "Sorry, sweetheart. But you dared me."

"You are so going to pay for that." I lunge, hooking an arm around his neck, and we both sink into the water, laughing as we splash around. The buoyancy and cold shock wash away the tension that's been clinging to me like a second skin. For a few blissful moments, it's just us—a couple of people playing in a lake, with no threats or break-ins or bad guys to worry about.

Eventually, we settle into a rhythm of gentle swimming, drifting away from the shore. The lake isn't huge, but it's big enough that we can't see the far side clearly. Tall pines ring the perimeter, and I realize it's kind of beautiful out here—like our own secluded paradise.

I'm treading water next to Boone, watching him tilt his head back to let the sun warm his face. There's a bead of water trailing down his cheek, and I have the sudden urge to lean in and kiss it away. So I do. I slip closer, cupping the side of his face, pressing my lips to that spot just above his jaw. He stills, eyes opening, and the intensity in his gaze makes my heart flip.

"Hi," he murmurs, voice low and husky.

"Hi," I echo, feeling heat rush through me despite the cold water.

He skims a hand across my waist, pulling me closer until I can feel the steady thump of his heart against my chest. "You're freezing," he comments, though his fingertips are warm against my skin.

"So warm me up." My challenge comes out breathy, half daring him, half pleading.

His laugh is soft as he dips his head and captures my mouth in a gentle kiss. My eyes drift shut, and I melt into him. The water cradles us, and for a moment, it feels like there's nothing else in the world but his mouth on mine, his arms wrapped around me.

He deepens the kiss, sliding his tongue past my parted lips, and I answer with a small moan. It's a slow, unhurried dance, our bodies buoyed by the lake's gentle current. Eventually, we break apart to catch our breath, forehead to forehead, breath mingling in the space between us.

"I could get used to this," he admits softly, running his hands up and down my sides.

My chest tightens with a familiar mix of hope and fear. I want to believe that once this is over, we'll find a way to keep this closeness, this odd paradise we've built in hiding. But a part of me can't quite trust it. Not yet.

"Me too," I whisper, my lips ghosting over his cheek. "But for now, I'll settle for a fun day in the water."

"Deal," he says, a grin tugging at his mouth.

WE SPEND the next few hours like kids on summer break—splashing, racing each other across the lake, diving for rocks on the lakebed (Boone wins that little competition, no surprise there). I even manage to climb onto his back and demand a piggyback ride through the shallow part, laughing so hard I nearly choke on the water.

We pause occasionally, drifting, letting the sun dry our arms and shoulders while the rest of us stays submerged. Boone cracks jokes about how this is probably the first time he's gotten to have fun in a body of water that wasn't crawling with potential threats or camouflage gear. I tease him that if he's so used to dangerous waters, maybe I should stage a surprise attack, and he narrows his eyes at me like he's considering the possibility.

It's the most carefree I've felt in weeks. The tension in my neck and shoulders unwinds, replaced by a soft glow that I can only describe as peace—at least for a little while. My troubles aren't gone, but they're overshadowed by the simple pleasure of sunshine and Boone's warm presence beside me.

Guarding What's Mine

Eventually, my stomach growls, and Boone laughs, patting his own abdomen. "We need food," he declares, water droplets glistening on his chest. "I feel like I could eat a whole pizza."

I grin. "Pizza, huh? You're talking to the right girl, but I don't think we have the supplies for a second pizza extravaganza. How about a couple of sandwiches back at the cabin?"

He pretends to think, tapping a finger against his chin. "Hmm, you are the pizza guru, but I guess sandwiches will do... for now."

We wade back to shore, my limbs heavy from the exertion of swimming. The midday sun beats down, drying our skin as we trudge up the short path to the cabin. Boone grabs two towels from the porch, handing one to me. I wrap it around my shoulders, grateful for the warmth.

Inside, we rummage through the fridge, pulling out cold cuts, cheese, lettuce, tomatoes, and whatever condiments we can find. The cabin's still quiet, the faint hum of the wind in the trees seeping through the windows.

Boone sets the bread on the counter. "So, I'm thinking a triple-decker."

I roll my eyes. "You and your enormous appetite. Go for it. I'll have a normal, two-slice sandwich, thanks."

"Suit yourself," he says, grinning. He glances at me, his gaze lingering on my damp hair and the beads of lake water still glistening on my arms. "You look... happy."

I tilt my head, smiling despite myself. "I guess I am. You gave me a day of normalcy. Or as close to normal as we can get."

He gives a shrug, carefully layering turkey and cheese onto his bread. "I just hate seeing you stressed out. You deserve a break from all the chaos."

A warmth blossoms in my chest at his sincerity. "Thank you," I say softly. "I needed it."

After we finish assembling our sandwiches, we settle at the small table near the window. The sunlight filters through, illuminating the dust motes dancing in the air. We eat quietly at first, hunger taking precedence. I savor every bite, the crisp lettuce and tangy mustard reminding me of simpler days.

Halfway through our meal, Boone's phone vibrates on the table, and my heart leaps into my throat. But when he checks it, he shakes his head. "Spam text," he mutters, laying the phone face down again.

I let out a breath I didn't realize I was holding. "I'm dreading the next call," I admit, picking at my crust. "Every ring feels like it could be more bad news."

He reaches across the table, placing his hand over mine. "Maybe it'll be good news next time."

The gentle pressure of his palm is reassuring, and I turn my hand over to intertwine our fingers. "God, I hope so," I whisper.

We finish eating, clean up the plates, and then Boone suggests we might do some reading or play cards to pass the afternoon. But I can't resist throwing a smirk his way. "Last time we played cards, you destroyed me. How about we read for a bit first, Mr. Poker Face."

He chuckles. "Fine by me."

THE REST of the day unfolds in a pleasant blur—reading in companionable silence on the porch, occasionally commenting on a line from our respective books, or pointing out a squirrel bounding through the underbrush. It's almost laughable how peaceful it is, given the chaos swirling in the outside world. But I hold onto it like a lifeline, like if I can etch these moments into my memory, I'll have something good to replay when the nightmares come creeping in.

When the sun begins to dip, painting the sky in lavender and gold, Boone stands and stretches, the muscles in his back shifting under his skin. "I'll start dinner," he offers. "Unless you have another grand pizza plan up your sleeve."

I laugh softly, closing my book. "I think you can handle it tonight," I say. "We have that leftover chicken and some veggies, right?"

"Right," he confirms, leaning down to press a quick kiss to my forehead. "You rest, I'll call you when it's ready."

I watch him disappear into the cabin, a swirl of gratitude and affection in my chest. It's strange to realize how close I've grown to him in such a short time. Stranger still to feel my heart flutter every time he calls me sweetheart or gives me that lazy half-smile.

Eventually, I stand and follow him inside, offering to chop vegetables while he sears the chicken. We chat about nothing in particular—favorite childhood TV shows, embarrassing high school moments (he had few; I had many), and a million other small details that people share when they're learning each other's corners.

It doesn't escape me that, for a day at least, I haven't been consumed by fear. I haven't cried once about the shop or railed about Charles. Boone gave me space to simply be, to remember that I'm more than just a victim or a target. He's seen me at my worst, yet still looks at me like I'm something precious he wants to protect.

As the sun sets, we eat our chicken and veggies by the dim light of the lantern and the soft glow from the fireplace. It's delicious in a homey, simple way—nourishing in more ways than one.

After dinner, I help wash dishes, and then we collapse on the couch, too comfortable to move much. I catch Boone stifling a yawn. "Tired?" I tease, nudging his side.

"It's been a busy day of victory laps in the lake," he shoots back, smirking. "And piggyback rides."

I roll my eyes, smiling at the memory. "A day well spent."

He turns toward me, draping an arm along the back of the couch. "You feeling okay?" The question is soft, but loaded. He's asking about more than my physical state.

I draw in a breath, letting my gaze drop to our joined hands. "I am," I say honestly. "Better than I have in a while. Thank you... for all of this. For letting me escape my own head, even if it's just for a day."

His hand tightens on mine. "I'd give you a lifetime of these days if I could."

My eyes mist at the sincerity in his tone, but I force a smile to mask the sudden rush of emotion. "One day at a time, right?"

He nods, and then leans in, pressing a soft kiss to my lips. I melt against him, letting the warmth and safety of his presence anchor me. And for one precious day, I let the nightmares and uncertainty stay locked outside, reminding myself that tomorrow—whatever it brings—will come soon enough. But for now, we have each other, and that's more than enough to keep the darkness at bay.

Chapter 27

Boone

I'm standing on the cabin's porch in the early morning light, sipping from a mug of coffee that's already gone lukewarm. A thin veil of fog stretches over the lake, and the first tentative rays of sunlight touch the treetops. Normally, I'd find the sight peaceful—the kind of moment that makes you take a deep breath and appreciate the stillness.

But my mind isn't on the scenery today. I'm thinking about Aubree, tucked inside the cabin, still asleep. Last night we lingered on the couch long after sunset, half-dozing in each other's arms. It was a good kind of quiet, a peacefulness I haven't felt in ages. Yet I can't shake the tension coursing through me, waiting for Dean to call, hoping for a breakthrough that'll let me get her life back on track.

That's when my phone buzzes on the small wooden table next to me. I snatch it up in one swift motion, heart pounding the second I see Dean's name flash on the screen.

I press the phone to my ear, not bothering with a greeting. "Dean?"

"Boone, got some news." His voice is clipped, the kind of tone he uses when he's got a lot to say and not enough time to say it.

I swallow, setting my coffee down. "I'm listening."

He exhales sharply. "We made a move on Charles—Aubree's stepfather. Finally pinned him. We'd been monitoring his accounts, and last night he made another large transaction. We traced it to a company that basically 'rents' out mercenaries or 'fixers' for a fee. You pay, they do whatever you want, no questions asked."

My jaw tightens. I have to take a second to calm the surge of anger that bubbles up. "So he was paying them to attack Aubree?"

"Looks that way," Dean confirms. "He also hired them to track her down. That's how they knew about the cabin. Remember that incident at your old place, the one by the Tennessee border? We pulled that attacker's prints from the site—got a match for a guy on the payroll of this shady company. Charles used information from Aubree's mother to find you two. Your location was compromised the second she told him Aubree was holed up somewhere in that region."

I rake a hand over my hair, feeling a grim satisfaction in finally having answers—and fury at the same time. "So that's how they found us," I say. "Damn it. So it was never a random guess. He knew."

"Exactly," Dean replies. "But here's the good news: we've got enough to bury him legally. We also confronted him with the evidence. Bravo Team cornered him at his office. He folded when we showed him the receipts and the testimonies from that company's contact. He's in custody. Aubree's mother wants nothing more to do with him."

A strange blend of relief and lingering tension floods me. "So... Aubree's safe," I say quietly, not quite believing we're finally here.

"She is," Dean confirms. "The cops are involved now. They've got Charles locked up, and it's looking like they'll press multiple charges—conspiracy, attempted assault, who knows what else they'll tack on. He won't see the light of day for a long time, if at all."

I close my eyes for a moment, soaking up the words. Charles is caught. The threat is over. Aubree's life can go back to normal. Part of me is still on high alert, waiting for the other shoe to drop, but Dean sounds certain. "That's... amazing news," I manage, my throat tight. "Does Aubree's mom know everything?"

"Oh yeah," Dean says. "She left him. I just got off the phone with her. She's furious, wants Charles prosecuted to the fullest extent. By the way, she's waiting back at Aubree's place right now, if you two want to head back into town."

"Of course." I take a moment to tamp down the fierce protectiveness that's so much a part of me. "Guess we're done here, then."

Dean lets out a breath, relief evident in his tone. "Yeah, partner, I guess we are. I hate that it went this far, but I'm glad it's resolved. You can bring Aubree home."

"Thanks, Dean. For everything."

He grunts. "Don't thank me yet. You've got to break the news to her. And hey"—his voice lightens—"maybe I'll see you around here soon, without guns blazing."

"Count on it," I say, cracking a wry grin.

Dean ends the call, and I let my hand drop to my side. My gaze drifts back to the lake, but I can hardly see it now through the adrenaline pumping in my veins. Charles is done—he can't harm Aubree anymore. She can go home. It's everything I've wanted for her since I first took on this job.

Yet beneath the relief, there's another emotion twisting in my gut: what happens next for us?

I find Aubree in the kitchen, her hair bundled in a messy bun, rummaging for breakfast. She turns the second she sees me, her eyes scanning my face. "You look… tense," she says, stopping with a carton of eggs in hand.

"It's good tense," I say, stepping forward. I rest a palm on her shoulder, feeling her warmth through the thin fabric of her T-shirt. "Dean just called."

Her eyes go wide. "Oh God, what happened?"

I squeeze her shoulder gently. "He's got proof—solid proof—that your stepfather orchestrated this whole thing. They confronted Charles. He's in custody. He confessed."

She sets the eggs down abruptly, covering her mouth with both hands. "He— so he's caught?"

I nod, watching as her emotions flit across her face—shock, relief, anger, sadness. "It's over. You're safe. You can go home."

Her eyes brim with tears, but this time, they're tears of relief. She exhales a shaky breath, stepping into me. I envelop her in my arms, letting her press her face to my chest. We stand there for a long moment, and I hear the soft hitch of her breath as she processes it all.

Eventually, she leans back, swiping at her cheeks with a watery smile. "I can't believe it. This nightmare is... done?"

"Done," I confirm. "Your mother's waiting for you at the shop, I think. Or your house. Dean said she left Charles—completely."

Fresh tears prick Aubree's eyes, but she nods fiercely. "Good. She deserves better. He— I can't believe he was behind it all. Hiring people to scare me, to— to harm me, just for money?"

I rub my hand up and down her back. "He wanted to control your mom's inheritance. Maybe he thought scaring you off would give him more leverage. We'll probably never understand all the details, but the important thing is he can't do anything else. The police have him, and Maddox Security has more than enough evidence to keep him locked up."

She drops her head onto my shoulder. "Thank God," she whispers.

We pack quickly. It's surreal, folding clothes and stashing them in duffel bags, knowing this time we're not fleeing to another safe house—we're heading home. Aubree's quiet, occasionally stopping to stare at something in the cabin—a throw blanket, the bed we've shared, the windows that overlooked the lake. There's a bittersweet undercurrent to it all. This place has been our sanctuary, our prison, and our weird little nest all at once.

After a final sweep, we load up the truck. I notice her lingering by the doorway, taking one last look at the cabin. I touch her elbow gently. "You okay?"

She lets out a breath, glancing at me. "Yeah. Just... a lot of memories here."

I don't say anything, just slip my hand into hers. We walk out together, and I lock up behind us. Then we climb into the truck, the engine rumbling to life. Aubree watches out the window as I steer us down the dirt road leading back to the main highway.

The drive feels longer than it should, maybe because we're both anxious about what waits for us. She fidgets with the hem of her shirt, glancing at me every so often with a mix of excitement and nervousness. I reach over, resting a comforting hand on her knee whenever the traffic slows enough that I can spare a hand from the wheel.

"Do you think... my shop's okay?" she asks at one point, voice trembling with the question.

I nod. "Dean said the cops were investigating, and they'll have it secured. It might need some repairs, but it's still yours. Nothing can change that."

She exhales, a ghost of a smile forming. "I really just want to walk inside, see it with my own eyes."

"You will," I promise.

We cross the city limits of Nashville by late afternoon, the once-familiar skyline greeting us with its mix of old and new buildings. I feel a pulse of adrenaline. It's strange to be back, knowing how much has changed since we left. Finally, I navigate the streets leading to Aubree's neighborhood.

We park outside her home—a modest one-story, white siding, with a small front porch. My hand hovers over the ignition, and I glance at her. "Ready?"

She swallows. "Yeah. Let's do this."

I kill the engine, and we step out. Almost immediately, the front door bursts open, and Aubree's mother—tall, poised despite the stress—is hurrying down the porch steps. Her eyes are red-rimmed, and she's clutching a tissue. The second she sees Aubree, she breaks into a sob.

Aubree rushes forward, and they collide in a tangle of arms, tears streaming freely. I hang back by the truck, giving them space, watching as the mother clings to her daughter, stroking her hair, murmuring apologies and relief. After a moment, I discreetly shift my gaze to the street, making sure no one's lurking. Old habits die hard.

Eventually, Aubree's mother beckons me over with a shaky smile. "You must be Boone," she says, voice watery. She reaches out to shake my hand. "Thank you. Thank you for protecting her."

I dip my head politely. "Just doing my job, ma'am. But… she's a strong woman. She did most of the protecting herself."

Aubree's mother exhales, her lips trembling. "I'm Lisa," she says. "And please—let's go inside. I have a lot to tell both of you."

Inside, the house is warm, cluttered with pictures and knick-knacks that give it a cozy, lived-in feel. Lisa leads us to the small living room, where we settle on a couch that's a bit worn but looks inviting. She sits in an armchair opposite us, tissues in hand.

She inhales, composing herself. "I've left Charles," she announces, though we already know. "After I found out everything, I… I couldn't stay with a man who'd harm my daughter. I'm pressing charges. He's in custody now, and I'll be cooperating fully with the police."

Aubree nods, still clinging to her mother's hand. "Mom, I'm so sorry you had to go through this."

Lisa shakes her head fiercely. "Don't apologize. This is on him. I'm just glad you're safe."

I watch them exchange a look that's thick with emotion—relief, grief, and a deep bond that not even Charles's betrayal could break. My chest tightens at the sight, a mix of protectiveness and a strange sense of pride that Aubree is returning to the life she deserves.

They talk for a while—Lisa explains how the police grilled her about Charles's finances, how they gathered proof of his intent to drive Aubree away for monetary gain. She's furious at him, and she's furious at herself for not seeing the signs sooner. Aubree keeps insisting her mother's not at fault, and I silently agree. Con men can be terrifyingly good at deception.

Eventually, Lisa pats Aubree's hand. "I hate to say this, but… I know you're dying to see your shop, right?"

Aubree's eyes sparkle with tears, and a small smile forms. "More than anything," she admits.

Lisa smiles back, rising from the armchair. "Then let's go."

SLICE SLICE BABY looks strangely untouched from the outside—same red-and-gray sign, same big display window that's finally been fixed. But as we step inside, I notice the faint lines of a new frame around the front door, where it must've been repaired after the recent break-in. My stomach clenches, imagining the damage that might be hidden behind the scenes.

Aubree takes a trembling step forward, running her hand along the counter where countless customers have ordered slices. "Oh my God," she whispers, eyes watering again. "It's… still standing."

I follow, hovering protectively at her side, scanning the interior. The floor is swept clean. I see a few spots on the walls where paint has been touched up, presumably covering whatever damage occurred. There's a faint smell of cleaning supplies mingling with the lingering scent of tomato sauce and dough.

Lisa steps up to us, pointing toward the back. "The police had it cleaned up, dusted for fingerprints. Nothing major was stolen. No big vandalism." She searches Aubree's face. "They're still looking for the guy who broke in, but it doesn't look like it's connected to Charles. Might've been a random burglary after all."

Aubree nods, tears filling her eyes again. "I can't believe it. I thought everything would be ruined."

"But it's not," I remind her softly. "You still have your place."

She turns to me, eyes shining with gratitude and relief. Then she throws her arms around my neck, hugging me fiercely. I freeze for a split second, not used to public displays like this, but then I wrap my arms around her, letting her trembling sigh wash over me.

Lisa clears her throat gently. "I'll... I'll give you two a moment," she says, slipping behind the counter, presumably to check on something.

Aubree pulls back and stares up at me, her hands still resting on my shoulders. "Thank you," she whispers. "For everything."

I brush a loose strand of hair from her face. "I told you, it's my job," I reply, my voice rough with emotion. "But... it was more than that. I'm just glad you're safe."

She smiles, leaning her forehead against mine. "So now what?" she whispers. "You go back to Maddox Security, pick up another job? And I just... run my shop?" There's a hint of fear in her eyes, like she's worried this is where we part ways.

My breath catches. I haven't entirely sorted out the answer for that question yet. Dean hasn't assigned me a new job. Technically, I'm free to do whatever I want, so long as the danger to Aubree is resolved. And it is, isn't it?

"We'll figure it out," I say quietly, pressing a reassuring kiss to her temple.

We stand here a moment longer, in the center of her shop, holding each other. The smell of fresh dough and tomato sauce seems to wrap around us like a promise of normalcy returning. Just a few days ago, we were hiding in a remote cabin, wondering if Charles would succeed in scaring her off for good. Now, with him behind bars and the shop still standing, the future feels open again.

Aubree clears her throat and lets go of me, though her hand slips down to entwine with mine. "So," she says, voice still slightly shaky, "let's start by making some pizza. I owe you a proper Slice Slice Baby pie, right?"

I chuckle, feeling a knot of tension unwind in my gut. "Damn right you do."

She grins, leading me behind the counter, where her mother waits with a relieved smile. As we pass the row of ingredient bins, Aubree stares at them like she's greeting old friends—pepperoni, olives, mushrooms. The dough mixer in the corner is silent for now, but I can already picture it whirring back to life under her skilled hands.

For the first time in weeks, I see her face light up with genuine excitement.

"Pizza?" she asks, meeting my gaze.

"Pizza," I confirm.

Her mother lets out a small laugh, rolling up her sleeves. "Then let's make the best damn pie this town has ever seen."

It's a fresh start—one she's more than earned. And as I watch Aubree grab a ball of dough, a bright new confidence in her eyes, I know that whatever happens next, we'll figure it out. Together. Because this time, there's nothing left to run from.

Chapter 28

Aubree

It's been a little over a week since I've been back in Nashville, and the rhythmic hum of Slice Slice Baby has come roaring back to life. At least, that's how it seems on the surface. The ovens are running hot all day, the high school crowd is spilling in after last period, and the laughter of friends sharing slices fills the shop just like it always did.

But there's a Boone-shaped hole in my life, and it's bigger than I ever expected.

This morning starts like any other. Stuart and I roll out dough in the back kitchen, the clatter of pans and the thunk of the dough press keeping me grounded. He kneads with strong, practiced hands—an old soul in a eighteen-year-old's body. I watch him with a little smile, remembering how unsure he was when I first hired him. Now, he's practically my right-hand man.

"You doing okay today?" he asks, sliding a fresh ball of dough across the floured counter toward me. The flour puffs up in a little cloud, making me sneeze.

"I'm fine," I say, sniffling. But Stuart raises an eyebrow in that telltale way. "Okay, so maybe I'm not fine, but I'm surviving," I admit, exhaling as I start to shape the dough into a circle. "Business is good, we haven't gotten any new threats, and people are pouring back in. So yeah, just... figuring out this new normal."

He nods, pressing his hands against the dough. "Is it... you know, Boone?"

The mention of his name makes my chest clench. "You're too perceptive for your own good," I mutter, carefully spinning the circle of dough. When I look up, I see sympathy in Stuart's gaze, and I offer a small smile. "I just miss him, you know? We talk every night, but it's not the same."

Stuart nods. "Long-distance sucks, huh?"

"Yeah," I admit, pressing a thumb into the center of the dough to even it out. "But he has his life in Saint Pierce, and I have mine here."

The door to the back kitchen swings open then, and my mom steps in, smelling faintly of that expensive perfume she's always worn. She's got a stack of newly printed menus in one hand—featuring our latest specialty pie, the "Safe Haven," which is basically a love letter to the comfort food that got me through the worst weeks of my life.

"Honey," she greets me, setting the menus on a nearby shelf. "I talked to one of the local paper's food columnists. They might want to do a feature on Slice Slice Baby. You feeling up for that?"

"Really?" I say, my spirits lifting just a bit. "That's amazing, Mom."

She smiles warmly, her eyes flicking to Stuart. "Hello, Stuart. Good to see you."

He nods, brushing flour from his hands. "Hey, Ms. Ryan." He excuses himself, heading out to the front counter, presumably to let us talk in private.

My mom turns to me, her brow furrowing with concern. "How are you doing?"

The question makes me set down the dough. "I'm okay." I swallow, forcing myself to speak the truth. "I miss Boone. A lot."

She nods, stepping closer and placing a hand on my arm. "Have you two talked recently?"

"Every night," I say with a half-laugh, hearing how pathetic I must sound. "We call, sometimes just for a few minutes, sometimes an hour or more. But it's so... different. Not seeing him every day, or waking up to his face, or even hearing him humming while he checks the locks ten times in a row."

Her expression softens. "You'll figure it out. He cared about you—anyone could see that."

I let out a shaky breath, glancing down at the flour dusting my fingertips. "I know. He says he's trying to arrange work in Nashville, some reason to come out this way. But that could take time."

"Sweetheart," my mother says gently, "you deserve to be happy. If Boone makes you happy, then... make a plan. A visit, at least. You're not stuck in Nashville, you know. You can take a weekend and go to Saint Pierce to see him."

I look up at her, startled by the suggestion. "I guess that's possible," I say, cheeks warming at the thought of surprising Boone, showing up at his place in Saint Pierce with a pizza in hand and a big grin. "I just… it's busy here. We're trying to recover from everything, and—"

She pats my arm. "Honey, life is always going to be busy. And so is his. You have to carve out time for the things that matter."

I sigh, turning back to the dough. Carefully, I ladle sauce onto the crust, spreading it in smooth, practiced circles. "I'll think about it," I promise. "It's only been a week since I got back, you know. We're still trying to fix the back door and restock the supplies, and the high school crowd has been insane. It's just… I get so tired at the end of the day."

Mom nods, stepping over to help me sprinkle cheese onto the sauce. "You are doing so well, though. Don't sell yourself short. The customers love your new Safe Haven pizza, and everyone's been eager to support the shop after what happened." She hesitates, then lowers her voice. "How are you holding up with everything else? Charles still…?"

"Still in custody," I reply, blinking hard to ward off any hint of tears. "The police say they have enough to keep him there for a while. There's no bail. And if he does manage to wiggle out, we have a restraining order. Plus, all of Maddox Security is on alert. If he tries anything, they'll know."

She nods, relief evident in her eyes. "Good. I can't believe I ever… ever trusted that man. But at least we're done with him." She sets down the cheese, straightening up. "And you, my love, can finally get back to making your life what you want it to be."

I finish assembling the pizza with a flourish—pepperoni, mushrooms, and a sprinkle of fresh basil. "This is the life I want," I murmur, sliding the pizza onto a sheet pan. "Mostly. I just… I wish Boone was here, too."

My mom squeezes my shoulder. "Have faith, honey. Sometimes the best things in life are worth a little distance and a little waiting."

I swallow, nodding. "Yeah," I say softly, lifting the tray and heading toward the oven. I slide it in, and the heat blasts my face. The comforting smell of rising dough fills the room. For a moment, I close my eyes, letting the familiarity of it ground me.

A little while later, I stand at the front counter, greeting the regulars who file in for their early dinner slices. The buzz of conversation spills through the glass door as high school students shuffle in, already trying to figure out where to sit. My heart lifts at the sight—this is the kind of normal I've craved for so long.

Stuart mans the register, flashing me a grin whenever we share a glance. He's settled back into his old rhythm, joking with customers about the new specialty pizzas and teasing them if they don't like olives (like he does with every single olive-hater, bless him).

The day zips by, full of orders and laughter and the occasional kitchen mishap. Once or twice, I catch a glimpse of my phone on the counter and wonder if Boone will text me something sweet, like he usually does around this time of day. But it stays silent.

By the time evening rolls around, I'm exhausted, but in that good, productive way. Stuart waves goodbye, promising to come in early tomorrow. Mom offers to stay and close with me, but I insist I can handle it, so she heads home.

Guarding What's Mine

I linger at the front, turning off a few lights and locking the door. The neon "open" sign goes dark with a soft click. The quiet hum of the fridge motors in the background as I gather up any stray trash and check the tables.

When I finish, I collapse into one of the booths, phone in hand. Sure enough, there's a missed call and a voicemail from Boone. My heart leaps, and I press the phone to my ear, barely noticing how my pulse pounds.

"Hey," his deep voice rumbles through the speaker. "I guess you're busy at the shop. I, uh, just wanted to say hi. Miss you. I might have a free weekend soon—wondering if we could figure out a time to see each other. Call me back, okay?"

I press the phone to my chest, a wave of affection and longing flooding me. I punch in his number, but it goes straight to voicemail, so I leave a breathless message of my own: "Hey, Boone, sorry I missed you. Been a crazy day. I miss you, too. Call me tonight when you can—I'll be home, probably taking a bath or something equally boring. Or if I can't wait, I'll call you first. I love—I mean, talk soon."

My cheeks burn at how close I came to blurting out the L-word. We haven't said it, not yet. It might be too soon. But my heart knows it's there, a simmering truth I can't deny.

Exhaling, I lock up the shop and step outside into the cool night air. The streetlights cast a warm glow over the familiar sidewalk. My gaze drifts to the sign above the shop door—Slice Slice Baby—and a pang of gratitude washes over me. I'm here, I'm safe, and life is slowly returning to normal.

But part of my normal, it seems, is missing. The part that I found hidden away in a remote cabin with a man who taught me how to feel protected and cherished at the same time. And even though it hurts, even though the distance is daunting, I cling to the hope that he and I will figure it out.

I cross my arms against the gentle breeze, heading to my car. I think about the future—maybe a weekend trip to Saint Pierce, or him finding work here, or somehow forging a life that lets us close that gap. Because missing Boone like this feels raw and aching, and I can't imagine letting it stay that way forever.

As I unlock the car and slip into the driver's seat, I let myself smile. Even if the days are hectic and the nights are lonely, I know where my heart is leading me. And that's back to Boone, one way or another.

Chapter 29

Boone

I'm sitting in Dean's corner office on the thirtieth floor of Maddox Security's headquarters in Saint Pierce, trying—and failing—to focus on the conversation. The ocean sprawls outside the floor-to-ceiling windows, sparkling in the late morning sun. Normally, I'd be transfixed by the waves, reminded of the early days of my career when I'd do oceanside drills and sweeps. But today, my mind's somewhere else entirely.

Aubree.

It's been over a week since I last saw her in person—since we packed up the cabin, drove her home, and handed her life back to her. I keep telling myself it was the right thing, that she needed to return to Slice Slice Baby and the town she loves. But every day since I left, I wake up missing her more than the day before. The phone calls help, but they're not enough. Her voice lights me up, sure, but it also makes the emptiness more apparent. I crave the soft press of her lips, the way her laughter feels in my arms.

I snap back to reality when Dean clears his throat pointedly. He's sitting behind his massive glass desk, eyebrows raised. "You still with me, Boone?" he asks, the edge of a smile tugging at his mouth.

"Yeah," I lie, giving a quick nod. "Sorry, just got lost in thought."

"Mm-hmm." He doesn't buy it for a second, though he doesn't push. Instead, he points at the folder on his desk. "So, I've been thinking about expanding. We've got a strong hold on the East Coast, Florida especially, but there's a market in the Midwest—Tennessee, Kentucky, the surrounding states. I've got some high-end clients sniffing around who'd love an office closer to home."

I turn my attention fully to Dean, interest piqued despite the buzzing in my chest that's still chanting Aubree's name. "That's a big move," I say.

He nods. "Sure is. But it's time. I've already scouted a few properties around Nashville for a potential office. The place is booming—corporate expansions, entertainment scene, politicians, country music stars. Plenty of folks with money who need premium security."

I blink, my thoughts jumping to the cabin I own just outside Nashville. The air, the pines, the streams... and Aubree, whose pizza shop is only a short drive from there. My heart thuds harder. "You're thinking about setting up a branch in Tennessee?" I ask slowly, trying to keep my voice even.

Dean leans back in his chair, arms crossing over his chest. "Yeah. And I need someone I can trust to head it up." He levels his gaze at me. "Someone who's proven he can handle a crisis under pressure, who's got the skill and the leadership. And quite frankly, I think you'd be perfect for it. You're already half living in the mountains up there anyway."

My mind goes blank for a moment, like it's short-circuiting. "Me?" I manage to say.

Dean smirks. "You. Unless you're not interested. But I seem to recall you have a certain fondness for the Tennessee woods—and maybe other reasons to be up there?"

Heat creeps up my neck. He's obviously referring to Aubree, though he's polite enough not to say her name. "I, uh... I'm definitely interested," I blurt, excitement thrumming through me. A chance to live near Aubree, to actually build something in Nashville while doing the job I love? It sounds like a dream I didn't know I could have.

Dean grins, pulling a sheet of paper from the folder. "Excellent. I've got a rough timeline. We'll want to secure an office space within the next month. Then we'll gradually transfer some of our key personnel, train up some newbies, and get the branch running. I'd want you to oversee all of that, including hiring decisions."

I flip through the pages he hands me. My head spins with the potential. Managing my own branch? Setting up a team? I've always been more of a field operative than an office guy, but the idea of building something from the ground up, doing it on my terms... it's a rush. "This is huge," I say quietly. "Thank you for trusting me."

He shrugs. "You've earned it, Boone. I need someone who's dependable, who'll keep a tight ship. And if that's in Nashville, well—it's a bonus that you're already fond of the area. You just have to promise to keep your head on straight. No letting personal matters get in the way of the job."

I know he's hinting at Aubree, but I can't even pretend to be annoyed. Because this changes everything. Instead, I nod, my chest tight. "I'll handle it, Dean. I won't let you down."

"Good. I'll send the formal offer to your email. Get your eyes on the contract, talk it over with whoever you need to."

"Right," I say, swallowing. I can't wait to tell Aubree—but a part of me wants to keep it a surprise. Something in me craves that moment where I show up in her pizza shop and say, "By the way, I'm moving here. Permanently."

Dean must see the wheels spinning in my mind, because he lets out a short chuckle. "I take it you're thinking about how to break the news?"

"You could say that," I admit.

He waves a hand. "Do it however you like. I'm giving you about a week or so to get your ducks in a row. Then we'll finalize everything. Sound good?"

"Sounds perfect," I say, standing up straighter. The ocean outside the window glimmers, but my mind's on a different horizon. "Thank you, Dean."

He gives a curt nod, then folds his hands on the desk. "Now get out of here. I've got another meeting, and you've got some planning to do."

I leave the skyrise with my heart hammering against my ribs. The midday heat hits me as soon as I step onto the sidewalk, but it doesn't bother me. My head's spinning with the best kind of chaos—logistics, tasks, and the thought of seeing Aubree again.

Over the next few days, it's non-stop. Dean sends me reams of documents to review—reports, budgets, recruitment strategies. I make calls to potential local contacts, cross-check a list of employees who might transfer. It's exhilarating, but all-consuming. By the end of each day, my phone is filled with missed calls and texts from old friends or colleagues.

And one missed text from Aubree each night—"Hey, sorry I missed your call, busy day. Miss you, or hope you're well, etc." And my heart wrenches every time. I want to call her back, tell her everything, hear her laugh when I describe how I'll run my own branch. But each time I check the clock, it's past midnight, or I'm knee-deep in a planning meeting. I hate it. Hate letting the days slip by without hearing her voice. But the payoff—surprising her in person—burns bright in my mind.

Finally, after nearly a week, I pack up my truck. It's still early morning when I hit the road, heading north out of Saint Pierce, the sky a wash of gold and pink. My overnight bag rides in the passenger seat, stuffed with enough clothes to last a few days. I called Aubree's mother last night, quietly letting her in on the secret. She agreed to keep her daughter busy and none the wiser.

A grin tugs at my lips as I merge onto the highway. This is it. I can't wait to see the look on her face when I walk into Slice Slice Baby unannounced, maybe right in the middle of lunch rush. I might bring her flowers, or maybe just show up at the counter and order a slice.

The miles stretch ahead, but my chest feels lighter with every sign that points toward Nashville. I turn on the radio, letting some old country songs fill the cab, ignoring the swirl of traffic. My mind drifts to the memory of holding Aubree's hand, the warmth of her gaze, the way she'd nudge me whenever I was too serious. In just a few hours, I'll be there.

She has no idea I'm coming. And I can't wait to change that.

Chapter 30

Aubree

It's late afternoon at Slice Slice Baby, and the usual hum of conversation and sizzling ovens is starting to wind down. School let out a while ago, so the rush of teenagers has tapered off to a quiet trickle of customers. I rub my temple, a dull headache forming from a day of slinging dough, mixing sauces, and managing the constant chatter of orders. My mother stands behind the counter, reorganizing our brand-new menus for what feels like the hundredth time.

"You need a break," she insists, her brow furrowed with maternal concern. "You can't keep burning the candle at both ends like this, Aubree. You've been back for a couple of weeks, and you haven't stopped once to breathe."

I sigh, busy punching an order into the system. "I'm fine, Mom. Really."

She gives me a pointed look. "That's what you always say right before you crash."

The computer beeps, confirming the order, and I tear off the receipt. "Well," I respond quietly, "I can't exactly take time off. Not when we're still picking up the pieces around here."

Her gaze softens, and she sets the menus down, coming around the counter to lay a gentle hand on my arm. "Aubree, I see how exhausted you are." She hesitates, then touches on the subject I've been avoiding all day. "And I know you haven't heard from Boone in a few days."

The mention of Boone's name sends a pang through me—like a needle prick in my heart. "He's been busy, I guess," I say, trying to keep my voice light. "I know he's got a lot going on in Saint Pierce."

Mom's expression turns sympathetic. "You miss him, don't you?"

I force a small laugh, feigning a casualness I don't feel. "Yeah. I do. I miss him… a lot. But maybe this is just the way it is, you know? We live in different places, and life is hectic. I can't expect him to put his whole career on hold just to call me every night."

She opens her mouth like she's about to protest, but then closes it. After a moment, she steps in and pulls me into a quick hug. I hug her back, inhaling the familiar scent of her perfume. I didn't realize until this moment how much I need the comfort.

"You'll figure it out," she murmurs, pressing a kiss to the top of my head. "One step at a time. Now, I have a meeting with our realtor about some changes to the house. You going to be okay closing up alone tonight?"

I step back and nod, forcing a smile. "Of course. Stuart's already headed home early for once, but I can handle it. There's not much left to do."

She gives me one last searching look before grabbing her purse. "Lock the door as soon as you're done, okay?"

"Will do, Mom."

———

ABOUT AN HOUR LATER, the last straggle of customers has left, and the shop is officially closed. I flip the OPEN sign to CLOSED, lock the door, and go through my usual closing routine. Wiping down the counters, putting leftover dough in the fridge, loading a small tray of unbaked pizza crusts into the walk-in cooler. Every so often, my mind flicks to Boone. Where is he now? Probably busy with some intense security job, or maybe he's just buried under a mountain of work. Part of me worries—what if he's drifting away? And I hate that I feel that dread creeping in, but I can't help it. Love can be terrifying when you don't know where you stand.

I push the thought aside and focus on brushing the last bits of flour off the stainless-steel prep table. The overhead lights buzz softly, casting long shadows across the now-empty dining area. I can't help but glance outside, at the dimly lit street. It's quiet tonight, just the glow of streetlamps and the occasional car passing by.

Finally, I turn off the majority of the lights, leaving only a small overhead bulb in the kitchen. I'm about to head to the back to grab my purse and keys when I hear it:

The jangling of the front door.

My heart jumps. I locked that door—didn't I?

"Sorry, we're closed!" I call out automatically, stepping out from behind the prep area.

The figure in the doorway is tall, and for a split second my stomach seizes with fear—someone's broken in before, it wouldn't be the first time. Then the silhouette steps forward into the faint glow of the light. My breath catches.

"Earl?" I say, surprised. He's clutching a baseball cap in his hand, his expression oddly tense. Earl's always been a loyal customer. He's older than me by a couple of years, thinning hair, kind smile. Usually harmless. He was here the night the brick was thrown through the window.

"Hey there, Aubree," he says, voice shaky. "Sorry to come by so late, I just… wanted to talk."

I exhale, forcing a smile despite the confusion roiling in my gut. "Well, we're closed, but for you, I can make an exception. Everything okay?"

He doesn't move from where he stands, just stares with an intensity that's putting me on edge. "I had to see you," he mutters, stepping closer. "You haven't been returning my calls."

Calls? I blink, shaking my head. "Earl, I don't… think I got any calls from you. I'm sorry. Things have been crazy."

His grip tightens on the cap, knuckles bleaching white. "I used to come in every day, you know. You were always so sweet. I asked you out once, remember?"

A faint memory tugs at me—Earl joking, something about "we should get coffee sometime." I brushed it off. A polite "maybe sometime," accompanied by a laugh, because he was a friendly regular, not someone I'd date. "That was… oh, Earl, I'm sorry if I led you on or anything. I just…"

His eyes narrow. "You turned me down," he corrects, taking another step. The overhead light in the kitchen catches on his face, casting harsh shadows that make him look older, angrier. "You laughed. And you told me you'd never date a customer."

I swallow hard, dread coiling in my stomach. "Earl, I don't remember that exactly, but if I offended you—"

He barks out a low, humorless laugh. "Offended me? No, not offended. Just heartbroken. I loved you, Aubree. More than you even realized. And you turned me down like I was nothing."

My mind whirls, struggling to keep up. "Earl… we never— I mean, I barely know you." My pulse quickens as something cold settles into my veins. This is not the Earl I thought I knew.

He stiffens, a strange mania in his eyes. "That's your fault," he hisses. "I tried to show you I could take care of you. But you wouldn't see it. You pushed me aside."

My breath catches. "Earl," I say slowly, raising my hands to try to keep him calm. "I— I'm sorry if you felt that way. But you can't just—"

"You didn't just break my heart," he says, voice trembling with anger. "You humiliated me. All those times I came in, tried to talk to you, and you brushed me off. That's when I decided to show you that you needed me. That you'd have nowhere else to turn."

My blood runs cold. "What do you mean?"

He shifts closer, looming over me, and I realize how tall he actually is compared to my average height. "All those letters, the brick through your window, the phone calls. That was me. Trying to scare you so you'd run to *me* for comfort." He tightens his jaw, eyes blazing with a twisted sense of hurt. "You never did, though. You had that meddling mother who hired security. And that scumbag stepfather tried to meddle too, but that wasn't me. I just wanted you to *need* me, Aubree."

A fresh wave of horror slams into me. So Charles hired people to track me, but Earl was also threatening me on his own? Is that why it felt so relentless, from so many directions? I step back, heart hammering. "You… you broke into my shop?"

His laugh is brittle. "It was easy. Your security system was all messed up after that fiasco with Charles. Figured I'd take another opportunity to scare you. And still, you didn't call me. You called him." He spits the last word, like referencing Boone is a bitter taste on his tongue.

My chest tightens, adrenaline surging. I need to get out, get away. But he's blocking the door, and my phone is in the back. "Earl, this isn't right," I say, trying to keep my voice calm, though my legs are shaking. "You're just upset. Let's… let's talk to someone, get you help—"

He snaps. Before I can register the movement, he lunges, gripping my wrist in a crushing hold. I gasp, trying to yank free, but his grip is like iron. "No more help," he snarls, spittle flying from his lips. "We're doing this my way."

"Earl, stop!" I twist, attempting to land a kick, but he anticipates it, sidestepping and jerking my arm painfully behind my back. A cry escapes my throat, sharp and terrified.

His breath is hot against my ear. "You could've had me, Aubree," he mutters, voice raw with desperation. "We could've been happy. But you never gave me a chance."

I grit my teeth, tears stinging my eyes at the pain in my wrenched shoulder. "You're hurting me!" I manage, trying to dig my nails into the arm that's pinning me.

He doesn't let go. Instead, he lurches us toward the back, where the kitchen lies. A million thoughts tumble through my mind—my mother, Boone, the helplessness of it all. How is this happening?

I bite my lip hard, trying not to scream in panic. If I can just get him to relax his grip for a second, I might slip free.

But Earl's bigger, stronger, and clearly unhinged. Before I know it, he's pulling something from his pocket—a coil of thick rope. My stomach drops. "No—don't—" I start, heart thudding wildly.

"Shut up," he hisses, forcing me to the floor. My knee hits the tile hard, sending a jolt of pain up my leg. He uses his weight to press me down, and I thrash, but it's no use. The rope snakes around my wrists, pinching the skin.

Terror floods every inch of me, my mind screaming at me to fight. I twist my head, trying to catch a glimpse of the exit, but he's half on top of me, pressing his forearm into my back. If I were calmer, I might recall the self-defense lessons Boone taught me, but right now, I'm choking on pure panic.

Within moments, Earl has my wrists bound, my ankles too, and I can't do more than squirm. Sweat drips into my eyes, and I blink it away, chest heaving.

Earl shoves me onto my side, face twisted with triumph. "You see?" he says, voice low. "You could've made this easier, but you forced my hand." He stands, glaring at me like he's deciding what to do next. "I can't leave you here now. You'll just call the cops, call that damn security company. No, we're going somewhere. Just you and me."

I shake my head violently, tears burning hot behind my eyelids. My voice catches in my throat, coming out as a ragged plea. "Earl, please... you don't have to do this."

He lifts me by my bound arms, ignoring my cry of pain, and starts dragging me through the back exit. I can feel the rough concrete under me as he half-carries, half-drags my body outside. The night air hits my face, but there's no relief in it, just the stench of garbage from the dumpster and the distant hum of traffic.

"Help!" I try to yell, but he clamps a hand over my mouth so hard my lips grind against my teeth, cutting them. The metallic taste of blood seeps in, and I gag.

"Shut up," he repeats, breath ragged. "You're mine now."

He stumbles with me toward a parked van that I barely register. The back doors are open, the interior dark. He hoists me onto the floor, and I land with a sickening thud. My vision blurs, spots dancing at the edges, and I hear the slam of the doors behind me.

The engine roars to life. My heart pounds in my ears so loud I can hardly breathe. I wriggle, trying to find any give in the ropes, but he's bound me tight. Above my panicked gasps, I hear Earl mumbling to himself, something about "finding a place where no one can stop us."

No. This can't be real. My mother is at home. Boone is away in Saint Pierce, not even answering his phone regularly. And I'm here, kidnapped by a man I thought was a harmless regular—a man who's been behind the threats all along.

The van lurches forward, and I tumble onto my side, tears streaming down my cheeks. My mind screams Boone's name, but my lips are too dry, too swollen. I can't cry for help. I can't fight. All I can do is stare at the dusty floor of the van and pray someone figures out what happened.

Because right now, I'm alone. Completely at Earl's mercy. And I've never been more terrified in my life.

Chapter 31

Boone

I swing my truck into the parking spot across the street from Slice Slice Baby, my heart thumping with a mixture of anticipation and nerves. It's late, and the moon hangs heavy in the sky. My mind buzzes with excitement—I've been waiting for this moment for days, planning how I'd surprise Aubree.

I can practically picture her wide-eyed gasp, the way her soft lips will part in a smile when she sees me. I'll walk in, she'll be behind the counter, maybe messing with dough, or closing up shop. I'll give her that cocky grin and say, "Sorry, ma'am, but is there a special on surprising the girl you love?" She'll laugh, her cheeks turning that faint pink I've come to crave seeing.

But the second I climb out of the truck and cross the street, something feels wrong. There's a stillness in the air, a heaviness that presses against my chest. The sign on Slice Slice Baby's door says "Closed," but the door itself is slightly ajar, letting a wedge of dim light spill onto the sidewalk. Aubree wouldn't leave it like that, especially not after everything that's happened. Anxiety sparks, rattling my nerves as I push the door open with more force than necessary.

"Aubree?" I call out, voice echoing eerily in the empty shop. Nothing. Not even the hum of ovens or the clatter of pans. I step inside, searching the rows of booths and tables. The overhead lights are half off, leaving the front area in deep shadow. My pulse quickens.

The shop is deserted—no Stuart, no Aubree, no Lisa. Just silence and the faint smell of fresh dough. I cross to the counter, scanning behind it. The place is deserted. My stomach knots.

She's not here.

I fight the flare of panic. This is the middle of Nashville, not the middle of nowhere. She could've run an errand, right? But she'd never leave the front door wide open, especially not after the break-in and all the threats. Something's off. All my instincts scream at me that something is very, very wrong.

I grab my phone, calling her, and I hear the distant sound of her ringtone. I move in the direction of it, spotting her keys, phone, and purse on the back table. Something's not right.

I hang up, and punch in Dean's number. He answers on the second ring. "Boone?" he says, sounding mildly surprised. "Aren't you supposed to be—?"

"Dean," I interrupt, my voice raw. "I'm at Aubree's shop. She's gone. The door's wide open, nobody's here. I need you to pull up the security feeds. Now."

"What?" Dean's tone snaps to attention, urgent. "You sure she's not just in the back?"

"I checked. She's left all her things. Her phone. Purse. Keys. Place is empty." My gaze roves around, searching for any clue or sign of a fight. I grab her keys. "This isn't normal, Dean. She wouldn't just up and leave everything like this."

There's a flurry of keyboard clacks on his end, the sound of Dean working fast. "Hold on... I'm logging into the cameras. We left the system in place after all that stuff with Charles. The main feed... oh, shit." His voice drops as he watches something I can't see yet. "Boone, the feed is glitchy, but it looks like someone came in after closing time."

My mouth goes dry. "Aubree was alone, wasn't she? Her mother probably left her alone knowing I'd be here soon. Goddamn it." I step around the counter, nearly tripping over a stool that's on its side. Fear spikes through me—why is it knocked over?

"Yeah," Dean says, still working. "I see a figure... big guy, maybe. He's... pulling her toward the back. That's all I can see from this angle."

A spike of anger and dread slams into my gut, so strong it almost makes me dizzy. "Dean, run the back alley camera. Maybe we got a better angle out there."

"On it," he mutters. More typing. A few seconds pass in brutal silence. "Got it. He's pushing her into a white van. No plate visible from this angle, though. Dammit, it's too dark."

I grip my phone, knuckles whitening. I pace behind the counter, stepping through the flour scattered on the floor. "Dean," I say, forcing my voice to steady. "Send me that footage. Now."

"Sending," he confirms, keys clacking. "Done. Pulling it up on my end, too. Trying to zoom in on the face. Wait... I recognize him from the first night at her shop, back when we were watching her more closely. Wasn't he a regular?"

My lips peel back in a snarl. "Earl," I grind out. It's like a punch to the gut, remembering that unassuming older guy who always seemed so friendly. We never had any reason to suspect him. But now, everything clicks into place. "He must have been behind some of this. Maybe he acted alone, or maybe not. But obviously, he got to her."

Dean's breath hisses through the line. "I'm tapping into the city's traffic cams next. Gonna see if we can track that van. You stay put, or—actually, do what you gotta do. But keep me updated. We'll find her, Boone."

"Goddamn right we will," I bark, ending the call. The rage swirling inside me is almost suffocating. I failed her. I was supposed to protect her, but I was holed up in Saint Pierce, tying up loose ends. If I'd come sooner—if I'd called more often—maybe I would've known something was wrong.

I swallow down the guilt and force myself to function. This is a crisis, and in a crisis, you don't shut down, you act. My phone buzzes with an incoming file from Dean—the security footage. I slip behind the counter and open it, watching with a sinking heart as the grainy image shows Earl dragging Aubree, her legs trying to kick, her face a mask of terror. The clip ends with him shoving her into a van. I freeze the frame, trying to glean any detail—a partial license plate, a unique dent, something. But it's dark, and his van looks painfully generic.

I exhale shakily, shutting off the video. All it does is stoke my fury. I picture her fighting him, screaming for help. That's all I can see in my head now. The fear in her eyes rips at my insides.

"Not happening again," I murmur under my breath. "I'm getting you back, Aubree."

I call Dean again. He picks up, out of breath like he's running between computers. "I'm into the city's transportation network," he reports. "Got a partial shot of the van heading west on Highway 70. Traffic's not too bad right now, but they'll have at least a ten or twenty-minute lead on you."

"I'm heading that way." I spin on my heel, striding to the front door. "Send me real-time updates. And do me a favor—ping the local precinct, see if they have any cameras near the highway. I want every possible angle."

"Consider it done. I'll funnel everything to your phone. We'll find them, Boone."

I kill the call, my heart hammering. Tucking my phone in my pocket, I step out onto the sidewalk, bracing myself against the evening breeze. The sign overhead glows with the bright red neon of "Slice Slice Baby," mocking me with normalcy. The shop was supposed to be where I surprised her. Instead, it's a crime scene.

I lock the door behind me, pocketing her keys, my chest tight. She might need the shop intact when she comes back. And I vow she will come back. Then I jog to my truck, yanking open the driver's side door. The engine roars to life, and I tear away from the curb, heading west. I retrieve my phone from my pocket and perch it on the dash, in case Dean calls again.

As I speed down the streets, streetlights whipping by in a blur, my mind churns with guilt. I should've been here. If I'd come just an hour sooner, I might have stopped this. Or maybe it's not about being early; maybe I should never have left her side after we took down Charles. The memory of her shy grin, her messy hair in the mornings, all of it squeezes my heart.

The phone rings again—Dean. I jab the answer button on speaker. "What's new?"

"I've followed the camera feed a bit further. The van got on the highway around exit twelve. I lost it for a moment, but I'm cross-checking other cameras. We need a better vantage point. The city's got scattered coverage—some cameras are out, some are pointed away."

"Just keep looking," I say, my voice tense. "I'm almost on the highway. Let me know if you get a direction. North, south, wherever."

"Got it. I'll call you back."

He hangs up. I let out a harsh breath, eyes scanning the road as I swerve onto the on-ramp. The radio is off, and all I hear is the roar of the engine and my own ragged breathing. I glance down at the speedometer—pushing eighty-five in a sixty zone. Don't care. If a cop tries to pull me over, I'll flash my security credentials and keep going.

I dial another number, pressing the phone to my ear. It rings twice before a deep voice picks up. " Thor speaking."

"Thor, It's Boone," I say, my words tumbling out. "I've got a situation. A friend—someone I care about—has been kidnapped. I need a team, fast."

Thor's voice instantly sharpens. "Kidnapped? You sure?"

"Dead sure," I growl. "I was at her shop. The security footage showed some asshole named Earl dragging her into a van. We have partial route intel, but no exact location yet. She's in danger, Thor. I can't do this alone."

"You won't," Thor says firmly. "I'm about an hour out of Nashville right now. Who else you want on this?"

"Garrett's local," I say, thinking rapidly. "He's got good recon skills. Let's bring him in. And any other guys we can trust, the ones who'll keep it tight-lipped. This is personal."

"Understood," Thor replies. "We'll keep it off the official grid if that's what you want."

"Absolutely," I confirm, jaw tight. "Dean's still working the tech angle, pulling traffic cams and city feeds. Once we pin down a location, I'll call you. We're going to need a strike team—small, quick, and ready for anything."

Thor exhales, the sound crackling over the line. "We got you. I'll call a few guys and get them mobilized. Send me the details once you have them."

I nod, even though he can't see me. "Thanks, man. I appreciate it." I end the call, relief flickering through the panic. Thor's reliable—he was my commanding officer's golden boy at one point. He's got the skills and the network.

Now for Garrett. I tap his number, heart still thrumming. He picks up, sounding casual at first, "Yo, what's—?"

"Garrett, it's Boone," I cut in. "I need your help. Now. Aubree's been taken. I have partial leads on a white van heading west out of Nashville. I've called Thor in, too."

He curses quietly. "I'm in, no question. Where do you need me?"

"Wait until I have a location," I reply, muscles tensing as I weave around slower traffic on the highway. "Thor's building a small team. We'll coordinate and figure out exactly how to move once we know where she is. She's my top priority, Garrett."

"Got it. I'll prep my gear and stand by. Don't do anything stupid alone, okay?"

My throat tightens. "No promises," I mutter, "but I'll try not to. I'll call you soon."

"Stay safe," Garrett says, then hangs up.

I toss the phone onto the passenger seat, gripping the steering wheel with both hands. The highway unfurls in front of me, taillights streaking by. My mind races, conjuring images of Aubree tied up, terrified, or worse. The thought is like a knife in my chest.

She must be so scared, I think, biting the inside of my cheek until I taste blood. This can't be happening. We'd already dealt with her stepfather's betrayal, and we'd thought it was over. Meanwhile, some unhinged regular who'd been lurking under our noses all this time was waiting for his chance. The idea that we never saw it coming makes me want to punch something.

A wave of guilt washes over me again—If only I'd arrived an hour earlier, if only I'd insisted on staying in Nashville from the get-go. But regrets won't help me now. I need to channel that energy into finding her.

The phone rings again—Dean. My heart jumps as I flip it to speaker. "You got something?" I bark.

"Tracked the van past exit 20," Dean says, voice clipped. "It took a turn onto a rural road about eight miles from the city boundary. The cameras aren't great out there, but we have it on a feed from a gas station. I'm scanning ahead, trying to see if there's another camera. This might be the best lead we've got for now."

"Good," I say, checking the next exit sign. "I'm coming up on exit 18. That means I'm close. Keep me updated. I'm calling in a couple guys to help."

"Good call," Dean says. "You want me to get the local cops on this? Or do you want to handle it privately?"

I hesitate, the thought of the cops launching a slow, bureaucratic response making me cringe. They'd mean well, but by the time they get a warrant, or figure out jurisdiction, Earl could vanish. "Let me handle it for now," I decide. "If we need them, I'll pull them in. Right now, speed is critical."

"Agreed," Dean says. He sighs, and I sense his frustration. "We'll do everything we can from this end, Boone. Just... be careful, okay? We don't know what this guy's capable of. I read a quick dive on his background—some petty crimes, but nothing major. Still, he's obviously escalated."

"He's got Aubree," I say, voice shaking with anger. "He's dangerous enough."

Dean's silent for a moment. Then, quietly, "I know what she means to you. We'll find her, man. Hang in there."

The call ends, leaving me with the roar of my engine as I push the speedometer past ninety.

I grit my teeth, swallowing hard. "Hold on, Aubree," I mutter, gripping the wheel. "I'm coming for you."

Because nothing—no distance, no unhinged stalker, no threat of violence—will stop me from bringing her home.

Chapter 32

Aubree

My head throbs, and my wrists ache from the tight cords binding them. I'm wedged in the back of Earl's van, the stale smell of oil and dust filling my nostrils every time I breathe in. Every jolt and rattle along the uneven road makes the rope bite harder into my skin. My heart won't stop hammering, a frantic drumbeat that roars in my ears.

I have no clue how long we've been driving. Minutes? Hours? The windows in this old, beat-up vehicle are covered with some kind of tarp, letting only slivers of light in. The darkness is suffocating, broken only by the dim glow from the front dash. I can vaguely see Earl's silhouette through a small gap in the seats as he navigates, his hands gripping the wheel.

Every so often, he mutters something to himself, so quiet I can't quite make out the words. I inch myself forward to try and unlatch the back doors. But the second I move, his gaze flicks to the rearview mirror, and I freeze, heart racing. He doesn't say anything—just sets his jaw like he's daring me to try it again. I see the mania swirling in his eyes, and it sends a cold shudder through me. I can't risk provoking him further.

Eventually, the van slows and bumps down a rutted path. The ride grows rougher. Every rock we drive over makes me grunt as I'm tossed about on the dirty floor. My stomach knots—where is he taking me? The overhead branches create a flickering pattern of light and shadow inside the van, telling me we're probably deep in the woods. Far from anyone who could help.

Then Earl kills the engine, plunging the interior into near-total silence aside from my ragged breathing. I feel my pulse reverberating in my fingertips, and for one wild second, I cling to hope—maybe he'll change his mind, maybe this is just a sick prank. But that hope vanishes the moment I hear him open the driver's door and stomp around to the back.

He yanks the double doors open, letting in a rush of cool, pine-scented air. The light outside is weak, but it still stings my eyes after the darkness in here.

"Get up," Earl commands, climbing into the back. I'm still bound at wrists and ankles, so standing is impossible. I try to push myself upright with my elbows, but he grabs me, hauling me against his chest with surprising strength.

A cry escapes my throat. I'm half-expecting him to let me walk or limp, but instead, he slings me over his shoulder like I weigh nothing. My stomach churns, the world spinning as we exit the van. I catch a glimpse of tall pines, tangled brush, and an old structure—a cabin, by the look of its sagging porch and boarded-up windows.

He stomps up the creaking steps, the boards groaning under our combined weight. The door swings open with a shrill squeak of rusted hinges, and a musty odor assaults my senses

—like damp wood and old cigarettes. He steps inside, kicking the door shut behind us with a dull thump that echoes in the enclosed space.

I blink, trying to adjust to the gloom. The cabin's main room is small, cluttered with dusty furniture. A battered couch slumps against one wall. A rickety kitchen area occupies the far corner, its counters piled with newspapers and empty cans. There's a flickering overhead light, its bulb so dim it barely chases away the shadows.

Earl sets me down near the corner of the room. My legs buckle, unsteady with fear and the rope pinning my ankles together. He grips my arm, lowering me with a gentleness that feels horribly out of place. But then his hand tightens, grinding bone against bone, a reminder that he's very much in control.

"This is where you'll stay," he says, a note of triumph in his voice. "Cozy, right?"

My breath shudders out. "Earl," I start, trying to keep the tremor from my voice, "you can't possibly mean—"

He pulls a coil of rope from a nearby table—like he's prepared this place in advance—and secures me to a thick wooden post, forcing me into a sitting position against the wall. The cord digs into my back and across my ribs. I gasp as he knots it, ignoring my weak attempts to wriggle free.

My mind races: How do I talk him down? How do I escape? "Earl," I say again, gentler this time, forcing myself to look up at him. His eyes glint with a strange mixture of anger and longing. "I— Listen, I know you're upset. But this isn't the way. People are going to notice I'm missing, they'll come looking—"

He barks a laugh. "They won't find you, Aubree." He paces a few steps, gesturing around the dingy cabin. "This place is mine. My grandfather left it, and no one's used it for years. It's miles from the nearest road. No one around. No neighbors, no passing cars."

I swallow, dread coiling in my stomach. "You can't keep me here forever," I manage, my voice thin. "Somebody will figure out where I am."

He turns sharply, his lips curling into a sneer. "Oh yeah? Like who? That pretty-boy bodyguard you had sniffing around your shop?" A wild gleam flares in his eyes, and I realize he's practically trembling with rage at the mention of Boone. "He's gone, isn't he? Left you behind, gave you space. He's not coming. And your mother? She won't know where to look." He lets out a mirthless chuckle, face twisting. "You're mine now."

Hot tears prick my eyes. I want to scream at him, lash out, but a wave of cold fear floods my chest. Reason—maybe that's my only weapon right now. "Earl," I say, trying to keep my voice calm. "This isn't you. Think about what you're doing. Kidnapping is a crime—"

"A crime?" he scoffs, crossing to the small kitchen. I watch helplessly as he pulls open a cooler, retrieving a can of beer. The metal crack echoes in the silent cabin, and a faint hiss escapes as he takes a swig. "You think I care about that? It's your fault, Aubree. You turned me down. You humiliated me. All I wanted was for you to see I could take care of you."

I stare, heart pounding. "So you threatened me?" I whisper, voice nearly breaking. "That was your idea of love? Throwing bricks, writing those awful notes—hurting my business?"

He slams the beer can on the counter, frothy liquid sloshing over the rim. "You forced my hand," he snaps, eyes wild. "If you'd just given me a chance—if you hadn't run off with your boyfriend—I wouldn't have had to prove how vulnerable you were. I wanted to make you see you needed me."

My throat works, tears now sliding down my cheeks. "And now?" I ask. "What—what do you think is going to happen here?"

He rakes a hand through his thinning hair, pacing again. The floorboards groan under his heavy steps. "We'll stay here, just us. No one to interfere. You'll learn to appreciate me." He gestures at the dingy walls, the filthy furniture. "Maybe I'll fix this place up. We can live out our days here."

A cold spike of terror stabs through my chest. He's serious. He thinks he can keep me hostage indefinitely, like some twisted fantasy. My eyes dart around, noting the windows—boarded, letting in slivers of dusky light. The door is behind him, blocked. My legs are bound, my wrists pinned together, plus an extra rope tethering me to the post.

"I'm sorry," I whisper, tears dripping off my chin. "If I hurt you—if I led you on. But this isn't the answer, Earl. You're going to ruin both our lives."

He swivels his head, eyes dark. "Don't say that. We can make it work. I love you, Aubree. Always have."

A shaky sob escapes me. Love? This is *not* love. This is obsession, delusion. But I bite my lip. Confronting him too harshly might push him to violence. I need to tread carefully. "What about my mother?" I say softly. "She'll be worried. She'll call the police. People will look for me. This can't last."

"She'll move on," he growls, coming closer, looming over me. I recoil as his shadow falls across my face. "Everyone moves on. You'll see. They'll forget eventually. We'll have each other, that's all we need."

I shiver, the reality of my predicament sinking in. I tug discreetly at my bonds—nothing. He's tied them expertly. My wrists burn from the friction. "Earl," I plead, swallowing the lump in my throat. "You can't do this. Please—"

He cuts me off by grabbing a remote from a dusty side table. There's an ancient TV on a stand in the corner, and he flicks it on. Static flares, then an old sitcom flickers into view. The laughter from the screen feels jarringly out of place.

"I'm done talking," he mutters, flopping onto the sagging couch. He cracks another beer, ignoring the sticky puddle on the counter. The cabin fills with the tinny sound of canned laughter, as if mocking this entire nightmare.

Tears blur my vision as I watch him, shoulders tense, eyes glued to the flickering show. Like we're just two people hanging out in his living room, except I'm tied to a post in the corner, trembling, heart pounding so loud I can barely think.

Inside my head, I scream at the unfairness of it, at the raw terror slicing through my veins. But I bite it down, forcing myself not to panic. Panicking does me no good. I remember Boone's words about keeping calm, about always searching for a way out.

I shift my wrists, feeling for any slack in the rope. It's tight. Maybe over time, if I keep working at it, I can loosen it. My eyes flick to Earl. He's not paying direct attention to me right now, but it won't take much for him to notice me fiddling with the knots.

Still, I have to try. I swallow the fear and begin slowly flexing my fingers, testing the cord's tension. I need to trust that Boone—or someone—will realize I'm gone, that they'll come for me. But what if they don't?

Stop it, I tell myself fiercely. Someone will notice. Right? I have to survive until then.

I cast a glance at Earl again. He stares at the TV, occasionally sipping his beer, like he's unwinding after a long day. The sheer normalcy of his action in this horrific moment makes bile rise in my throat. But I hold it down, forcing myself to breathe quietly.

I cling to hope—hope that I can find a way out, or at least delay whatever twisted plan Earl has. My wrists burn from the ropes, and my body aches, but I grit my teeth and keep testing the knots, praying for a miracle.

Because right now, in this dim, musty cabin with an unstable man holding me captive, I have nothing else to hold onto but hope.

Chapter 33

Boone

I'm parked under the glaring fluorescent lights of a rundown gas station, the last confirmed surveillance spot for the white van that took Aubree. The night air is thick with tension, and my mind buzzes with a singular focus: get her back. Nothing else matters.

Around me, the men I've assembled—Garrett and Thor, plus two others we've worked with in the past—stand in a loose circle, eyes trained on a large county map draped over the hood of my truck. We're lit by the overhead fluorescent lights of the gas station, casting dancing shadows across the asphalt. Our tactical gear is strapped tight: black cargo pants, chest rigs, sidearms, and rifles. Each of us is bristling with the pent-up energy that comes before a rescue operation.

"Dean, you're on speaker," I say, raising my phone so the men can hear.

"Good. I can see your location on the map," Dean says. "The gas station's cameras lost sight of the van just down that county road. I'm cross-referencing property deeds within a twenty-mile radius. We know Earl's from around here, so I'm trying to find any property his family might've owned."

Thor, a mountain of a man with a braided blond beard, taps the map with one thick finger. "We've got forest and farmland in every direction. If he turned off the road, there could be a hundred places to hide someone."

Garrett, lean and wiry, nods. "He's not going to risk a busy area. He'd want somewhere isolated."

My jaw tightens as I stare at the lines on the map. My stomach churns with guilt and rage—Aubree could be anywhere in these backwoods. I call up every memory I have of the last time we had intel on Earl. We never pegged him as a threat, but now I realize how little we knew. "Dean," I say, forcing calm into my voice, "any luck with those deeds?"

"Yeah—hang on." There's a flurry of keyboard clicks in the background. "I found something: an old cabin owned by an Earl Branson Sr. near Pine Hollow Road. Property records are outdated, but it's only about six or seven miles west of your current location, up in the hills. It hasn't been sold, so it might still belong to the family."

Thor glances at the map, zeroing in on that area. "That's rough terrain. Only a couple logging roads going up that way."

"Perfect for someone who wants to hide," Garrett murmurs.

Dean's voice cuts in again. "I'm sending coordinates to Boone now. The place is about two miles off a main road, then you gotta take a dirt track. I'm scouring for any other possible leads, but this is our best bet."

I check my phone, a dull beep letting me know the coordinates have arrived. My hands tremble with urgency. "We'll head there right now. Dean, stay on standby. Keep scanning for any new intel—if the place has multiple buildings, if you see movement from overhead satellites, anything."

"Understood," Dean says. "Boone… bring her back safe."

"I will." My voice is tight, loaded with a promise I intend to keep. I end the call and look at my team. Adrenaline thrums in my veins, but I force my shoulders to relax. "We have a single target, Earl, plus Aubree as a hostage. We don't know if he's armed, but we have to assume he is. She's top priority."

Garrett nods, flipping his rifle's safety off, then on again, a nervous habit. "We'll approach quiet, set up perimeter coverage, and do a quick breach."

The two other men, Daniels and Vega—both ex-military with solid track records—shift in closer, scanning the map. Daniels points to Rain Ridge Road. "That logging trail is pretty narrow. We might have to park and move on foot once it gets rough."

"Better that way," Thor says, voice low. "We don't want him hearing engine noise from a mile off."

I fold the map and tuck it under my arm. "All right," I say, meeting each of their eyes in turn. "Let's move."

We depart the gas station in a small convoy—my truck in the lead, Garrett and Thor in an SUV behind. The drive takes us along a desolate county road, the moon slung low over thick pine forests. A sign for Rain Ridge Road appears, battered and half-hidden by tall weeds. I flick on my brights and turn onto the narrower pavement, which soon degrades into gravel.

Ahead, the path snakes uphill through dense trees, branches scraping the side of my truck. Finally, I spot a wide turnoff where we can stash our vehicles behind some brush. I park, cut the engine, and the men pull up behind me. The darkness here is thick, the air cool, and the only sounds are distant crickets and the soft rustle of pines.

We gather near the SUV's open hatch, pulling out extra gear: night-vision goggles, suppressed pistols, short-barreled rifles for close quarters. Each man checks his weapon, loads mags, and tests his comm gear. My heart pounds, each beat echoing with the thought of Aubree—somewhere up that trail, alone with a psychopath.

Thor hands me a suppressed rifle. "We keep it quiet as long as possible," he says. "No sense giving him time to hurt her if he hears us coming."

"Agreed." I sling the rifle over my shoulder and step in front of the group, the glow of a small tactical flashlight giving just enough light to see each face. "Here's the plan: we move up this logging road on foot. Garrett, you take point. Keep an eye out for any sign of the cabin. Once we see it, we fan out. Thor, you and Daniels circle around the left side, find a vantage. Vega and I will move right, see if there's a back entrance or side window. We go in together on my call. Everyone clear?"

Four nods answer me. Good. These men are professionals, men I trust. They won't panic. They know how to handle a hostage situation.

I swallow hard, forcing down the knot in my throat. I have to stay calm for Aubree's sake. "Let's go."

The hike up the trail is slow and silent. We keep our footsteps careful, avoiding dry twigs that might snap underfoot. Garrett uses a small thermal scope to check for any heat signatures ahead, but the dense foliage limits visibility. The darkness is nearly absolute, except for thin moonlight filtering through the treetops.

After maybe fifteen minutes, Garrett raises a fist, signaling us to stop. We drop to one knee, hearts pounding. He points through a gap in the pines, and I see a faint glow—like a dim porch light or maybe the flicker of a single bulb inside a building.

"That's gotta be it," I whisper, inching forward to peer between branches. Sure enough, a small cabin emerges from the gloom, an old structure with a sagging roof. One window glows weakly, and there's a battered van parked nearby—my gut twists, recognizing the white van.

Biting back a wave of anger, I motion for the men to split up. Thor and Daniels slip off to the left, rifles at the ready, vanishing into the trees. Vega and I circle right, creeping through tall grass and around the side of the cabin. My heart pounds loud enough that I worry it'll give us away.

We converge near the cabin's rear corner. A single broken window sits at shoulder height, boards nailed across half of it. Dim light seeps out, enough for me to see a dirty interior. I catch a glimpse of movement—someone walking across the room. Could be Earl. I can't see Aubree yet.

I tap my earpiece. "Thor, you in position?"

His voice crackles quietly. "Yeah, we've got eyes on the front door. Looks like it's barred from the inside. No direct line of sight to the occupant, though. Wait for your signal."

I wave Vega forward, and we inch closer to the window. Carefully, I angle my head to peek through a gap in the boards. My breath catches: in the murky lamp light, I see Aubree. She's tied to a post in the far corner, looking pale and terrified. Her wrists are bound, and a coil of rope snakes around her waist, securing her to the wooden beam. She's shaking, tears drying on her cheeks.

Then I see Earl. He's half-sitting on a sagging couch, a beer can in one hand, some kind of small handgun resting on the cushion beside him. My jaw clenches so hard it hurts. He looks half-drunk, flipping channels on a battered old TV. Every so often, he glances at Aubree, muttering under his breath. She doesn't speak—just trembles, eyes darting toward the windows. Probably praying for a miracle.

Time for that miracle to arrive.

I tap my earpiece again, voice calm. "We have visual on Aubree, hostage in the south corner. Earl is inside, armed with a pistol. Looks intoxicated. We'll breach on my mark."

Thor responds instantly, "Roger. We'll come in from the front, draw his attention. You get Aubree out."

I lock eyes with Vega, who nods, gripping his rifle. "Cover me," I whisper. We shift along the wall, finding the rear door—a flimsy wooden thing with a rusted handle. I test it gently. Locked. I expected that. But from the look of the frame, it won't hold up to a well-placed kick.

"All teams, stand by," I say softly. My heart jackhammers against my ribs. I picture Aubree's face when I finally free her, the relief in her eyes. One chance to get this right. One chance to make sure no one gets hurt.

I raise my foot, bracing for the breach. "Three… two… one… breach."

Thor and Daniels must do the same up front, because I hear a tremendous crash from the other side of the cabin. At the exact moment, I slam my boot into the door. The old wood splinters with a deafening crack, the lock giving way instantly. Vega and I rush in, rifles up, adrenaline flooding my system.

Inside, the cabin is all chaos and flickering light. Earl leaps off the couch, eyes wide, beer can clattering to the floor. He scrambles for his handgun. My finger tightens on the trigger, but I hold my fire—Aubree's too close behind him, and I can't risk a stray bullet.

"Freeze!" I bellow, voice echoing in the cramped space. "Drop the weapon!"

From the front, Thor and Daniels burst in, rifles aimed. Earl spins, wild-eyed, the pistol in his hand. For a split second, I think he might open fire. Then Thor rams the butt of his rifle into Earl's wrist, knocking the gun free with a metallic clatter. Earl staggers back, howling.

"Down on the ground!" Daniels shouts, training his sights on Earl's chest.

Earl tries to lunge for his weapon again, but Thor decks him with a single massive punch. He collapses like a rag doll, hitting the floor with a thud that rattles the furniture. Vega rushes in to secure him, pinning Earl's arms behind his back, wrestling him into restraints.

Meanwhile, I sprint across the room to Aubree. She's shaking, eyes wide with disbelief. "Boone?" she whispers, voice raw and quivering.

I drop to my knees beside her, fumbling with the ropes. My hands won't stop shaking. "I'm here. It's okay." My heart twists at the sight of raw chafing around her wrists and ankles, the tear tracks on her cheeks. She gasps, tears welling again.

One of the knots is tight, so I grab a knife from my belt and carefully slice through the rope. "It's all right," I murmur, more to myself than her. "You're safe now."

Her hands come free, and I gather her into my arms, crushing her against my chest. She sobs once, then grips me like a lifeline, burying her face in my shoulder. Relief washes over me in a dizzying wave, and for a heartbeat, I close my eyes, letting her warmth steady me. She's alive. She's here.

In the background, I hear Thor's voice. "Suspect is secure. Good job, guys."

Garrett hustles in from the front, rifle at the ready. He does a quick sweep of the room. "Clear," he announces, stepping over debris.

I pull back slightly, cupping Aubree's face to check for injuries. Her lip is cut, probably from a fall, and her wrists are raw, but otherwise, she seems unharmed. "Does anything else hurt?" I ask, voice trembling with concern.

She shakes her head, tears spilling anew. "Just—my arms, my legs… I'm okay. You came."

"Of course I came," I whisper, pressing a trembling kiss to her forehead. "I'll always come for you."

She lets out a shaky exhale, trying to form words. "He—He said nobody would find me. I was so scared."

I tuck her hair behind her ear, leaning my forehead against hers. "He's done," I promise, feeling the raw edge in my own voice. "He'll never hurt you again."

Behind us, Earl groans, pinned face down on the floor while Vega cuffs his wrists. Thor looms over him, muttering something about how lucky he is we didn't shoot. The battered old TV flickers with some infomercial, bizarrely oblivious to the drama unfolding.

Finally, I help Aubree to her feet, keeping an arm around her waist. She's unsteady, leaning heavily against me. I glance at Thor, who nods. "Let's get her out of here."

We guide her outside, into the crisp night air. The men drag Earl—cuffed and bleeding from a split lip—along behind us. Daniels carries his confiscated pistol in a plastic evidence bag. My chest still pounds, but every breath feels like a gift now that I'm holding Aubree. She trembles, and I adjust my grip to support her better.

We move away from the cabin, stepping through the pine needles until we reach our vehicles. Garrett takes point, scanning the trees for any signs of an accomplice, but it looks like Earl was alone. Good. No more surprises.

At my truck, I open the passenger door and help Aubree inside. She winces, holding her wrists gingerly. "We'll get you to a hospital," I murmur. "Check for sprains. Then you can rest."

She blinks, tears still clinging to her lashes. "Thank you," she whispers, voice trembling. "You saved my life."

My throat tightens. "I'm sorry I didn't get here sooner," I say, brushing my knuckles against her cheek. "I should've been there to stop him in the first place."

She chokes back a sob, lacing her fingers through mine. "Don't," she manages. "You're here now. That's all that matters."

I press my forehead to hers, inhaling the scent of her hair, letting relief course through my veins. Around us, my team loads Earl into another vehicle, presumably to hand him off to the cops. Thor and Garrett coordinate on the phone with Dean, letting him know the situation is resolved. But all I can focus on is Aubree—her breath against my neck, her grip tight as if she's afraid I'll vanish.

"I promise," I murmur, tears burning my own eyes, "I'm not letting go of you again."

Guarding What's Mine

She just nods, leaning into me, and for a moment, we remain locked in that quiet pocket of relief. The hush of the forest wraps around us, broken only by distant chatter from the men. In the end, all that matters is that she's here, safe in my arms.

Tomorrow, we'll deal with the aftermath—police statements, hospital checks, a thousand questions. But tonight, I'll hold her close, knowing we made it out alive. And as I help her buckle in, pressing a gentle kiss to her temple, I vow never to leave her side again.

Chapter 34

Aubree

I'm sitting on a stiff hospital bed, an ice pack resting gingerly on my sprained wrist, and I can't stop staring at Boone. He's perched on the narrow chair in the corner, arms folded across his broad chest, gaze fixed protectively on me. Every so often, a nurse passes by the open door, and Boone's head swivels, as if expecting a threat to jump out of the hallway. It makes me smile, even though the day's terror still clings to my nerves.

"Does it hurt too much?" he asks, nodding at the bandage wrapped around my wrist.

I shrug, biting back a wince at the movement. "A little. The doctor said it's not broken, just a bad sprain from when Earl knocked me down." My throat catches at the memory—how helpless I felt, how certain I was that no one would find me.

Boone leans forward, resting his forearms on his knees. "He's in custody now. And from what Dean said, the cops have more than enough evidence to put him away for a long time. Turns out Earl hid his tracks very well, but they were able to uncover some very damning evidence."

I nod, relief a warm glow in my chest. "I heard. They found all those files, drafts of the creepy letters he sent me. Even pictures from my shop. It's so… it's so surreal that he was behind everything. Not just the threats, but the break-in too. I thought I was finally safe, and then…"

My words trail off. Boone stands and crosses to my bed, placing a reassuring hand on my uninjured arm. "I know," he says softly, his brown eyes filled with empathy. "I'm just sorry I wasn't here sooner."

I blink back a sting of tears. "Don't say that. You saved me."

"But I should've been here," he insists, voice low and earnest. He squeezes my shoulder. "I was planning on surprising you. In fact, that's exactly why I came to the shop tonight."

I tilt my head, curiosity piqued. "Surprising me?" My heart flutters at the thought—when I was trapped in that cabin, I could only dream that he'd come for me. And now it turns out he was on his way anyway?

He nods, a small smile tugging at his lips. "Dean offered me a new position—he's expanding Maddox Security into the Midwest. Nashville specifically. And… he asked me to head up the new branch."

My jaw drops, a rush of happiness flooding me. "You're moving to Nashville?" I whisper, hardly believing it.

"Yeah," he says, slipping his hand into mine, careful not to jostle my injured wrist. "My cabin is the perfect place to live while running the new location. I was hoping to tell you in person." He exhales, laughter mingling with relief. "Didn't think I'd be rescuing you on the same night, but I guess life had other plans."

Tears prick my eyes—this time, tears of joy, relief, and a dozen other emotions I can't name. "Boone," I manage, "that's... that's amazing. You don't have to leave me again?"

He shakes his head, and I see the old worry etched on his features easing. "Nope," he murmurs, giving my fingers a gentle squeeze. "You're stuck with me."

Before I can respond, the door to my little hospital room bursts open, and my mother rushes in, eyes brimming with concern. "Aubree!" she cries, flinging her arms around me in a careful hug. "Oh my God, are you all right? The nurses wouldn't let me back here for ages."

I let out a choked laugh, burying my face in her shoulder. "I'm fine, Mom. I promise."

She steps back, scanning my wrist and the bruises forming on my arms. Her eyes fill with worried tears. "Honey, I was so terrified. Boone called me, told me everything. I came as fast as I could."

Boone clears his throat softly, a polite gesture to remind us he's here. My mother spins toward him, reaching out to pat his arm in gratitude. "Thank you for saving my daughter. Again."

He ducks his head, looking slightly bashful. "Just doing my job, ma'am."

She glances between us, her expression shifting from relief to something more pleased. "Well, I'm glad you'll be living here full time so you can watch over my Aubree-dear."

I can't help but grin at how she zeroes in on that detail. Boone laughs under his breath. "Yes, ma'am. Dean asked me to run a new branch of Maddox Security. I'm moving up here permanently."

My mother's face lights up, and she casts me a knowing glance. "I'm as happy as I was the first time you told me." She laughs. Then, as if unable to contain herself, she throws her arms around Boone, hugging him tight. He stiffens for half a second before relaxing, patting her back awkwardly. I can't help but giggle; I'm used to my mom's big displays of affection, but Boone clearly isn't.

When she pulls away, she gives him a teary smile. "You have no idea how grateful I am," she says, dabbing at her eyes. "Between Charles' mess and then this psychopath Earl… I just want Aubree to be safe."

Boone's jaw tightens, his protective streak flaring. "She will be," he says firmly. "And the police are all over this now. Dean told me they traced every single threatening email to Earl's computer. He'd used a VPN to mask his IP address and that's why it took a while. He'd been acting alone, feeding off the chaos Charles created."

My mother sighs, relief and exhaustion weighing her shoulders. "I can't believe all this… it's finally over." Her gaze drifts to me, and she gives a watery smile. "You should rest, sweetie. Let the doctors make sure your wrist is going to heal right."

I nod, sinking back against the pillows. "I will, Mom. Thank you." Then I hesitate. "Are you… did you want to stay?"

She glances at Boone, then back at me, understanding lighting her eyes. "I think I'll just step outside and talk to the nurse about the discharge papers," she says. "Let you two have a moment."

I bite my lip, a fresh wave of gratitude washing over me for my mother's thoughtfulness. "Thanks, Mom. I love you."

She smiles, patting my leg gently. "I love you too, honey." With that, she slips out of the room, closing the door behind her.

Now it's just me and Boone again, the quiet hum of hospital machinery filling the space. He pulls the chair closer to my bedside, resting one hand on the rail. "So," he says, letting out a shaky breath, "here we are."

"Here we are," I echo, my heart twisting. Despite the bandages and bruises, I feel lighter than I have in weeks. "I can't believe you're really moving here."

He grins, warmth flooding his features. "I was hoping to take you out on a proper date, you know. Maybe show up at your shop unannounced with flowers, something romantic." He gestures vaguely. "But fate had other ideas."

I let out a short laugh, reaching over to thread my fingers through his. My wrist twinges, but I ignore it. "You saved my life. That's pretty romantic in its own way."

He brushes his thumb over my knuckles, his gaze gentle. "I promise I'm done with the big rescues, though. I'd like to just... live normally. With you, if you'll have me."

Emotion wells in my chest. "Boone, that's all I've wanted since this whole thing started. I mean, ever since you showed up, telling me to close my shop and stay with you in that cabin, I've felt safe around you. I trust you with my life."

His expression softens. "I won't let you down. I'm here for good. Dean's expansion deal is real—he'll have me hiring a new team, which is half of the guys who helped rescue you tonight. We'll set up an office downtown. I'll still get to protect people, but... I'll also get to have a real life with you." He glances away, suddenly shy. "If that's what you want."

My throat grows tight as I watch him fumble. This big, strong ex-military man who's saved me from multiple threats now,

Guarding What's Mine

looking so earnest and a bit unsure. "Of course that's what I want," I manage, my voice thick. "I— I want you, Boone."

He exhales, relief washing over his face, and I lean forward, pressing a gentle kiss to his lips. It's short, but sweet, and I taste the salt of my own tears. He cups the side of my face, stroking his thumb along my cheek in a gesture that feels like home.

When we pull apart, a knock sounds at the door. A nurse peeks in, offering a polite smile. "Hi there, just need to check that wrist for a moment, make sure everything's all good, then we'll get you out of here."

Boone stands, giving me room as the nurse comes over. She gently unwraps the bandage, prodding the area with delicate hands. I wince, but she assures me it's just a sprain, nothing broken. "We'll give you a brace to wear for a week or so," she says. "Ice it, take anti-inflammatories, and rest as much as you can."

I nod, thanking her through a wince. Boone watches intently, like he's memorizing every instruction. Once she's done, she leaves the room, promising to grab my discharge papers.

Boone clears his throat, the hint of a smile on his face. "You're going to be okay."

I let out a shuddering breath. "Yeah," I say softly, finally starting to believe it myself. "I am. Everything's going to be okay now."

A moment later, my mother reenters, a packet of paperwork in hand. "They said you can leave in a little bit. We just have to finalize these forms." She sets them on the small rolling table. "You'll be home tonight. We can order some takeout, maybe watch one of those cheesy reality shows you like."

I arch an amused eyebrow. "Mom, you hate those shows."

She laughs, leaning in to squeeze my shoulder. "I'll do anything to see you smile right now."

Boone, standing at my other side, dips his head. "I might join you if that's okay."

My mother's eyes sparkle knowingly. "Oh, I'd be insulted if you didn't."

Heat warms my cheeks. I mumble something like "Thank you," and inside I'm touched by her acceptance. After the nightmare of Charles and Earl, I think we all just want a quiet, safe place to land.

The door swings open again, and this time it's a man packed with just about as many muscles as Boone, phone in hand, his tie slightly askew like he's been running. He gives me a quick nod. "Aubree, I'm glad to see you're up. How're you feeling?"

"Tired, bruised, but good," I say with a small smile. "Thank you."

Boone clasps the man on the shoulder. "This is Dean. Without him we'd never have found you." Boone turns his attention on Dean. "You got here quick."

Dean chuckles lightly. "Flew private as soon as I knew she'd been kidnapped. I wanted to be here."

Boone shakes his hand and they do that bro hug men do. "Thanks, man. I appreciate it."

Dean winks at me with a smile. "Besides, I had to meet the woman who could bring Boone to his knees."

I laugh as Boone blushes deep red. "Thank you again, Dean."

Dean waves me off. "Hey, I just pointed Boone in the right direction. He did the hard part."

I glance at Boone, who offers a modest shrug. I know better—Dean's remote surveillance and coordination made all the difference. "So," I ask, curiosity prickling, "any more news?"

Dean slides his phone into his pocket. "Police have Earl in custody, and they're building a case with all the evidence we uncovered—his computer, the footage, the break-in logs. It's airtight. No way he's slipping through. And with Charles still locked up for his separate crimes, I'd say you're officially free of psychos."

An enormous weight lifts from my shoulders, and I feel like I can finally breathe. "That's… thank God," I murmur. "I can't wait to get back to Slice Slice Baby without fearing someone's going to snatch me off the street."

My mother's face brightens. "And with Boone moving here, you'll have some extra backup, right?"

My gaze flickers to Boone, who gives me a gentle, reassuring grin. "Absolutely," he says. "Although I'll try not to hover too much. I have an office to run, after all."

I smile, warmth flooding my chest. I can see our future in that grin—quiet mornings at my pizza shop, stolen kisses behind the counter, maybe even a routine jog along the Tennessee trails. Real life, not just a crisis.

Dean clears his throat, nodding at Boone. "Whenever you're ready, let me know. We'll lock down the Nashville location. I've already got half the paperwork done. Should be operational in a couple of weeks."

Boone nods. "I'll be in touch first thing tomorrow, once I know Aubree's settled."

"Good," Dean says, then pats my shoulder. "Take care, all right? You've been through the wringer."

I nod gratefully. "I will."

He waves and steps out, presumably to finalize more details. My mother flips through the paperwork, humming in relief that there's not much to sign. Then the nurse returns with my new wrist brace, and Boone carefully helps me slide it on, his touch gentle but sure.

I fight back tears again—this time, tears of overwhelming gratitude. So many people rallied to protect me, and Boone, my savior in more ways than one, is staying. Really staying.

Once the brace is in place, my mother finishes signing the discharge forms. "All done," she says, gathering them up. "We can go."

Boone offers me his arm, and we walk out of the hospital room. The hallway is bright and smells of antiseptic, but I don't mind. It's just another step away from the darkness Earl trapped me in. Another step toward freedom.

In the parking lot, under the glow of street lamps, Boone opens the passenger door of his truck. I climb in, feeling the dull ache in my limbs. He buckles me in, and I let out a sigh as he circles around to the driver's side. My mother slides into her car, promising to meet us back at my place.

As Boone starts the engine, he glances my way. "So," he says, a hint of a smile on his face, "how about tomorrow, after you rest, we head to your shop? I can help you open up. Maybe we can even make a special pizza to celebrate the end of all this."

My chest tightens with affection. "I'd love that," I say softly. I reach over, placing my good hand on his. "Thank you, Boone. For saving me, for everything... for choosing to stay."

He threads his fingers through mine, eyes warm. "I'd choose you a hundred times over, Aubree," he murmurs, squeezing gently. "No matter what."

Guarding What's Mine

I curl my fingers around his, letting the sweet promise of those words settle into my heart. The truck rumbles forward, and we drive off into the Nashville night, heading to a future that finally feels bright and free of fear. And in this moment, even with my wrist throbbing and my body sore, I feel more at peace than I have in a long, long time.

Because I'm not alone—and I never will be again.

Epilogue

Boone

The fluorescent lights hum overhead in the Nashville office of Maddox Security, illuminating the large mission board tacked to the wall. On it are photos, maps, red string linking a half-dozen leads about a kidnapped heiress. It's late, the rest of the city caught in the lull of evening traffic, but for me and my team, there's no such thing as off-hours. Not when someone's life hangs in the balance.

I stand at the head of a long conference table, scanning the faces of the men who've become my new Nashville crew. Garrett flips through a file, brow furrowed, while Thor—John Hansen, that towering hulk of a man—leans against the wall, arms crossed over his chest, nodding along to the plan. Two other guys, Daniels and Vega, exchange quick glances, each wearing the same no-nonsense expression they wore the day we rescued Aubree.

I clear my throat, and their attention snaps to me. "All right, so the target is eighteen-year-old Fiona Chambers. Family's got major political ties in Kentucky. She was taken sometime yesterday evening from her university campus. We have reason to believe the kidnappers want a ransom, but we also suspect they might not be in this for the money alone. Could be a power play against her father's upcoming election. Regardless, our job is to get her back safely."

Garrett taps his pen on the file. "You said campus security last spotted her near the library, then all cameras went dark?"

"Exactly," I confirm. "Which tells me these guys know how to work around standard security systems. We need to assume they're professionals. Dean got some intel that points to an abandoned warehouse on the outskirts of town. We'll check that first."

Thor pushes off the wall. "And we're coordinating all ground teams from here?"

"Yup," I say, flipping through the mission dossier. "We have two mobile units ready to converge. I'll quarterback from the office—watching the cams, feeding you all real-time updates. If there's any sign of movement or suspicious activity, I'll direct you. This is a hostage retrieval, so caution is key." I look each man in the eye. "I want zero casualties on our side and minimal risk to the girl. Understood?"

Four heads nod in unison. We run through a final gear check and timeline. Once I'm satisfied, I close the folder with a snap. "All right, get moving. Let's bring her home."

They break away, gathering their tactical bags and heading for the elevator. Garrett pats my shoulder as he passes. "We've got this, Boss."

"Be safe," I tell them. "I'll be on comms the whole time."

They disappear down the hall, and the heavy office door clicks shut behind them. For a brief moment, I inhale, letting the hum of the overhead lights fill the silence. I glance around the conference room—my conference room. Since moving to Nashville and setting up this branch of Maddox Security, I've poured everything into making it top-tier. We're still growing, but the team is strong, and Dean's regular updates confirm we're heading in the right direction.

A small grin tugs at my lips. I never expected to have roots anywhere—always figured I'd bounce from one high-stakes job to another, living on the edge. But everything changed the day I met Aubree. This office, this city… it's ours now. I grab my jacket from the back of a chair and head for the exit, flipping off the conference room lights. The mission will unfold in real time, but I can coordinate from home just as effectively as I can here—plus, I've got good reason to hurry back.

The drive from downtown Nashville to my cabin in the hills takes about twenty minutes, winding along back roads flanked by tall pines. The night is cool, the sky dotted with stars. My phone rests on the console, set to speaker so I can jump onto comms if Garrett or Thor calls. Thus far, it's been quiet. They're still en route to the warehouse, probably scouting vantage points.

Finally, I pull onto the familiar gravel path that leads up the slope toward the cabin. As I crest the last turn, the warm glow of porch lights greets me, and my chest tightens with contentment. This place has changed so much since Aubree moved in. It used to feel too big, too lonely. Now, it's home.

I park, kill the engine, and step out, relishing the cool night air. The faint aroma of pine and woodsmoke drifts across the yard. And then—my stomach rumbles—the distinct smell of tomato sauce and cheese. She's making pizza. My mouth waters instantly.

Inside, the cabin glows softly with low lighting. My boots thud against the wooden floor as I call out, "Aubree?"

"In the kitchen!" she answers, her voice carrying a playful lilt.

I round the corner, grinning at the sight that greets me: Aubree at the counter, wearing a simple tank top and jeans dusted with flour. She's got a dough circle spread out, sauce ladled on, and a bowl of shredded cheese at the ready.

"You cooked at the shop all day, and now you're making pizza at home?" I tease, leaning against the doorframe.

She laughs, brushing back a stray lock of hair. "We closed early, and I was feeling inspired. I want to make something special for us." She lifts an eyebrow, eyeing my tactical jacket. "Long day?"

I drop the jacket on a nearby chair, stepping forward to rest my hands at her waist. The familiar warmth of her body seeps into me. "Always. We've got a new mission—some heiress got snatched. But the team's on it." I dip my head, kissing her cheek softly. "I'll coordinate once they reach the location."

A flicker of worry passes through her gaze, but she hides it quickly, focusing on the pizza. "Well, at least you're not charging off into danger this time."

I chuckle, pressing closer. "Don't worry, I'll leave the fieldwork to my team tonight. I prefer being here with you."

She tilts her head, offering me a warm smile that lights up her face. "Good. Because I have mozzarella that's practically begging to be tasted, and I need a test subject."

"Oh, I volunteer," I say, and before she can protest, I lean in, capturing her lips in a lingering kiss. She tastes like fresh basil and the sweetness that's entirely her. For a moment, the outside world fades—the mission, the kidnappings, the stress. It's just us, the quiet hum of the oven, and the press of her body against mine.

She sighs happily when we break apart. "Boone," she whispers, sliding her arms around my neck. "I love you."

My chest tightens with emotion. I gather her closer, the edge of the countertop digging into my stomach, and kiss her again, deeper this time. My pulse quickens, warmth sparking through my veins. She responds eagerly, her fingers threading into my hair, and I let a soft groan slip free. Even months later, the taste of her still drives me wild.

We break apart only when the oven timer buzzes—an urgent beep that draws a laugh from her throat. She turns, shutting off the timer, and I rest my hands on her hips. "Saved by the bell," I tease, voice husky.

She winks over her shoulder. "If the pizza burns, you'll never let me hear the end of it."

I help sprinkle the last of the cheese and slide the pizza into the oven. Then I take her hand and pull her away from the heat, backing her up against the kitchen island. My heart thrums with desire, the memory of nearly losing her months ago making every moment that much more precious.

Her eyes glow, and she tugs me down for another kiss—this one more heated, our lips parting, breath mingling. My world narrows to the feel of her, the soft moan that escapes when I deepen the kiss, the way her fingers clutch the front of my shirt like she can't get close enough. I slide my hands under her shirt, palming the bare skin of her waist, and she arches against me.

A faint beep from my phone's comm app intrudes, and I swallow a frustrated groan. Duty calls, even in the midst of bliss. Aubree must hear it too, because she gives me a regretful smile, cheeks flushed.

"Go," she murmurs, smoothing her palm over my chest. "I know they need you."

I press my forehead to hers. "One minute. Then I'm all yours," I promise, stepping back reluctantly.

She gives me a playful smirk and leans against the counter. I grab my phone, checking the update. Garrett's text: "In position. Warehouse quiet. No sign of the girl yet." I exhale, swiftly typing a response: "Stay put. Wait for my signal."

Setting the phone aside, I turn back to Aubree. She arches a brow. "Everything okay?"

"Yeah," I say. "They're starting the recon. I'll keep an ear open, but for now…" I slip my arms around her again, voice trailing into a low murmur. "Let's focus on us."

She leans in, pressing her lips to the corner of my mouth. "That's exactly what I had in mind."

The cabin is quiet, save for the ticking of the oven, the soft rush of our breaths. We steal another few minutes of slow, heated kisses, hands roaming, hearts pounding. The intensity of it all leaves me breathless and grateful—grateful that she's safe, that we've built a life together, that we can live like this, free of the fear and danger that nearly tore us apart.

Eventually, the oven timer goes off again, and we disentangle with a shared laugh. She slides the pizza out, the rich aroma filling the kitchen. I snag a piece before it cools, ignoring her mock-scolding about burning my tongue.

As we sit at the tiny kitchen table, side by side, devouring the fresh pizza, I can't help but look around the cabin—the place that once felt so empty is now brimming with little touches of Aubree: a throw blanket draped on the couch, photos of us pinned on the wall, a row of pizza-related cookbooks on the shelf. My chest warms at the thought of how much has changed in just a few months.

After dinner, we settle on the couch, her head tucked under my chin. My phone buzzes intermittently with mission updates, but the situation seems under control. Garrett's last text said they spotted movement, but they're waiting for the kidnappers to make a move. In a few hours, they'll probably move in for the rescue. And I'll be guiding them from afar, confident they can handle the ground operation.

In this moment, though, I choose to soak up the peace— Aubree's soft breathing against my chest, the crackle of the fireplace, the security of a home that's truly ours. She shifts, curling her arms around my torso, and I stroke her hair, pressing a gentle kiss to her temple.

"Boone," she whispers, her lips curving into a satisfied smile. "Thank you for… everything."

I smile into her hair. "You never have to thank me."

She tilts her head up, touching her mouth to mine again. The kiss starts slow, building in warmth, her hands sliding over my chest. I lose myself in it, the rush of desire mingling with a profound tenderness. When she finally pulls back, breathless, her eyes shine with love and contentment.

And in that instant, I know: this is it—my happily ever after. We've survived threats, kidnappings, family betrayals. And we've come out stronger, bound by a bond forged in danger and sealed with devotion. From now on, we face the world together—a dynamic duo, always ready to lean on each other no matter what chaos unfolds outside these cabin walls.

I cradle her face, letting my thumb brush her cheek. "I love you," I say simply, feeling the weight of the words sink in.

Her smile is radiant. "I love you too."

Guarding What's Mine

Outside, the night settles deeper, and in the hush of our sanctuary, we share another tender kiss. The future beckons—filled with missions, pizzas, laughter, maybe even more than that somewhere down the line. But for now, we're just here, in this perfect, ordinary-extraordinary moment. And we wouldn't trade it for the world.

Bonus Epilogue

Aubree

It's nearly ten o'clock at night, and I'm still at Slice Slice Baby. I don't usually linger this long, but we had a huge catering order for a graduation party this afternoon, and the kitchen is a disaster—flour footprints from the prep station to the walk-in, half-empty cans of tomatoes stacked by the sink, sauce splattered on the steel counters. My staff all went home hours ago. I insisted, actually; they worked hard, and I felt like I had enough energy to tidy up alone. Of course, that was before I realized how late it would be when I finished.

The overhead lights are on half-power, casting a warm glow across the empty dining area. I take a moment to enjoy the hush. During the day, this place bustles with customers—teens after school, families grabbing a quick bite, even the occasional traveling musician. It's my pride and joy, my life's work. But right now, it's a quiet sanctuary where I can count the squeaks of my sneakers on tile.

I mop the last sticky patch near the counter, leaning on the handle and blowing a stray curl from my forehead. "Done," I

Bonus Epilogue

announce to the empty shop. My voice echoes off the walls. I smile wryly—Boone would tease me for talking to myself again.

Boone. Just thinking his name warms my chest. It's been a while since he joined me in Nashville with Maddox Security's new branch, but sometimes I still can't believe we share a life here—no more living in fear, no more kidnappings or dangerous secrets. We're truly free to be together, and it feels surreal.

I shake my head, swallowing a grin as I roll the mop bucket toward the kitchen. The big overhead clock reads 10:08. He usually checks in if I'm staying late to make sure I'm safe or he begs me to lock up early. But he hasn't called tonight, which is odd. Maybe he's tied up with a mission briefing or coordinating something for Dean. He's got a million responsibilities as the head of the new Nashville office. Still, the silence makes me a little uneasy.

As if on cue, a sudden noise rattles from the back hallway—like a metal pan crashing to the floor. My heart leaps. I freeze, gripping the mop handle tight enough to whiten my knuckles. It's probably just something shifting on a shelf... But the memory of being ambushed, months ago, still lingers in my bones.

I set the mop down, forcing calm. "It's nothing," I murmur, though my pulse hammers. Another faint sound—like shuffling footsteps—sends a chill through me. Immediately, I pull out my phone.

Scrolling to Boone's number, I think, *Better safe than sorry.*

"Aubree? Pull yourself together," I whisper to myself. Even though I'm armed with new self-defense moves Boone taught me, my heart still spikes with adrenaline whenever I'm startled like this. *Just check it out, or call him.*

Bonus Epilogue

My thumb hovers over the Call button. But before I can press it, the swinging kitchen door pushes open. I jump, nearly dropping the phone.

"Surprise!" a chorus of voices booms from the shadows—voices I recognize. My heart practically catapults out of my chest as the overhead lights flick on to full brightness.

Standing there, half-hidden by the door, is Boone—grinning from ear to ear, a cupcake with a lit candle in his hand. And behind him is a crowd of familiar faces: Ranger with his arm around Tory, Orion with Briar on his left, Dean and Sophia, Asher and Lincoln, Dean's sister Isabella, and a handful of other dear friends. My mother is among them, holding a box of decorations, her eyes shining.

"Happy birthday, Aubree!" Boone exclaims, stepping forward, candle flickering dangerously close to his short hair. He quickly sets it down on the nearest table.

I stare, mouth agape. My pulse is still thrashing from the scare, and now it's thrashing for a completely different reason—shock, delight, absolute disbelief. "You guys… oh my gosh," I manage, pressing a hand to my chest. "You scared me half to death!"

My mother crosses the tile in a few quick strides, wrapping me in a warm hug. "We're sorry, darling," she says, laughing. "But we had to catch you off-guard. It was Boone's idea."

Boone slides the cupcake away so he doesn't accidentally burn something, then shrugs, all sheepish. "Guilty." But his eyes dance with mischief. "I had to make sure you couldn't suspect a thing. Hence the silence all day."

I let out a breathless laugh. "I was about to call you—thought someone broke in! You're lucky I didn't throw a rolling pin at your head."

Bonus Epilogue

He grabs the cupcake, holding it out to me. "Make a wish." He smirks. "And no wishing to hit me with the rolling pin."

I laugh, and then close my eyes. I've got everything I could ever wish for, so I blow out the candle, wishing for more precious moments like this. "Thank you."

Dean steps forward, Sophia by his side, both looking very pleased with themselves. "We cleared the idea with your mom," Dean explains, slipping an arm around Sophia's waist. "Figured you'd be alone this evening."

Sophia, radiant as ever, nods in agreement. "Besides, we can't let your birthday slide by without a fuss. After everything you've been through, you deserve a real celebration."

A wave of gratitude and affection floods me. These people—my family, my friends, the security crew—are all here for me. I blink back tears, though I can't wipe the huge grin from my face. *A surprise birthday party,* I think, shaking my head in wonder. "You guys are incredible."

Ranger, his dark hair tousled, smirks. "Yeah, yeah. Enough with the sentiment. Let's get some pizza going." He pats Tory's shoulder, who flashes me a bright smile. "Tory's been dying to learn your technique."

I laugh, feeling the tension drain from my body. "Sure, absolutely. Let's… do you all want to make your own?" My voice brims with excitement. *Pizza-making party,* it's a concept so close to my heart. I always loved the communal energy of kneading dough and sprinkling toppings with friends.

"Yes, please," Orion chimes in, flicking a playful glance at his girlfriend, Briar. She's tall, with a long brown hair that flows halfway down her back. "Briar claims she can out-pizza me. We'll see."

Bonus Epilogue

Briar snorts, elbowing him. "Even Jeb can out pizza you, buddy." Yes. her African-gray parrot, Jeb. He's a real character.

Smiling ear to ear, I gesture them all toward the back, where the big dough mixer and giant prep tables stand. "Let's do it! I'll show you how to knead the dough, shape it, top it. That is, if you're all prepared to get flour everywhere."

"We've been warned," Garrett says. He looks slightly more relaxed than usual—back when he first joined Maddox Security Nashville Team, he was always so serious. Now he's letting Thor talk his ear off about some new training regimen.

Dean laughs, pressing a quick kiss to Sophia's temple. "We brought wine, by the way. Not sure if it pairs with pizza, but we'll make do."

Boone's eyes meet mine as everyone filters into the kitchen, the tension in my chest replaced by a warm, giddy feeling. I mouth *thank you* to him. He winks, trailing his fingers down my arm lightly—a simple touch that sends a thrill through me.

⸺

Soon, the back kitchen buzzes with chatter and laughter. We set out bowls of shredded cheese, sauces—marinara, Alfredo, even a pesto option—plus an array of toppings: pepperoni, sausage, mushrooms, onions, bell peppers, olives, pineapple for the brave. My mother helps me measure out lumps of dough so everyone can start shaping their own pies.

"Okay," I say, voice raised to be heard over everything. "First step: flatten the dough into a disc. You can use your hands or a rolling pin. Don't be shy with the flour."

Bonus Epilogue

Tory, wearing an oversized apron, watches me with wide eyes. "Wait, I do *this*?" She tries to press the dough with her palms and nearly sticks it to the table. "Oh no, it's all sticky!"

Ranger laughs. "You're just not used to getting your hands dirty, Princess." She swats him with a flour-dusted hand, leaving a white print on his black T-shirt. He yelps, and we all laugh.

Next to them, Orion and Briar engage in a playful dough-throwing war. Briar flicks a pinch of flour at Orion, and he retaliates by tapping her nose with a sauce-dipped finger. "Hey, no fair!" she protests, though her laughter undercuts any real complaint.

Dean and Sophia, more subdued in their mischief, share a single piece of dough, shaping it together. Every so often, I see them pause to whisper or exchange a soft kiss. They look so content—married life suits them perfectly.

Garrett and Thor stand at the far side of the table, quietly following my steps, though Thor occasionally cracks a joke that makes Garrett roll his eyes. They're an interesting duo—both laser-focused when they want to be, but also comfortable enough to banter.

Isabella, Dean's sister, edges closer to me with a conspiratorial grin. "I've always wanted to know your secret sauce recipe. Dean raves about it." She tucks a strand of hair behind her ear. Isabella's come a long way since we first met—she used to be so guarded, but now she's blossomed in her own right.

I wave a sauce-stained wooden spoon. "Oh, that's top secret. But maybe, if you're nice, I'll let you watch me make it next time."

She laughs. "Deal. Just let me handle a ladle or something."

Bonus Epilogue

Boone stands near the dough mixer, arms folded, grinning like a proud conspirator. It's obvious he's enjoying this scene—everyone he cares about, all in one place, celebrating my birthday in the simplest, most meaningful way: making pizza.

At one point, my mother sidles up to me, eyes sparkling. She sets down a wine bottle on the metal counter. "I think it's time we pop one of these open, don't you?"

I glance at the label—some fancy red blend. "Ooh, yes. Let's see if it pairs with mozzarella."

She chuckles, rummaging in a drawer for a corkscrew. "I had no idea that boy was planning such a big surprise," she muses. "But he's obviously gone to great lengths to gather everyone."

A wave of affection sweeps through me. "He's wonderful," I say softly, watching Boone lean over to help Tory flip her dough without wrecking it. "I never thought I'd find someone so… committed and sweet and protective, all at once."

My mother smiles, patting my arm. "You deserve it, darling. And he deserves you."

I help her open the wine, and soon enough, glasses are distributed. People sip, some swirl, others just dive in. The kitchen warms with laughter. The entire vibe is joyous, safe, and fun—completely different from the tension we all knew when Charles and Earl were looming threats.

It doesn't take long for the pizzas to start emerging from the ovens, each one unique: some with extra pepperoni, some loaded with veggies, one with pineapple that Garrett rolls his eyes at. We set them on cooling racks, the air filling with the mouthwatering aroma of fresh dough, garlic, basil, melted cheese.

Bonus Epilogue

Ranger proclaims, "We've officially discovered the best way to celebrate a birthday. Screw cake, pizza is where it's at."

Tory bumps his hip. "We can have dessert pizza, too, you know?"

I grin. "Don't tempt me. I've got a Nutella and strawberry recipe that'll blow your mind."

Boone, a glass of wine in hand, sidles up behind me, slipping an arm around my waist. "You realize the second you mention dessert pizza, these animals will never leave," he teases, jerking his chin toward the group, who have already devoured half the first pizza.

"Well, that's the point," I reply, leaning into him. "If I never let them leave, this party never ends."

He chuckles, pressing a soft kiss to my temple. The simple gesture makes my pulse flutter. "Happy birthday, Brie-cheese," he murmurs, brushing his lips against my ear.

I groan, burying my face in Boone's chest. He laughs, gently prying me away to address the group. "Aubree's old nickname from high school was Brie-cheese. As in the cheese."

Immediately, my mother giggles. "Yes, well, my daughter was obsessed with cheese on everything when she was younger, so a few friends started calling her that."

Orion nearly chokes on his wine. "Oh, this is golden." He raps a fist on the table. "Brie-cheese, indeed. She's the pizza queen, it all comes full circle."

Briar, eyes shining with amusement, points a tomato slice at me. "So, do we all get to call you Brie-cheese now?"

I shoot a mock glare at Boone. "No. Absolutely not."

But Dean just laughs. "Too late, Brie-cheese."

Bonus Epilogue

I throw my hands up in mock despair as everyone breaks into giggles or smirks. Boone slips an arm around me again, nuzzling my temple. "Sorry," he mouths, though he looks anything but apologetic.

"Traitor," I mouth back, but my grin betrays me. I can't stay mad at that face.

Once we've all had our fill of pizza—at least four or five pies demolished—someone finds a stereo in the front, and soon soft music floats through the shop. We gather around the dining area, which Dean and Sophia have festooned with colorful streamers. My mother has a small cake, too, because apparently you can't have a birthday without at least a slice of something sweet. She sets a single candle on it—like a nod to tradition. Everyone gathers, softly singing "Happy Birthday" as I blow out the candle, cheeks burning at all the attention.

Ranger's girlfriend, Tory, compliments me on the "best birthday idea ever," and I remind her, "It wasn't my idea, but I'll take credit anyway."

We pop open another bottle of wine, and the conversation flows. We talk about everything: how Orion and Briar are thinking of adopting a rescue dog, how Garrett is toying with the idea of going undercover in a big upcoming job, how Thor has decided to coach a kids' soccer team in his off hours, how Isabella is busily helping grow the Maddox Security teams. Dean and Sophia recount a hilarious story about the time they had to fake-marriage themselves into a mission, which sends everyone into peals of laughter. It's amazing how many inside jokes and stories we've all accumulated in such a short time.

Bonus Epilogue

Eventually, the shop quiets a little. Some of the group starts drifting toward the front, gathering their coats and leftover slices. It's nearing midnight, and even this crowd has limits. My mother winks at me, saying, "I'll see you tomorrow, honey. I'll leave you with your friends." She hugs me tight, whispering, "Happy birthday, dear," before stepping out.

Ranger and Tory are next to leave, followed by Orion and Briar, who promise to text us about that rescue dog. Dean and Sophia stick around for a bit, helping me and Boone gather empty cups and plates, while Garrett and Thor engage in a quiet debate about whether pineapple belongs on pizza. (They never settle it, obviously.)

Finally, with the place mostly tidied and the leftover wine corked, Dean and Sophia wave goodbye. Garrett and Thor leave with Isabella—someone mentions going out for a late-night coffee. In a matter of minutes, the shop returns to silence, lit only by the overhead lights and a few decorative strings of white bulbs around the windows. The clock reads nearly one in the morning now.

I let out a contented sigh, leaning against a booth seat. Boone steps toward me, his eyes bright with affection and maybe a hint of mischief. "You okay, Bree?"

"I'm fine, Boone." My voice softens. "Thank you for... everything. For the surprise, for getting all our friends together. For making today so special."

He tucks a strand of hair behind my ear, his touch sending shivers down my spine. "You deserve it. It's your first birthday in a long time where you're not looking over your shoulder."

I swallow, remembering the terror of the past—kidnappings, threats, heartbreak. Now, it's replaced by laughter and pizza. "I never thought I'd be so... happy," I admit, voice trembling with emotion. "It almost feels unreal."

Bonus Epilogue

Boone steps closer, warm hands resting on my hips. "It's real," he murmurs, voice low. "We made it real. You and me."

Our gazes lock, and I see the reflection of the overhead lights dancing in his dark eyes. My heart clenches with a fierce love I can hardly put into words. I slip my arms around his neck, pulling him closer. "I love you," I whisper, the words tasting sweet and certain on my lips.

He smiles, the corners of his eyes crinkling. "I love you, too. You have no idea how much."

Then he dips his head, capturing my mouth in a tender, lingering kiss. I melt against him, my body warming under his touch, my mind swimming with the sensation of his lips exploring mine. There's no fear, no tension—just pure contentment and a slow-burning passion.

I tighten my grip around his neck, leaning up on my toes as the kiss deepens. His hands press firmly into my lower back, pulling me flush against him. The low hum of the fridge motors fades away, replaced by the pounding of my heart and the soft sound of our ragged breathing.

Breaking apart, I rest my forehead against his, our chests rising and falling in sync. "Where'd you learn to kiss like that, tough guy?" I tease breathlessly.

He laughs softly, brushing his nose against mine. "Must've been that extra cheese you keep shoveling into my dinners. Gave me power."

I roll my eyes again, but I'm smiling so hard it hurts. He nudges my chin, kissing me lightly again, and I can't resist letting out a giddy sigh.

We stand there for a moment, wrapped in each other, until the overhead lights flicker—an automated timer set to nighttime mode, reminding us it's after hours. "Guess we better lock up,"

Bonus Epilogue

I murmur, stepping back to glance around the shop. The tables are tidy, the leftover decorations drifting in a half-deflated balloon pinned to the corner. The faint smell of tomato sauce and melted cheese still lingers. It's comforting, homey.

Boone nods, hands slipping from my waist reluctantly. "Let's do that. Then we can head back to the cabin. I've got one more surprise for you."

I arch an eyebrow. "Another surprise? You're relentless."

He just grins, grabbing the keys from the counter. "A man's gotta keep his girlfriend guessing, right?"

My heart flutters. I can't believe this is my life: teased and treasured by the man who once rescued me and took me to a cabin in the woods. Now we share that cabin as our home, building a future that grows more certain each day.

I step into the cool night air, turning to lock the glass door behind us. Boone stands at my shoulder, scanning the quiet street. Ever the protector. Once I'm done, he guides me gently by the elbow to his truck, parked by the curb, and opens the passenger door for me. I climb in, tucking my hair behind my ears, the afterglow of the party still making my cheeks warm.

As he slips into the driver's seat, I ask softly, "Can you at least give me a hint about this last surprise?"

He glances my way, the overhead dome light illuminating a playful glint in his eyes. "Well... it involves a certain leftover Nutella and strawberry sauce we forgot to use tonight."

A laugh bubbles out of me. "That's not a surprise, that's just dessert."

He leans over, pressing a quick, mischievous kiss to my lips. "Trust me, Bree, it's gonna be sweet."

Bonus Epilogue

I can't help but grin as he starts the engine. The truck rumbles to life, headlights slicing through the darkness. We pull away from Slice Slice Baby, the neon sign flickering behind us. My chest feels full, brimming with gratitude for my friends, my mother, the new life we've carved out in Nashville—and, most of all, for Boone.

As we drive, I let my hand rest on his thigh, a silent thanks. We talk in hushed tones about the night's events; Orion's flour fight, Ranger's sauce mishap, my mother's quiet laughter as she watched it all unfold.

Eventually, the city lights fade, giving way to the moonlit pines that line the road to our cabin. Boone turns off the main highway onto the gravel path, and I roll down the window, inhaling the crisp forest air. It's such a different world from the day we first found ourselves holed up in a cabin, me terrified for my life. Now, it's a place of safety and love.

When we finally arrive, Boone parks, cuts the engine, and we sit for a beat in the hush of the wilderness.

"Give me a minute or two to set up," Boone says, kissing my hand before hopping out of the truck.

I follow him to the front porch and wait while he rushes inside. I hear the distant hoot of an owl, and my heart aches with contentment.

Boone opens the front door, reappearing by my side with a big smile, and it nearly takes my breath away. He takes my hand and leads me inside. The cabin interior is cozy, lit by a single lamp in the corner. I notice the coffee table is cleared, replaced by a soft blanket spread across it, and on top sits a small tray of the leftover Nutella sauce and a container of fresh strawberries. I laugh softly, turning to Boone. "So, this is your big plan? Dessert after the big pizza party?"

Bonus Epilogue

He smirks, shrugging off his jacket. "Hey, you said you love sweet pizza combos."

I watch as he dips a strawberry into the Nutella and offers it to me. My breath hitches, and I lean forward, taking a bite. The taste is divine—rich chocolate, ripe berry. But the real sweetness is the way he's looking at me, eyes full of adoration.

We feed each other a few more strawberries, giggling when a drop of chocolate lands on his finger. I wipe it off with my thumb, and he catches my wrist, guiding my hand to his mouth so he can kiss my fingertips. The moment thickens with an undeniable tension.

He sets the tray aside and pulls me gently into his arms. "Happy birthday," he murmurs, voice husky. "I hope it was everything you wanted."

I lay my hands on his broad chest, feeling his heartbeat steady under my palms. "It was perfect," I whisper. "But you made it that way."

He slides a hand into my hair, tilting my head so our eyes meet. "I'd do anything to see you smile like that—like you're free of every worry. That's all I want."

Emotion clogs my throat. I close the distance, pressing my lips to his in a slow, deep kiss that conveys all the gratitude and love I can't put into words. He returns it just as fervently, arms circling my waist, drawing me flush against him. A soft sound escapes my throat as his mouth moves with mine, tasting of chocolate and strawberry and promise.

Time stretches, and the only things that matter are his lips, his warmth, the quiet hush of the cabin that envelops us. His hands roam my back, and I thread my fingers into his hair, losing myself in the closeness. We break away only to catch our breath, foreheads touching.

Bonus Epilogue

"You're mine," he murmurs, voice trembling with devotion. "And I'm yours."

I grin through the tears threatening to spill, nodding. "Forever," I say, letting the word settle between us like a vow.

He eases me down onto the plush blanket, the Nutella tray forgotten on the table. Our kisses grow languid, a heady mix of passion and tenderness. The entire day—the surprise party, the laughter, the silly teasing about my nickname—culminates in this moment, where everything is right in the world.

Eventually, we drift into a slower pace, curling against each other, legs tangled, hearts beating in unison. He tucks me under his chin, stroking my hair. The lamp's glow casts dancing shadows across the cabin walls, and I wonder if life can get any better than this.

In that stillness, he leans down to whisper against my ear. "Thank you for letting me love you, Bree."

I smile, shifting so I can look into his eyes. "Thank *you* for loving me enough," I say softly, then my voice softens. "Boone, this is everything I've ever wanted. I'm so happy. I feel safe. And I just... I can't wait to see where we go from here."

He brushes his thumb across my cheek. "Wherever we go, we go together."

I snuggle closer, letting my eyes slip shut. The gentle thump of his heart lulls me, reminding me how far we've come—through danger, betrayal, heartbreak—and how we emerged stronger, building a life so filled with warmth and joy that my heart could burst.

Outside, the wind rustles the pine trees, and somewhere, an owl hoots softly. But within these walls, all is still, and I'm home. Wrapped in the arms of the man I love, stomach full of pizza, head full of laughter, and a future that glows as

Bonus Epilogue

brightly as the stars. If this is a dream, I never want to wake up.

I lift my head for one final kiss, a soft brush of lips that seals this perfect night. "I love you," I whisper again. It never gets old, speaking those words.

Boone smiles, eyes shining. "I love you, too, Aubree."

We settle back into each other's arms, letting the night envelop us. And in the quiet hush of our cabin, I realize that this—this shared joy, this unwavering trust, this simple, everyday magic—is my happily ever after.

Thank you for reading Boone and Aubree. Keep reading for the first chapter of Taking What's Mine, Book #4 in the Men of Maddox Security Series. >>>>>>

Patreon

Calling All Romance Lovers!

Ready for exclusive perks, behind-the-scenes access, and swoon-worthy surprises? Join **Logan Chance's Patreon** today!

Here's what you'll get:

• **Sticker of the Month Club** – Collect your favorite characters and moments in adorable sticker form.

• **Signed Paperbacks** – Delivered straight to your door, just for you.

• **Exclusive Giveaways** – Win books, swag, and more.

• **Bonus Content** – Unreleased scenes, steamy extras, and secrets from your favorite stories.

• **Character Interviews** – Get to know Logan's characters like never before.

• **Sneak Peeks** – Be the first to dive into upcoming books and projects.

Patreon

And that's just the beginning! There's SO MUCH MORE! Logan's Patreon is packed with romance reader delights you won't want to miss.

Sign up now and get access to all the swoony goodies today!

CLICK HERE, or visit www.patreon.com/loganchance

Your next favorite romance moment is waiting for you.

Sneak Peek Taking What's Mine

Chapter One

Lincoln

"I know she's my sister, but you're the only one I trust to keep her safe," Dean says, his gray eyes pleading with me to understand.

When Dean asked me to show up to the monthly meeting for Maddox Securities early, I never expected him to say this. I thought maybe he'd appreciated my work, and wanted to promote me to a top level executive or something. Someone who could oversee the jobs being dealt out, instead of the ones always performing them.

Sure, I love security work. I was a Navy SEAL, and when I retired, I wanted to play an active part in keeping people safe.

Being a SEAL, I was sought after by many companies to do just that.

However, Dean pays the best.

We've also grown into great friends since I've been working here.

Dean Maddox runs one of the most successful security companies in all the world. He gets clients from all walks of life, and we do whatever we have to do to keep the paying customer safe.

The Atlantic Ocean shines through the floor-to-ceiling wall as I try to understand Dean. "You want me to... what exactly?"

"Just take her to your house. Keep her safe while a few of my men and I check into who's been threatening her."

The thought of Isabel Maddox being threatened pisses me off. I've known Isabel for years. Ever since Dean brought her on to work here with us. She's like a second boss, and has been running things while Dean was on a manhunt, looking for the dangerous Bishop Blackstone.

"What does she think about it?"

Dean's eyes dart toward the ocean. "Uh, well..." his words fall away.

"You did tell her about the plan, right?"

"Not exactly."

I sigh, running my hand through my hair. "What exactly did you tell her?"

Dean winces, like he's afraid of his own sister. Which I don't blame him. She's a real firestarter. Especially when she's angry.

I've seen her angry once. I highly recommend against it.

"I texted her that she needs to stay with you for a while."

"Texted her?" I shake my head. Dean can't be serious here.

"Yeah, she'll be fine. Listen, whether she likes it or not, she needs to stay with you. You have to keep her safe."

There's a few folders on the table in front of where Dean sits, and I stare at them for a moment while I think about what he says. He's right.

Isabel's in danger, and we have to keep her safe.

It shouldn't matter that I've had a thing for her since I met her. That every time I stare into her deep gray eyes I get struck dumb and can't form a complete sentence. It's not her fault I'm an idiot when she's around.

I can do the job he's asking of me.

And even though I've wanted to know how sweet her lips taste, or how silky her skin feels, I won't let that temptation enter my mind while I do the job at hand.

"I'm the man for the job," I say, shaking his hand.

At that very moment Ranger steps through the doors. "Hello," he quips out.

Dean and I nod, and Boone enters just as Ranger takes a seat beside me.

"I'm here, the meeting can begin now," Boone says in his usual casual manner, as he runs his hand over his beard. He sits and stares at Ranger. "Sorry to hear about your sister."

Ranger only nods. "It's fine."

"If you need me to knock out the mother fucker, just let me know," Boone says, always ready to get into a fight.

I ask, "Knock who out?"

"My sister had a rough go with her ex. He ended up cheating on her, and really bringing down her self-worth. "She's been devastated ever since. It's probably why I'll never fall in love," Ranger says.

"Love isn't all bad." Dean smiles.

"I'm surprised you're even here today," Boone boasts.

"Hey, I'm not sorry I fell in love. Sophia means the world to me. We had to pretend to be married to catch Bishop. It wasn't easy, but when you know, you know." He's nervous, I can tell. "Actually it goes along the same lines as the job I'm giving August today." He laughs a little as he turns his attention onto the papers on the table.

The door swings open, and Orion steps through looking a little worse for wear.

"Why do you have the meetings so early in the morning?" He glares at Dean.

"It's nine am. I wouldn't call that early." Dean grins.

Orion slumps down into the seat nearest the door.

"Someone had a rough night," Boone says in his overzealous way.

Orion grumbles as he lays his head on the table.

August steps through the door, looking a little unsure if he's in the right place. He's a lot younger than the rest of us, and is the newest member on the team, but I haven't heard any complaints, so he's good in my book.

"Thanks for being here. I know the past couple of months have been tough with me searching for Bishop. I'd like to thank all of you in the hand you all played in finding him." Dean thumbs through the files on the table. "Hopefully now we can finally have some peace."

I listen as he speaks to everyone in the room. I personally wasn't around for the Bishop fiasco, as I was still in the service, but I get what he means about everyone pitching in.

"I know Isabel has been helping out a ton, and I'm lucky to have such an awesome sister," Dean says, his eyes meeting mine. "Now, I have some assignments that have come up, and wanted to hand out each one."

"Ranger, I'll start with you first. The G-Summit Meeting is this weekend and this is, Tory Ann," he says, handing him a file.

He opens it, staring at the file in his hands. "Is she attending the summit?"

"No, she isn't. Her father is a world renowned scientist Fredrick Malser, and he'll be a keynote speaker. He'll be attending and will have his own personal security watching over him."

I zone out on the rest of the meeting, thinking about my assignment to watch Isabel. How am I ever going to be able to keep my mind from traveling to the same place it travels to every time she's around?

I don't know if I will be able to even concentrate on the task at hand. I have to, however, because there's no letting Dean down. And more importantly, there's no letting anyone harm one precious brown silky strand of Isabel's hair.

It's been a long time since I've been alone with a woman, not really making dating a priority, but to be honest, I've always kind of had a thing for Isabel. I've never made a move on her because I respect Dean too much. I respect my job. I respect what I'm doing here.

I've expressed my want of becoming more than security detail to Dean, and now I'm just proving my worth until he decides to promote me.

It's a big deal that he's asked me to be the one to watch his sister. It shows that trust building.

And I'll be damned if I'm going to do anything to fuck it up.

Dean asks August to stay behind at the end of the meeting, and the rest of us head out into the hallway.

"We all need to catch up soon," Boone says. "It was fun last time."

Even though I keep to myself on most days, I still like to let loose with the guys every once in a while. And these guys are more than co-workers to me, they're like my brothers.

"Maybe once I'm done protecting a girl from her ex, we can do a guy's poker night."

"I'm down with that," Ranger says with a hearty laugh.

I laugh along with everyone else. Sure, the card shark he is would love to take more money from us.

"I'd love some more free money." Ranger finishes.

"No, I'm not playing poker with this guy again," I say. "Besides, my job isn't an easy one." I'll have to work extra hard on keeping Isabel safe, and who knows for how long.

Ranger slaps my shoulder. "I figured when Dean brought you in before everyone else."

I breathe in deep and let it out on a sigh. "It's Isabel. She's being threatened."

All the men get visibly angry at this news, and I don't blame them. Isabel is like family to all of us.

"Who is it?" Boone asks.

I shrug. "Not sure. Dean's got some leads. I just need to keep Isabel safe while he checks on a few things."

"Good luck. She can't be too happy about that," Orion says with a laugh.

At that very second Isabel heads down the hall, her heels clicking with every step. Her gray eyes zero in on me as everyone else scatters.

"You." She points at me.

I point to my own chest. "Who me?"

"Yes." She pokes me in the chest with her finger. Which kind of hurts a little, so I step back. "I can't believe you and my brother are doing this to me."

She goes to poke me with her finger again but I stop her, holding onto her hand. "You can't believe we're protecting you?"

She parks both hands on her hips. "Care to explain yourself, Lincoln?"

"Explain what?"

The fire in Isabel's eyes is palpable. She's angry, this much is obvious, but she can't think we wouldn't protect her.

"Isabel, you have to know your brother and I only want what's best for you."

This rages her further. "I can take care of myself."

"No you can't."

And now she's full on pissed. My god, I've never seen anyone's eyes turn red in an instant before. "Are you saying I can't look after myself?"

Sneak Peek Taking What's Mine

I step closer, pinning her to the wall to calm her down. "I don't care if you think you can look after yourself or not. I was given the job to protect you, and that's what I'm going to fucking do. Understood?"

⸻

Taking What's Mine releases April 8th, CLICK HERE!

About the Author

Logan Chance is a USA Today bestselling author who specializes in high-octane romantic suspense with a touch of humor (or more). Known for weaving intense, pulse-pounding plots with sizzling chemistry, Logan's novels captivate readers from the first page. He was nominated for Best Debut Author Goodreads Choice Awards in 2016. He crafts tales filled with steamy romance, gripping twists, and heart-stopping action.

When he's not writing, Logan can often be found watching great movies, devouring his ever-growing TBR pile, or brainstorming his next captivating series. He currently resides in South Florida, where he continues to pen stories that keep readers on the edge of their seats—and always craving more.

Check out Logan's website: loganchance.com

Also by Logan Chance

Men of Maddox Security
PROTECTING WHAT'S MINE
SAVING WHAT'S MINE
GUARDING WHAT'S MINE
TAKING WHAT'S MINE
DEFENDING WHAT'S MINE

The Magnolia Ridge Series

DON'T FALL FOR YOUR BEST FRIEND, Paxton and Hartford's Story

DON'T FALL FOR YOUR BROTHER'S BEST FRIEND, Anya and Griffin's Story

DON'T FALL FOR YOUR GRUMPY NEIGHBOR, Shepherd and Felicity's Story

DON'T FALL FOR YOUR FAKE BOYFRIEND, Brock and Willow's Story

DON'T FALL FOR YOUR EX-BOYFRIEND'S BROTHER, Tripp and Millie's Story

DON'T FALL FOR YOUR GRUMPY HUSBAND, Callum and Violet's Story

The Gods Of Saint Pierce
SAY MY NAME
CROSS MY HEART
CLOSE YOUR EYES
ON YOUR KNEES

Magnolia Point

TEMPTING MR. SCROOGE

LATTE BE DESIRED

THE UMPIRE STRIKES BACK

The Taken Series

TAKEN BY MY BEST FRIEND

MARRIED TO MY ENEMY (BOOK ONE)

MARRIED TO MY ENEMY (BOOK TWO)

STOLEN BY THE BOSS

ABDUCTED BY MY FATHER'S BEST FRIEND

CAPTURED BY THE CRIMINAL

Men Of Ruthless Corp.

SOLD TO THE HITMAN (As featured in the hit Netflix Movie: *Hitman* starring Glen Powell)

Harmony Hills Series

RUIN'S REVENGE

STEP-SANTA

HOLIDAY HIDEOUT

HATED BY MY ROOMMATE

HARD RIDE

The Trifecta Series

HOT VEGAS NIGHTS

DIRTY VEGAS NIGHTS

FILTHY VEGAS NIGHTS

Vampire Romance

Wicked Matrimony: A Vampire Romance

A Never Say Never Novel

NEVER KISS A STRANGER

The Playboy Series

PLAYBOY

HEARTBREAKER

STUCK

LOVE DOCTOR

The Me Series

DATE ME

STUDY ME

SAVE ME

BREAK ME

Sexy Standalones

THE NEWLYFEDS

COLD HEARTED BACHELOR

Holiday Romance Stories

FAKING IT WITH MR. STEELE

A VERY MERRY ALPHA CHRISTMAS COLLECTION

MERRY PUCKING CHRISTMAS

Steamy Duet

THE BOSS DUET

Box Sets

A VERY MERRY ALPHA CHRISTMAS COLLECTION

ME: THE COMPLETE SERIES
FAKE IT BABY ONE MORE TIME
THE TRIFECTA SERIES: COMPLETE BOX SET
THE PLAYBOY COMPLETE COLLECTION
FILTHY ROMANCE COLLECTION
THE TAKEN SERIES BOX SET: BOOKS 1-3
THE TAKEN SERIES BOX SET BOOKS 4-6

Made in the USA
Las Vegas, NV
21 March 2025

19894678R00177